The
Unlocking
Season

GAIL BOWEN

The
Unlocking
Season

Published by ECW Press
665 Gerrard Street East
Toronto, Ontario, Canada M4M 1Y2
416-694-3348 / info@ecwpress.com

Cover design: Michel Vrana
Author photo: © Madeline Bowen-Diaz

Two of the pieces of art made by the character, Sally Love, have been described in *Murder at the Mendel*, an earlier novel in the Joanne Kilbourn-Shreve series.
Pages 95-96: Sally Love's Perfect Circles
Pages 190-191: Sally Love's self-portrait
First published by McClelland & Stewart Ltd., 1991
First M&S paperback edition, 1992

Joanne's description of Zack's paraplegia appears in *Kaleidoscope*, page 198, published by McClelland & Stewart, 2012.

This is a work of fiction. Names, characters, places, and incidents either are the product of the au-thor's imagination or are used fictitiously, and any resemblance to actual persons, living or dead, business establishments, events, or locales is entirely coincidental.

LIBRARY AND ARCHIVES CANADA CATALOGUING IN PUBLICATION

Title: The unlocking season / Gail Bowen.

Names: Bowen, Gail, 1942– author.

Series: Bowen, Gail, 1942- Joanne Kilbourn mysteries.

Description: Series statement: A Joanne Kilbourn mystery

Identifiers: Canadiana (print) 20200234412
Canadiana (ebook) 20200234420

ISBN 978-1-77041-528-7 (hardcover)
ISBN 978-1-77305-583-1 (PDF)
ISBN 978177305-582-4 (ePUB)

Classification: LCC PS8553.O8995 U55 2020
DDC C813/.54—dc23

The publication of *The Unlocking Season* has been generously supported by the Canada Council for the Arts which last year invested $153 million to bring the arts to Canadians throughout the country and is funded in part by the Government of Canada. *Nous remercions le Conseil des arts du Canada de son soutien. L'an dernier, le Conseil a investi 153 millions de dollars pour mettre de l'art dans la vie des Canadiennes et des Canadiens de tout le pays. Ce livre est financé en partie par le gouvernement du Canada.* We acknowledge the support of the Ontario Arts Council (OAC), an agency of the Government of Ontario, which last year funded 1,737 individual artists and 1,095 organizations in 223 communities across Ontario for a total of $52.1 million. We also acknowledge the contribution of the Government of Ontario through the Ontario Book Publishing Tax Credit, and through Ontario Creates for the marketing of this book.

PRINTED AND BOUND IN CANADA

PRINTING: FRIESENS   5   4   3   2   1

MIX
Paper from responsible sources
FSC® C016245
www.fsc.org

For Jack David,
for having faith in the Joanne Kilbourn series
and in me

and

Nathaniel Bowen,
for making it possible for his Dad and me
to continue living great lives.

CHAPTER ONE

On the Saturday morning before Easter, when I opened the front door and saw Georgie Shepherd on our porch, I felt a twinge of unease. Georgie was the executive producer of *Sisters and Strangers,* a six-part TV series based on the tangled relationships of my family. We had solid scripts for the first two episodes, but we were still struggling to finish the rest. Georgie's appearance at my house on a holiday weekend did not augur well.

Our dogs, Esme and Pantera, were sniffing Georgie's knees, making sure she passed muster before she stepped over the threshold. Luckily, it appeared that Georgie was a dog lover. "You have a bullmastiff *and* a Bouvier," she said. "They're beauties, but wow, they *are* big. You must be a fan of the giant breeds."

"We are, but Pantera and Esme chose us. Our son, Peter, is a vet. Pantera's owners brought him to Pete's clinic to have him neutered and never picked him up. When Pete called them, they told him they bought Pantera because he was cute, and now he was just big. Esme belonged to Pete's sister-in-law. When she died, Esme needed a home, and we needed a Bouvier."

"So happy endings all around," Georgie said, giving the dogs one last pat. There was an uneasiness in her tone. "Joanne, I apologize for barging in like this. I did try to phone, but my calls went straight to voicemail."

"My phone was turned off," I said. "Zack and I are dyeing eggs with our grandchildren."

The sulphur scent of boiling eggs lingered in the air. Georgie sniffed and grimaced. "I didn't know anyone still did that."

"We're old school," I said. "Come in and join the party."

"Sign me up for next year," Georgie said. "There's a problem we need to talk about."

Sisters and Strangers was about Douglas Ellard, the father who raised me, and his lifelong friend, the artist Desmond Love, who was my biological father. Telling their story fully and honestly mattered to me, and I had been working with the writer, Roy Brodnitz, on the script. At sixty, the chance to understand and accept a part of my life that until a year earlier had been shrouded in secrecy was a gift, and the chance to be involved in a process that meant stepping into a new world was seductive, but after a promising start, things fell apart.

I led Georgie into the living room. "The kitchen windows are open, and I've put out dishes of vinegar, so we'll be able to breathe soon. I'll let my family know you and I are talking."

When I returned, Georgie was sitting in an easy chair by the window that overlooked the creek behind our house. Her scrubbed, blond good looks, fine, precise features and cleanly marked jawline suggested a woman with a sunny, uncomplicated view of life, but Georgie's grey eyes were knowing, and her lips had a way of curling in private amusement at the vagaries of human behaviour. My grandmother would have said that Georgie Shepherd "was nobody's fool," and my grandmother would have been right.

Our forsythia had just bloomed. The bush's gold, bell-shaped flowers were a welcome burst of colour in the grey late-winter palette, and Georgie had half turned to gaze at them. "That forsythia is glorious," she said.

"A harbinger of spring," I said. "And a good omen."

"Let's hope," she said, "because there's troubling news. You know that Roy flew up north with the production team to scout locations for *Sisters and Strangers*."

"I talked to Roy yesterday," I said. "They'd just arrived on the island at Emma Lake where Ernest Lindner had his studio. Roy was ecstatic. One hundred and eighteen acres of virgin forest and a log cabin constructed in 1935 — exactly what they need for the outdoor shots."

Georgie winced, and when I saw the pain in her eyes, I sank into the chair across from hers. "Something's happened," I said.

She nodded. "Everything was fine. The production team rented vans in Saskatoon, drove to Emma Lake and hired boats to carry them and their gear out to the island. They had a shore lunch and then split up to explore the terrain. It was a gorgeous day, and at five o'clock, the team met back at the boat dock as planned."

"But Roy wasn't there?" I said. My pulse was racing. Our family had known Roy for less than a year, but he had been a good friend to us.

Georgie's gaze shifted back to the forsythia and stayed there, as if she wanted to hide among the blossoms. "Everyone assumed he'd lost track of the time, but when he wasn't there by half past five, they separated and started scouring the island. This time of year, the sun sets around seven thirty that far north. The crew knew they'd never find Roy in the dark, so they called the police in Prince Albert. It was close to ten before Ainsley and Kyle Daly, the production designer, spotted Roy. He was alive, but in Ainsley's words, he was in 'a state of mortal terror.'"

The image of the Roy Brodnitz I knew flashed through my mind. He was an elegant and fastidious man. At the beginning of his career, Roy had been a dancer, and after twenty years of sedentary life as a writer, he still moved with a dancer's grace. "I can't believe any of this," I said. "When I spoke to Roy yesterday, he was fine — better than fine. He sounded like his old self."

Georgie shook her head. "According to Ainsley, when she finally found Roy, he didn't recognize her."

"How could that be?" I said. "The two of them have been inseparable since they were fourteen."

"Ainsley said Roy was drenched in sweat; his clothes were filthy, and his fingernails looked as if he'd been clawing at the ground. He was muttering gibberish. He seemed desperate to make the others understand, but before they could make sense of what he was saying, he started gasping for breath and collapsed. Apparently, he suffered a massive heart attack."

"Where is he now?"

"Nick Kovacs and one of the police officers carried him out of the woods to a clearing where a helicopter could land and take him to a hospital in Saskatoon."

"What do they think caused the heart attack?"

"They don't know," Georgie said. "The doctors are waiting for more test results. When I raised the possibility that Roy might have been using cocaine again, Ainsley ripped my head off."

"Roy's been clean for over four years," I said. "I know that after his husband, Lev-Aaron, died, Roy hit bottom, but he made it through and went on to have the greatest success of his career."

She nodded. "*The Happiest Girl.*"

"It's still playing to packed houses on Broadway, and everyone who worked on the film adaptation says Roy's script is brilliant. He'd have no reason to use again."

"Are you certain of that?" Georgie said, and her tone was measured. "I've barely seen Roy since I arrived in Regina.

When Ainsley asked me to take over as executive producer of *Sisters and Strangers* after Gabe died, I had to hit the ground running. Roy and I haven't even had a cup of coffee together — his choice, not mine, and believe me, I gave him plenty of openings."

"Why would Roy need an opening to have coffee with you?" I said. "I thought the friendship among the three of you went way back."

"It does." Georgie's eyes met mine. Her gaze was penetrating. "You're a hard person to deceive, Joanne, so I'm going to lay it all out for you. After Gabe's death, Ainsley believed that she and Fawn could cope without bringing anyone else in. Gabe had made all the decisions about cast and crew, and as director, Ainsley had been part of all those decisions. Fawn had years of experience managing productions day-to-day. With one exception, it was in great shape for pre-production."

"And that exception was the script," I said. "When Roy and I agreed to what we referred to loosely as a collaboration, we were both so excited that the first two episodes seemed to write themselves."

Georgie nodded. "That's the way the scripts read. That opening with Sally and Joanne at fourteen, together on the raft is a flawless introduction to their idyllic summer."

"It *was* idyllic," I said. "One of the many perfect summers we shared growing up — all of them filled with blue skies and the fishy-weedy smell of the lake and Sally and me lying side by side on the raft with the sun pressing down on our backs like a hand. We thought it would always be that way."

"But it ended," Georgie said gently. "The scene where

Joanne goes to the Loves' cottage and discovers the family in the dining room — Des dead, Nina apparently near death and Sally lying face down in her own vomit — is heart-wrenching." Georgie reached out and squeezed my hand. "And you survived it."

"Barely," I said. "When I stood on the dock that night and watched my father drive the boat carrying Des's body and Nina and Sally across the water to the mainland, my world shattered. And it got worse. My father was a physician. He was also Des's oldest friend, and he told me he believed that after Des suffered the stroke that paralyzed his right side and ended his career, he must have felt he had no reason to live. He killed himself, and he attempted to take Nina and Sally with him by poisoning their drinks. Sally carried that assumption with her till the day she died. Months after her death, I discovered the truth — that it was Nina, unwilling to face a future with an invalid husband and a daughter she hated, who had poisoned the drinks. By then, of course, it was too late for Sally and too late for Des." I took a deep breath. "Working on *Sisters and Strangers* gave me a chance to right the terrible wrong that was done that night."

Georgie's voice was strong. "And you can still right that wrong. That's why I came over here today. No matter what state he's in, you're the only one who can give Roy what he needs to finish *Sisters and Strangers*."

"But I don't know what he needs. I've tried everything I can think of to bring Roy back to the way he felt when he wrote the first two episodes. Nothing I do works."

She turned to me. "What happened, Joanne?"

"I honestly don't know," I said. "But I do remember the exact moment when everything changed between Roy and me. It was not long after Gabe Vickers died. We had all just learned that Gabe was a sexual deviant who knew how to get what he wanted from innocent young women. Ainsley had a brilliant future as a director, but as long as Gabe was in the picture, that future was clouded. Roy was open about his relief that Gabe was out of her life."

"Roy's emotions were always close to the surface," Georgie said. "And sometimes that was problematic."

"His response to Gabe's death was definitely one of those times. When Gabe fell from the balcony of the penthouse he and Ainsley sublet, he'd been drinking heavily, and the assumption was that the fall was accidental. Of course, the police can't operate on assumptions, and as part of their investigation, they were looking into Gabe's relationships with those who had something to gain from his death. On more than one occasion, I'd heard Roy say that Gabe's death diminished no one because Gabe was a man without a conscience. His lack of discretion worried me, and I advised Roy to watch what he said. My intent was simply to caution him, but Roy concluded that I was pointing the finger at Ainsley, and he exploded. He told me that he and Ainsley had been together every second of every minute of every hour the night Gabe died, and then he tore out of my house and slammed the door behind him.

"That was before Christmas, and I didn't speak to Roy again until early in the New Year. By then, the police had discovered that Ainsley had gone to the penthouse she and Gabe shared and although they'd quarrelled, she had played no part in his death. Once it was clear Ainsley was innocent, I waited for Roy to get in touch so we could resume work . . ."

"But he didn't," Georgie guessed.

I nodded. "And at the end of the first week in January, I called and suggested that we meet in our old workplace, the writers' room at the production studios, the following Monday morning."

"And he agreed?"

"It was an offer he couldn't refuse," I said. "Roy's contract for *The Happiest Girl* gave Gabe the right of first refusal on Roy's next project. On December 1 I told Roy the story behind *Flying Blue Horses*, a painting Sally made when she was twelve. As soon as Roy heard the story, he knew he had the seed that would grow into the script that ultimately became *Sisters and Strangers*. He pitched the idea to Gabe Vickers, and he was keen to option the project. Zack drew up the option agreement and Gabe signed. The entire process took less than a week."

"I've seen that option agreement," Georgie said. "It's watertight. It gives you the whip hand. As owner of the material the series will be based on, if you're dissatisfied with the direction in which the project is developing, and you and the executive producer of *Sisters and Strangers* can't reach agreement, the option will be declared null and void." Georgie was clearly incredulous. "I still can't believe Gabe signed that agreement."

"Gabe needed to move quickly," I said. "The actors he wanted, Vale Frazier and Rosamond Burke from *The Happiest Girl*, were both available the following June; Ainsley was keen to direct; Roy was eager to write the script; the Saskatchewan Production Studios were available; and Gabe could hire the crew he was using for *The Happiest Girl*. All the stars were aligned. At that point, no one, least of all me, saw any reason why I would be dissatisfied with the direction the production would take."

Georgie took a deep breath and exhaled slowly. "Man plans, and God laughs."

"So it seems," I said. "Anyway, Roy had no choice but to show up on Monday morning. He didn't even sit for our meeting. He came through the door and announced that we were changing our approach. He said he would write outlines for the remaining episodes and we would 'flesh them out' with dialogue later, and then he left."

"And you accepted that?"

"I did. Roy had been our friend. I knew he was fragile emotionally, and I thought he needed time to work out whatever was troubling him. Anyway, I waited a full month."

Georgie's eyes widened. "A full month? My God, Joanne. Friendship does have limits."

"You're right, of course, but I kept hoping. Anyway, yet again, there was no real meeting. Roy came into the writers' room the day after I called him, handed me the binder containing the outlines and left. When I opened the binder, I felt as if I'd been kicked in the stomach."

"I can imagine," Georgie said. "I've seen the outlines.

There's nothing there — just numbered scenes with a list of the characters and locations needed for each scene."

"Ainsley was in the Living Skies offices, and I took the binder to her. She took one look at it, suggested it might be best if Roy and I worked separately for a while, and promised to take care of the problem."

"That must have been the day she called me," Georgie said. "In theory, I was hired as executive producer to work with Fawn Tootoosis on pre-production, but my real job was to be the safety net."

"The writer who could take over if Roy shut down completely." My heart sank. "This is all so sad."

Georgie nodded. "And to add to the sadness, Roy hasn't been fooled by the subterfuge. He knows why Ainsley brought me in, and the truth is killing him."

"So where do we go from here?"

Georgie ran her fingers through her smart shag haircut. "I honestly don't know. You said Roy was his old self when he called you yesterday."

"It was as if the clouds had cleared," I said. "Roy sounded carefree again. He used a phrase that was part of a kind of shorthand we shared. I'd had no experience with screen-writing, and it didn't take long for me to realize that if the characters are people you love, facts can get in the way. The first time Roy altered the facts to give a scene more power, I bristled. He said, 'This tweak makes the scene truer to life than life itself.' And he was right.

"Yesterday, he said the Lindner cabin was perfect for the Ellard family cottage, but the set carpenters would have to build something for the Loves. I hated the idea of adding a fake cottage to that untouched island, and when I didn't respond, Roy knew exactly what I was thinking. He asked me how long it had been since I'd seen our cottages on MacLeod Lake. It had been forty-five years. MacLeod Lake was in the centre of Ontario cottage country. I knew that by now there wouldn't be a square inch of the land that hadn't been developed. Roy had made his point. I said, 'Let's go with truer to life than life itself,' and we both laughed. It was like old times."

Now it was my turn to gaze out the window at the forsythia.

"But within hours of that talk, Roy was in 'a state of mortal terror,'" Georgie said. She picked up her cardigan and shrugged into it. "I wonder if we'll ever know what happened?"

We walked together to the door. When I reached to open it, Georgie touched my arm. "I'm glad we talked. There's truth in that old adage that a burden shared is a burden halved."

She sounded as miserable and confused as I felt. "We're having people for lunch here tomorrow," I said. "It will be mostly family, but Ben Bendure, the filmmaker who made *The Poison Apple*, the documentary about Sally Love, is coming down from Saskatoon for the day. He knew Sally and me all our lives, and he was part of all our summers at the lake. I realize this is a last-minute invitation, but I'm sure you and Ben will enjoy each other. We'll be eating around one, but if you want to catch the Easter egg hunt, come earlier."

Georgie didn't hesitate. "I accept," she said, "and I'll be early."

* * *

The news about Roy had shaken me, and I waited for my head to clear before I returned to the kitchen where the egg decorating had moved into high gear. The grandchildren each had a dozen hard-boiled eggs to work with, and the adults shared another four dozen. Our eighteen-month-old grandson, Charlie, had made quick work of his quota. He'd given all twelve eggs a speedy dip in the bowl of red colouring. Now forgotten, the eggs were back in their carton drying, and Charlie was hammering pegs into holes in a board from his tool set. His twin, Colin, was still moving his first egg carefully from one bowl of colour to the next, seemingly mesmerized by the changing colours.

Our daughter-in-law Maisie, our daughter, Mieka, and her daughters, Madeleine and Lena, were wrapping squares of silk cut from old neckties and blouses around raw eggs, boiling them for twenty minutes in water and vinegar and hoping for the dazzling results promised in the DIY video.

Madeleine, who was eleven, squinted at the boiling eggs. "Do you think these are really going to turn out?"

Lena said, "If Taylor was here the eggs would turn out. Everything she does ends up looking the way it's supposed to."

"That's because she's an artist," Madeleine said. "Remember how good she was at making pysanka? All the fancy patterns she could make with the wax?"

"Yeah, ours weren't as good as Taylor's, but they were still really nice," Lena said. "Do you think Taylor and Vale are making pysanka today out at the lake?"

"Why don't we FaceTime them tomorrow and see?" I said. "We could show them our eggs too."

Lena brightened. "That would be good."

"Not as good as having Taylor here with us," Madeleine said. "But we're going to have to get used to her not being here all the time. She and Vale are moving into their new condo as soon as the movie Vale's in is finished."

"I wish things could just stay the way they are now," Lena said.

"So do I," Zack said, "but Mimi says Taylor and Vale are starting a new life together and they need their own space."

"I guess that makes sense," Lena said.

"I guess it does," Zack said. Then he sighed and turned his wheelchair back to the butcher block table where he, our son, Peter and Charlie Dowhanuik, Mieka's new husband and godfather to the son Peter and Maisie had named for him, were wrestling with the twins' gifts from us: "easy to assemble" balance bikes.

It was a warm and comforting scene, and when Zack gave me a questioning glance, I tried for a reassuring smile.

Maisie and Peter were taking the twins to a birthday party at a vegan pizzeria, so after they'd packed up their eggs, and we'd snapped final pictures, they headed out, and I heated soup for the rest of us. After we'd eaten, Mieka and the girls went to April's Place, one of the two café play centres Mieka owned, to supervise yet more egg decorating, but I asked her new husband, Charlie D, to stay behind. There was something I wanted to talk to Zack and him about.

* * *

I had known Charlie Dowhanuik since the day he was born. His father, Howard, was premier of our province, and he was away politicking on the day his son came into the world. I drove Marnie Dowhanuik to the hospital, and I was in the delivery room with her. As a rule, even health care veterans meet the arrival of a newborn enthusiastically, but except for Charlie's howl, during his first minutes of life, the room was silent. The necessary tasks were performed — the umbilical cord was tied and cut; the baby was cleaned and placed in his mother's arms — but after seeing the port-wine birthmark that covered the left half of the newborn's face like a blood mask, no one said a word. Marnie Dowhanuik kissed her new son and said, "We'll handle this," and they had. After she'd explored every medical possibility and learned that nothing could be done, Marnie stood back and let Charlie live his life.

Like his mother, Charlie was physically stunning except for that mark: he had her strongly carved features and her beautiful coal-black wavy hair, and like his mother he was fearless. He was a wild child, a danger freak who was always surrounded by admirers, and his mother's wry assessment that Charlie didn't have friends, he had fans, proved prophetic.

Blessed with impeccable cadences and a voice as soothing as dark honey, Charlie D had parlayed his quick wit and deep well of empathy into a stellar career as a radio personality. For twelve years, his national call-in show, a blend of cool music, edgy riffs on life and a deep understanding of his listeners, maintained enviable ratings, notably with the fourteen to twenty-five demographic. At the end of his twelfth season, Charlie checked into a hospital renowned for its laser treatment success and the blood mask disappeared, but Charlie's visceral knowledge of what it felt like to walk down the street and see strangers avert their eyes remained, as did his tender heart.

Despite his media success, Charlie D had never lost touch with Peter and Mieka. As kids, the three of them had spent countless hours playing together in drafty small-town halls while their fathers politicked, and Marnie and I helped the local ladies dish up cabbage rolls and pierogies. They had taken a blood oath, nicking their fingers, pressing their fingers together and pledging kinship — the kind of things kids did in those days that they would never allow their own kids to do now. I had never been as innocent as Mieka believed me to be about the sexual attraction between her and Charlie D. I knew their almost primal bond had caused tensions in Mieka's short-lived first marriage, and when Charlie D moved back to Regina in January, and he and Mieka announced their engagement, I wasn't surprised.

They had a quiet family wedding, and Charlie D had begun hosting a two-hour national interview program, *Charlie D in the Morning*, for MediaNation. I had long since given up assessing or judging other people's relationships, but Charlie D and Mieka had the warm glow of two people who knew that they had found what they'd been waiting for. Madeleine and Lena embraced Charlie D's presence in their lives as easily and fully as he embraced their presence in his. It seemed the universe was unfolding as it should.

The March ratings for *Charlie D in the Morning* that had come out earlier in the week showed that, after a strong start, the program was gaining traction. U.S. programmers had taken note and the show was being picked up by a score of radio stations in desirable media markets. Charlie knew how to do an in-depth interview, and as his reputation for giving his subjects the chance to reveal their truest self was growing, he was landing some high-profile guests.

One of those high-profile guests was Roy Brodnitz. Charlie D had interviewed him earlier in the month, and the two men bonded. As Charlie said wryly, "Roy's demons and mine recognized each other immediately."

Now, as we sat in our sunny kitchen and I told them the news about Roy, Charlie's face, like Zack's, was somber.

When I'd finished, Zack wheeled his chair closer to me. "This doesn't make sense," he said. "How could Roy be fine when you talked to him just before noon and within hours be so terrified he was unreachable?"

Charlie D took out his phone. "I'll call the newsroom in Toronto and see if they've heard anything." The call he made was brief and clearly unsatisfactory. "Nada," he said. "But they aren't letting any grass grow under their feet. The interview I did with Roy was scheduled for broadcast in April, but the network is now considering playing it on Easter Monday."

"If Roy doesn't recover . . ." I said.

Charlie D was resigned. "That's the way of the world, Jo," he said. "The trailers for *The Happiest Girl* hit theatres this week, and in his interview with me Roy is candid about his lifelong struggle with depression and his fear of failure."

"I'm surprised he talked to you about that," I said. "He's always struck me as a very private person."

"Roy was not in great shape the day I interviewed him. Twice he became so emotional, I asked him if he wanted to stop, but he refused. I tried asking questions about his career — soft lobs, nothing emotionally charged — but Roy kept steering the conversation back to his failings. It was clear he needed to talk, so I let him go. You'd be amazed at how often an interview becomes a character excavation for the person being interviewed."

My body stiffened. "Do you think Roy might have hurt himself — not deliberately — perhaps by taking the wrong combination of medications?"

Zack's voice was gentle. "He has a history, Joanne, and Shakespeare was right — too often, the past is prologue. Roy used drugs before to stop his pain."

Charlie D was a journalist, but he was also my son-in-law, and when he asked whether *Sisters and Strangers* would be scuttled if Roy died, his voice was soft with concern.

I shook my head. "The project is too far along," I said. "Shooting starts in ten weeks. Georgie Shepherd told me when she was here that although she is nominally the series' executive producer, Ainsley hired her as backup in case Roy wasn't able to finish the scripts."

24

Zack turned to me. "How would you feel about that?"

"Fine, I guess," I said. "I haven't had a chance to think about it. Everything has happened so fast. But that's been true from the beginning."

"One morning Roy appeared with proof that Desmond Love, not Douglas Ellard, was my biological father, and within days Roy was talking about collaborating with me on a six-part series about my family and Des's."

"Then in the blink of an eye, you were drafting the legal papers, and Gabe was arranging the financing. When everything fell into place so quickly, Roy and I thought the gods must be on our side."

Charlie D leaned forward. "I've been curious about that. A six-part series usually takes months, even years, to get as far as pre-production, and *Sisters and Strangers* is almost ready to shoot. How did that happen?"

"Honour to whom honour is due," I said. "Gabe Vickers may have lacked a moral compass, but he knew how to get the money to put a project on its legs, and he knew who to hire on- and offscreen to create something people wanted. He moved fast. By the time he approached potential backers for *Sisters and Strangers*, Gabe was able to point out that, in addition to an amazing story and the brilliant writer/director collaboration that had produced *The Happiest Girl*, he had already signed a renowned actor, Rosamond Burke, and Vale Frazier, a young actor on the verge of becoming a major star. It must have been an easy sell."

"It wasn't entirely smooth sailing," Charlie D said. "My research for the Brodnitz interview referred to a six-part series that was about to get the green light from the network, but the final contracts hadn't been signed, so Gabe used dark magic and knocked that project out of the box to make way for *Sisters and Strangers.*"

"That sounds a little bizarre. Do you have any idea what Gabe did?"

Charlie D shook his head. "No. The head of the entertainment division at MediaNation suggested that I look into the history behind *Sisters and Strangers'* rapid ascent but the production company that got the boot wasn't protesting the network's decision, and Gabe's project was moving along smoothly. Until now, there didn't seem to be any reason to dig around."

Zack was quick to pick up on Charlie D's inference. "But if Roy dies under seemingly mysterious circumstances, there will be a reason to dig."

"You bet," Charlie D said. "Especially given Gabe Vickers's sudden and dramatic demise."

My nerves tightened. "The coroner called Gabe's death 'death by misadventure.'"

Our son-in-law's hazel eyes were troubled. "I know. I checked, and when I was doing my homework, I learned that 'death by misadventure' describes a death that is primarily due to an accident caused by a dangerous risk taken voluntarily."

Zack's response was matter of fact but firm. "I'm sure you also learned that the Vickers file is closed."

"I did," Charlie D said. "And let's hope it stays closed. There are still many unanswered questions about Vickers's death, Zack. Anyway, I'll be in New York this week. It's the epicentre of rumours and gossip, and if a dragon somewhere has crawled out of its lair I'll hear about it."

"It's always useful to know if a dragon is headed in our direction," Zack said with a half smile.

I wasn't as sanguine as my husband. I had been the prompter for Bishop Lambeth School's production of *Macbeth*, and the second witch spoke a line that always disturbed me. "By the pricking of my thumbs, Something wicked this way comes." It had been over forty years since I'd thought of that line, but seemingly, it had not lost its power to make my blood run cold.

CHAPTER TWO

The image of a vengeful dragon is not easily dispelled, but that evening Zack and I did our best. Our martini glasses were a little fuller than usual, and we dined by candlelight. Mieka had brought us moussaka: my only task was to pour on the béchamel; sprinkle the extra nutmeg and cheese on top and bake the dish for an hour. Zack made a green salad; I opened the wine and turned on Norah Jones. It was perfect — except we were two instead of three.

Zack served us both, then looked at his plate mournfully. "Moussaka is one of our daughter's favourites."

"Everything is one of Taylor's favourites," I said. "She's a trencherwoman."

"What do you suppose she and Vale are having for dinner tonight?"

"Well, they went straight from the airport to the cottage, so I imagine Taylor will pull something out of the freezer. They haven't seen each other for almost a month, and they're in love. I don't imagine food will be at the top of their agenda."

Zack sipped his wine. "You know I'm still having a hard time getting my head around this."

"The fact that Taylor's beloved is a young woman?"

"No, I'm fine with that. I'm just finding it difficult to believe that Taylor has a beloved at all." Zack raised his hand in a halt gesture. "And you don't have to tell me that our daughter is happy. I've seen her face. But she and Vale are only eighteen."

"They've both had to learn how to live with extraordinary gifts," I said. "Taylor sold her first painting when she was thirteen, and Vale has been acting since she was a child. They've both discovered the importance of making wise career decisions. This is the first love for both of them," I said. "The attraction was there from the beginning, but they haven't rushed into a relationship. They're working it through. Now eat your moussaka before it gets cold."

It was a quiet evening. We lit a fire. Zack worked on his opening statement for court Monday morning, and because I was thinking of Roy, I read the script for *The Happiest Girl* in which Vale was one of the leads. The film she was working on now was on hiatus for a week, and she and Taylor were staying at our cottage forty-five minutes from Regina. Vale was also playing the young Sally Love in *Sisters and Strangers*, and I'd been hoping she'd find time to come into the city and let Roy and me hear her read some of the dialogue Roy had written.

I was still hoping for that, but when our land line rang, I drew a ragged breath and ran to answer. It was Taylor, and the relief washed over me. "Just calling to say goodnight to you and Dad," she said. "I knew you'd want to hear that we were fine."

"You know us well," I said. "Is everything all right?"

"Everything's perfect," she said, her voice soft with contentment.

"Your dad wanted to know what you had for dinner."

She laughed. "Bacon and eggs. When we got to the lake, we were both starving. Vale hasn't had much experience putting heat to food, so I made our old standby. Is Dad there?"

"Right beside me. As soon as he realized it was you on the line, he wheeled over."

"Better hand him the phone or he'll drive out to the lake to count my fingers and toes for himself."

* * *

Zack and I decided to make an early night of it. I'd just finished brushing my teeth when the phone rang. Once again, I tensed. Roy and Taylor had always had a special fondness for each other, and I'd justified not telling her about Roy's collapse by reminding myself that the outcome was still uncertain. If the news was grim, she'd have to be told sooner rather than later.

However, my caller was not Georgie Shepherd with news

of Roy, it was my old friend, Ben Bendure. The documentaries Ben made often raised painfully troubling questions, but he was a comforting presence, and I was looking forward to seeing him the next day. Normally, Ben's deep and melodious bass was filled with energy, but that night his voice was a rasp, and he sounded weary.

"Are you okay?" I said.

"Yes, but Joanne, I won't be able to come to lunch tomorrow. I felt a cold coming on, and at eighty I take no chances. Pneumonia may be the old person's friend, but I'm not prepared to go gentle into that good night quite yet."

"Good," I said. "Because I'm not prepared to let you go. I'm glad you nipped this in the bud."

Ben's laugh was wry. "I might have been wiser to let nature take its course. On the way to the pharmacist's I slipped and broke my ankle. I just got out of the ER."

I groaned. "Oh Ben, I wish I lived closer, so I could at least make you chicken soup."

"Thanks, but my friends in the building will take good care of me."

"That's reassuring," I said. "Try to get some sleep, and I'll be in touch tomorrow."

"Wait. There's something else. Roy Brodnitz called me last night."

"Last night?" I said. "Do you remember the time?"

"Not sure. When my land line rang, it awakened me. I'd taken something for my cold, and I was groggy, but I did notice that it was after dark."

"Do you remember anything Roy said?"

"No, just that he wasn't making any sense. Roy and I have talked on the phone at least a dozen times since you introduced us before Christmas. Whenever he had questions about one of the DVDs I gave him of your family and the Love family, he'd call. We always had a substantive talk. The relationship between two filmmakers who make movies on the same subject can be contentious, but Roy was always charmingly tolerant of my suggestions."

"But he was different last night."

"He was obsessive. He kept talking about decay and the intensity of the colours and the white light that was every-where holding things together. I asked him to explain, but I couldn't get through to him. I was feeling punk, so I gave up, broke the connection and went back to sleep. When I called Roy this morning, there was no answer. I assumed he was sleeping it off."

"So you think that when Roy called you he'd been drink-ing?"

"That's what I thought at first. But tonight I checked my cell and saw that yesterday afternoon Roy had sent me some photos. They were close-ups of forest undergrowth, fallen branches, tree bark, lichen. They were exquisite — as intri-cate as a tapestry."

"That sounds like Ernest Lindner's work," I said. "Roy and some of the crew from *Sisters and Strangers* were scout-ing locations yesterday, and they were exploring the island where Ernie had his cabin and studio."

"Ernie was fascinated by the natural cycle of decay and regeneration," Ben said. "If Roy was on Ernie's island that might explain some of what he was trying to say. But Roy's an articulate man. Something must have happened . . ."

"You're right," I said. "And Ben, I wasn't planning to worry you with this, but Roy collapsed last night. He's been hospitalized in Saskatoon. Discovering exactly what did happen might be critical."

"Oh God. How bad is it?"

"I don't know, but you might have been the last person he spoke to. Any insight you have on what possibly happened could help."

"All I can offer is conjecture," Ben said. "I know Roy had a problem with cocaine, but the mania when he called me last night — especially all the raving about colour and the light that holds everything together — doesn't fit the pattern." Ben fell silent. Certain he had more to say, I waited. Finally, he cleared his throat and continued. "His behaviour does fit the pattern for someone using a hallucinogen."

I was taken aback. "I can't reconcile that with the man I knew."

Ben's voice was gentle. "Roy was no longer the man you knew, Joanne. He was suffering from writer's block, a bad one that was crippling him creatively. He'd called me about it two weeks ago. I didn't tell you because he swore me to secrecy. That promise doesn't matter now. Roy told me that when he began writing *Sisters and Strangers* it was as if he'd been given the gift of a story he was meant to share. And then, without warning, the gift was taken away."

"You think Roy believed using a hallucinogen might be a way of getting the gift back?"

"I think it's possible. People like the Beatles and Steve Jobs experimented with mind-expanding drugs like LSD and peyote because they believed that intensifying their sensory experiences fed their creativity. For some people it does. I've known visual artists who said that when they dropped acid, they had to work at full capacity just to keep up with the images that flooded their minds. The drugs banished their inhibitions and their fears. They removed everything that kept them from making the art they wanted to make."

"The possibility that a psychedelic drug would free him to write again might have been impossible for Roy to resist." I was close to tears. "But Ben, it didn't work for him. It might have destroyed him."

"Everyone who uses hallucinogens is aware that the outcome might not be positive," Ben said. "Sometimes, they just roll the dice. Joanne, call me if there's news. I'm fond of that young man."

"So am I."

* * *

When my conversation with Ben ended, Zack was in the shower. Had he been in the room, I would have asked him about the wisdom of calling Ainsley Blair and telling her about the possibility Ben Bendure had raised. But since he was in the shower, I called Ainsley and delivered a précis of my conversation with Ben and said I felt it was important for Roy's doctors to have any information that might be germane to his treatment.

As the silence between us lengthened, my body tensed. When Ainsley spoke, her words were a warning. "I'm handling this," she said. "Roy is my concern not yours. And Joanne, don't mention your theory about Roy using hallucinogens to anyone else. Words have wings, and the damage you could do to Roy's reputation through careless speculation would be irreparable."

* * *

When the dogs and I returned from our run on Easter morning, Zack was at the side of the house with the pruning shears snipping forsythia. I bent to kiss the top of his head.

"There were vases on the kitchen counter, and I figured you wanted to fill them with something," he said.

"You're not just a pretty face," I said. "There are tulips in the fridge, and the pussy willows that Maddy and Lena brought back from their school field trip are in the mud room, waiting to be snipped. The table will be glorious."

Zack grinned. "You're looking pretty glorious yourself this morning."

"It's sweat," I said. "You're experiencing an endorphin contact high."

"I'll take it," Zack said. "Spring is in the air. Pantera and Esme are panting with joy, and except for Angus, all our family will be with us today."

"The only cloud on the horizon is Roy's condition."

"Anything new on that?"

"Nothing," I said. "I'm still stewing over my call to Ainsley last night."

"You did the right thing. The standard tests for drugs in blood and urine do not include testing for hallucinogens unless doctors suspect a patient ingested something that would cause them to hallucinate. Giving Roy's doctors a possible explanation for what happened may have supplied them with a vital piece of information."

"Only if Ainsley passed it along," I said. "And I doubt that she did. She made it clear that she did not want me sullying Roy's reputation. She's shielding Roy the way he shielded her when he lied to me about her whereabouts the night Gabe died."

"They see you as an outsider," Zack said. "That relationship is too complex for us to contemplate on a beautiful Easter morning. Let's go inside where I can wipe you down, sniff your towel, snip pussy willows and jam this forsythia into vases."

I raised an eyebrow. "Are we still just talking about flowers?"

"That's up to you," Zack said.

"It will take two minutes tops to get the forsythia in water," I said. "The pussy willows can wait."

* * *

Christmas Eve and Easter morning are peak times for church attendance, and by the time Zack and I arrived, the cathedral was already full. Peter, the most organized of our children, had texted to say he and Maisie had already staked out two pews near the back of the church for our family. Taylor and Vale were each holding a squirming twin and laughing. Clearly, their reunion had been a happy one. Mieka's daughters were both servers: which meant they would play an active part in the service. Madeleine was the crucifer, so she would be carrying the cross and leading the processional, and Lena was the senior server. Charlie D already had his camera at the ready to get photos of the girls in their robes.

Charlie and Colin liked to sing, and when the service began and the choir processed up the centre aisle singing Handel's "Thine Be the Glory," the boys chimed in with their favourite — Raffi's "Peanut Butter Sandwich." Their duet was a hit in our immediate area, but when the prayers started, Charlie's and Colin's interest waned, and their dad and Charlie D took them downstairs to the playroom.

According to the prayer book Easter is a time to be "inflamed with new hope," and as the congregation sang the old hymns and I heard the promises of fresh beginnings, I felt a bloom of peace and gratitude.

When we were leaving, I noticed three young girls casting surreptitious glances at Vale. Finally, two of the girls pushed the third towards her, and the girl, blushing, asked Vale if she'd been Mandy, the teenager who committed suicide in the movie *Butterflies*. Vale said she had played that role. "It *is* Mandy," the blushing girl announced in a high and carrying voice. Suddenly Vale was surrounded by adolescents, phones in hand. The race for selfies was on.

Lena and Madeleine had been changing from their robes into their street clothes. When they joined us, and Lena saw the activity around Vale, she was clearly puzzled. "What's up?" she said.

Madeleine lowered her voice to a whisper. "Vale is famous." She shifted her gaze to Taylor. "Do you think she minds?"

"No," Taylor said. "It's part of her life."

I turned to our daughter. "It's going to part of your life too. Are you up for that?"

"As long as Vale and I go home together, I'll be fine." Taylor's expression was thoughtful. "Jo, Vale and I know how lucky we are. When we look at the pieces that had to fall into place to bring us together, it's hard not to believe in kismet. Roy Brodnitz saw my grandfather's painting *Aurora* in the window of a Manhattan gallery and felt his depression lift. Roy was grateful to have a second chance, and he wrote *The Happiest Girl*. When he was mayor, Dad spearheaded the movement to bring the Saskatchewan Production Studios back to life. *The Happiest Girl* was filmed here in Regina, and Vale and I met the person we were meant to be with forever." Our daughter's lips curved into a self-mocking smile. "And all because Roy Brodnitz glanced into a gallery window and saw a painting."

Throughout the service, Roy had been on my mind. Vale had worked with him, and Taylor regarded him as a cherished friend. They deserved to know what had happened. But when I looked at Taylor's face, I knew I couldn't shatter her quiet joy, so I swallowed hard and squeezed her shoulder.

* * *

As exceptional as everyone in our family believed the twins to be, their behaviour fell well within the normal range for eighteen-month-olds. Like the girl with the little curl right in the middle of her forehead, when Charlie and Colin were good, they were very, very good, but when they were bad — look out. Thankfully, Easter turned out to be one of their very, very good days. The weather was mild enough to have the egg hunt outdoors, and we were on our way to the backyard when the doorbell rang. Mieka gave me a questioning look. "Aren't we all here?"

"We are, but I invited Georgie Shepherd to join us. Ben Bendure was supposed to be here too. *Sisters and Strangers* deals with much of the material about Sally Love that Ben explored in *The Poison Apple*, and I thought he and Georgie would enjoy comparing notes."

"But Ben's not coming?" Mieka said.

"No, he had to cancel. He called last night to say he'd broken his ankle."

Mieka's brow pinched with concern. "Poor Ben," she said. "A broken ankle is never fun, but at his age, bones take longer to heal. And poor Georgie Shepherd. She'll have to survive the kids, the dogs and the rest of us without a kindred spirit to turn to."

"Georgie won't be hard pressed to find a kindred spirit," I said. "Come with me, and see for yourself." From the moment Georgie walked through the door in her crisp white cotton shirt, ankle length jeans, black cardigan and

39

eye-catching Burberry trainers, handed Mieka a large festively wrapped basket filled with Bernard Callebault chocolate rabbits and said, "Which way to the egg hunt?" it was obvious that Georgie Shepherd's driver's licence might have said she was forty-four, but she had come to play.

The party was non-stop zany. The boys tore around the backyard exploring every nook and cranny and Charlie D, Peter and Georgie were their willing accomplices, running along with them, snagging eggs that were beyond reach and making certain each twin's basket was filling at the same rate. Standing on our deck in the sunshine with Mieka watching the five of them was so blissful I was almost able to forget that Roy was lying in the ICU at Royal University Hospital in Saskatoon.

"This is the first year my daughters haven't been racing around with their own baskets," Mieka said.

"They were eager to take the dogs for a walk," I said. "It's possible one of the neighbourhood kids hasn't heard yet that Maddy and Lena are going to New York for spring break."

Mieka laughed softly. "Anyone in Regina who hasn't heard about our daughters' big adventure must have been living under a rock. The girls can't stop talking about it. I just hope they aren't disappointed."

"You have tickets for *The SpongeBob Musical*," I said. "How could they possibly be disappointed?"

"A Broadway show is exciting," Mieka agreed. "And proof as if I needed it that my daughters are growing up. They're great kids, but sometimes I wish the merry-go-round didn't go round so quickly. Charlie D and I didn't do the Easter Rabbit at our house this year. We decided the girls were probably past that."

"The Easter Rabbit came to Peter and Maisie's," I said. "Pete told Maisie and the boys how when you guys were little, the bunny always got into the flour canister at our place and when you woke up there were rabbit tracks all over the place."

"Dad always threatened to turn that rabbit into stew," Mieka said.

I smiled at the memory. "This year I guess Peter got to be the bad guy."

Mieka shook her head. "Charlie and Colin may be very young, but they know Peter is a softie. Maisie's a trial lawyer — I imagine she was the one who held up the stewpot and brandished the big spoon."

* * *

Lunch was a noisy, happy affair. It was a good meal — all the standard spring family favourites. Conversation topics were light, and there was plenty of laughter. Every so often, Zack or Georgie would glance my way and, remembering Roy, our smiles would fade. What had happened to Roy Brodnitz on the island was beyond imagining, and his future was uncertain, but the combination of a spring dinner with kids and dogs and the prospect of chocolate rabbits augmenting Mieka's lemon meringue pie for dessert lifted our spirits.

Madeleine and Lena had shopped, tobogganed, skated and just hung out with Taylor and Vale over the Christmas holidays, but the selfie scene after church had perplexed our granddaughters. Vale was no longer just one of Taylor's friends, she was a celebrity, and when the four of them sat across from one another at lunch, I noticed that the easy camaraderie they shared in December had given way to an anxious hesitancy from Madeleine and Lena.

Vale noticed too. She and Taylor made several attempts to ease the tension, but when it continued, Vale rose from her place at the table and went over to the girls. "Is something the matter?" she said.

Madeleine lowered her eyes. "No. It's just — suddenly you're famous, and we don't know how to act."

"A lot is changing for Taylor and me," Vale said. "But I'm the same. I'm still a beanpole, I still have freckles" — Vale took a strand of hair between her thumb and forefinger — "and I'm still a ginger. Let's just go back to the way we were before. Would that be okay?"

Madeleine and Lena exchanged a quick glance. Lena said, "Yes, because there's a lot we want to ask you — like do you know any of the actors in *Riverdale*, because *Riverdale* is made in Vancouver, and your movie is being made in Vancouver, and you're all actors, so we thought maybe . . ."

"Actually, I do know the actors who play Archie and Veronica," Vale said.

"And Jughead?" Lena said.

Vale nodded. "He's a really nice guy. We had coffee together last week."

Lena mock-swooned, and they all laughed.

"Instead of me just telling you about everybody, why

don't you visit me in Vancouver and see for yourself," Vale said. "Taylor's coming at the end of the month. If it's okay with your mum and Charlie D, we'll get you tickets on the same flight. I've been working, so I really haven't seen much of the city. It would be fun to spend the weekend exploring with you, and I promise that you will not leave Vancouver until you've spent serious time with Jughead."

Lena's eyes were saucers. "That would be epic." She cringed. "Sorry, Maddy, I know you hate that word."

"I don't hate the word. I just think you should use it more carefully." Maddy's grin came slowly, but it was wide. "Like right now," she said. "Going to Vancouver to meet the cast of Riverdale would be epic. It might even be beyond epic."

* * *

Georgie stayed behind to help clean up. When the dishwasher was chugging and the pots and pans were scrubbed and drying on the dish rack, I poured us each a glass of iced tea. I handed Georgie hers. "Let's take a breather," I said.

The grandkids and their parents were out in the backyard, so Georgie and I sat at the butcher block table.

"We haven't mentioned Roy today," I said. "Have you heard anything?"

Georgie shook her head. "Ainsley isn't taking my calls," she said. "I've been in touch with other members of the crew, but they say that Ainsley's shut them out. She's the only one who speaks to Roy's doctors, and she's not sharing information."

"That doesn't seem right," I said. "Roy has good friends on the crew."

"Including me," Georgie said. "Not knowing what's going on is unsettling."

"Everything about this is unsettling," I said. "Last night when Ben Bendure called to let me know he couldn't come to lunch he told me that the night before, he'd had a phone call from Roy."

Georgie tensed. "The night before last?" she repeated. "Did Ben remember the time?"

"No," I said. "Ben had been sleeping, and he was groggy. He did remember that it was dark outside. Ben said Roy was incoherent — talking obsessively about decay and the intensity of colours and the white light that was holding everything together. When Ben tried to get Roy to clarify, he became agitated, and the call ended.

"Yesterday morning, Ben tried to phone Roy, but there was no answer. Ben assumed Roy had been drinking the night before and was sleeping it off, but later when he checked his phone, Ben saw that Roy had sent him at least a dozen exquisite close-up photos of trees, undergrowth and rotting stumps. Ben said the photos were as intricate as a tapestry."

"Roy must have taken those photos in the afternoon, but a few hours later he was on all fours, scratching at the earth, barely human." Georgie leaned towards me. "What could have happened to him in those hours?"

"Ben thinks it's possible that Roy used a hallucinogen and had a bad reaction."

"Roy wouldn't have used drugs."

"That was my response too," I said. "But apparently Ben and Roy had talked frequently in the past few weeks. Roy was suffering from a severe case of writer's block. He was desperate, and Ben's theory is that he might have tried to use a hallucinogen to get past the block."

"Why didn't Roy talk to one of us?" Georgie was clearly exasperated. "We could have made sure he got the help he needed. Jo, I can't believe he wouldn't have told Ainsley."

"He might have," I said. "I made the mistake of calling Ainsley last night and telling her about Ben's theory. I thought if Roy had used a hallucinogen, the doctors treating him should be aware of it. Ainsley reminded me that Roy was her concern, not mine, and said that if I mentioned the possibility that Roy had used drugs, the damage to his reputation would be devastating."

"I'm surprised she picked up," Georgie said. "I imagine she won't next time."

"So we wait, and we hope."

"That's about it," Georgie said. "Would you mind if I said my goodbyes and went back to the office? I'm trying to make sure I'm on top of everything."

"That makes sense," I said. "Georgie, I'm really glad you came today."

"So am I," she said. "There aren't many kids in my world. They're kind of fun, aren't they?"

"They are, and Georgie you're always welcome here. I hope you know that."

She reached out and gave me a quick hug. "Thanks for everything."

* * *

By three o'clock, the Kilbourn-Dowhanuiks and the Crawford-Kilbourns, churched, fed and ready for the next adventure, had headed home with leftovers and fancy chocolate rabbits, but Zack and I had asked Vale and Taylor to stay behind so we could tell them about Roy.

It was a task I did not relish. Both women were fond of Roy. As Taylor said, Roy had brought Vale and her together, but even before that he had found a special place in her life. When he learned of the connection with Desmond Love, Roy invited our family to New York to see *The Happiest Girl.* The trip was Zack and my present to Taylor when she graduated from high school. Roy had been a generous host, and he ruefully admitted, "Taylor had me at a glance." As a dancer who left Regina at seventeen with Ainsley Blair to begin his career in musical theatre, Roy's advice to Taylor about building a career in the arts was solid, and she and Roy stayed in touch.

Since grade eleven, Taylor had planned to attend OCAD, an art, design and media university in Toronto, but when September rolled around, our daughter announced she'd decided to take a gap year. Taylor had inherited her birth mother's prodigious talent as a visual artist, and at seventeen, her work was already being purchased by knowledgeable collectors. Roy pointed out that Taylor already had the career that for many first-year students at OCAD would still be a distant dream, and there were other possibilities she might consider.

That winter the film adaptation of *The Happiest Girl* was being produced in Regina, and Roy encouraged Taylor to take advantage of the opportunity to see how a movie was made. Filmmaking was a new world for Taylor, and she was intrigued. When she and Vale Frazier, who played the lead role in the film, developed a romantic relationship, another new world opened for our daughter.

As the four of us sat at our kitchen table now, and I told Vale and Taylor about Roy's disappearance on the island, his bizarre behaviour when the crew found him and the decision to airlift him to Royal University Hospital in Saskatoon, I attempted to keep my tone matter of fact. But there was no way to minimize the horror of what had happened, and the expressions on the young women's faces shifted from concern, to disbelief and finally to shock. When I said that Roy's prognosis was uncertain, Vale reached across the table to take Taylor's hand.

"They have no idea what happened?" Vale said.

"None," Zack said. "The tests show he suffered a massive heart attack — clearly related to what went on in the hours he was separated from the others, but no one knows what actually transpired."

"Ben Bendure suggested one possibility," I said. When I told them, Taylor's head shake was vehement. "No. Roy told me he came close to destroying his life with drugs. He would never have gone down that path again."

"He might have believed LSD would lead him down a different path — a positive one," Zack said.

"Ben told me something that bears that out," I said. "The afternoon Roy was lost, he sent Ben photos: close-ups of forest undergrowth that were much like Ernest Lindner's work."

Taylor's dark eyes were troubled. "Last week Roy called and asked me about magic realism in visual art. It had been so long since I'd heard from him, I jumped at the chance to connect. I told him I had a book about Lindner's life and work, and I'd bring it by his apartment. I was hoping that Roy would invite me in and we could talk the way we used to, but he just took the book, thanked me and closed the door." The smile she gave Vale was rueful. "Now I wish I had the book. There aren't many illustrations in it, but there are enough to give you an idea of what we're talking about."

"All is not lost," Zack said. "We have some limited-edition prints of Lindner's work. I know exactly where they are, and I'll get them."

"Jo and Ernest Lindner were friends for years," Taylor said. When my daughter's lips twitched mischievously, I knew she was trying to lighten the mood. "Jo, why don't you tell Vale how you met Ernie?"

I turned towards Vale. "It was not my finest hour," I said. "It was during a provincial election, and I was door-knocking in the Nutana area of Saskatoon because they were short of volunteers. On the voters list Ernie had listed his occupation as painter. When I knocked at his door on 9th Street, I explained who I was and then I said, 'Exactly what do you paint?' Ernie invited me in, and when I saw the art on his walls, I could hardly breathe. He made me a cup of the best coffee I've ever had, and we talked about his life in Austria and his art."

"Until he retired, Ernest worked as an instructor at a technical collegiate," Taylor said. "His work has the kind of precision you see in architectural drafting."

Zack wheeled back in and placed the print of Ernie's painting of a decaying tree stump on the table. When Vale leaned in to look more closely, her shining auburn hair fanned across her pale cheek, and it was clear why the camera loved her. Her study of the drawing was intense. "He takes you inside that tree stump," she said finally. She straightened. "We're still in our world, but our world has expanded to include the colours and the textures of the world inside that stump."

"The magic is all around us," I said. "That's what Roy wanted to show in *Sisters and Strangers*."

"And he was doing it," Vale said. "That scene at Saugeen Reserve where Sally and her father are sitting on the hill overlooking the lake and the band of wild horses suddenly appears and streaks downhill to the water is amazing. But it's the way Roy shows how Sally perceives the scene that makes it magic. The horses are just a few metres away from her and from her viewpoint the horses' coats really are so black they're almost blue, and their hooves really do move so fast they barely touch earth." As Vale described the scene, her turquoise eyes shone and her face was radiant. "And then," she said, "comes that heart-stopping moment of absolute silence and Sally sees that the blue horses truly have lifted into the air and they are flying. Of course, the moment doesn't last. When the horses reach the lake, they're earthbound again — just ordinary horses, splashing and whinnying. But Sally knows that what she saw was real."

Vale's voice, always low and husky, had a thrilling intensity. "Roy knew how to make an audience feel the wonder. That was his gift. I understand why he would risk everything to have the gift returned to him."

Her words struck a nerve with our daughter. "What would you do if you knew you could never act again?" Taylor said, and there was a note of urgency in her voice.

Vale looked puzzled, and I realized that for her the answer to Taylor's question was self-evident. "I'd die."

Taylor's dark eyes searched her lover's face. "What about us?"

"If I couldn't act, there'd be no 'me' for you to love," Vale said. She shook herself as if shedding the words she'd just uttered. "I'm sorry, Taylor. I thought you understood that." She offered Taylor her hand. "Now, we really should get back to the lake if we're going to take that walk around the bay."

CHAPTER THREE

After I promised we'd call if there was news of Roy and we said our goodbyes, Zack and I watched at the door until Taylor's Volvo turned onto Albert Street.

"Vale is a complex young woman," I said.

"She is," Zack said. He turned his chair towards the hall, but he didn't move. "Do you think Vale loves Taylor?"

"I do," I said after a moment's consideration. "They've been involved for over a year. I don't think Vale knows how to handle her own feelings. She hasn't experienced much love in her life. Her father moved to Los Angeles when Vale was a baby. He's an actor in a soap opera. He married again and has a new family. Vale's mother is an actor in New York. She and Vale shared an apartment, but I think that, except for her agent, Vale's always been pretty much on her own."

"When Vale said that if she couldn't act, there would be nothing in her for Taylor to love, I thought of the first night she came to our house for dinner and told that harrowing story about how she was playing Tiny Tim in *A Christmas Carol* and the actor playing Bob Cratchit was carrying her on his shoulders, and he was so drunk, he lost his grip and let her fall to the stage."

"And how before she was carried offstage and taken to the hospital she adlibbed a line about Jesus always being especially gentle with children because he knew how easily children break," I said.

Zack had a reputation as a courtroom Prince of Darkness, but he was vulnerable to children. "Seven years old and already the consummate professional," he said, and I could hear the pain in his voice. "Vale deserves to know love. And if anyone can show her what love is, it's our daughter."

"I agree." I yawned. "I think the last forty-eight hours just caught up with me. I could use a nap."

We slept for an hour and then we made love. When we'd finished, Zack drew me close and said, "No matter how bad things get, this always makes life better."

"All is for the best in this best of all possible worlds?"

"No," Zack said. "This world is far from perfect, but when you and I are together like this, it's pretty damn good."

We settled back, and we must both have been half-dozing when I heard Charlie D calling our names. I slipped into my robe and still barefoot, made my way up the hall.

Charlie D took one look at me and lowered his eyes. "I'm sorry, I should have rung the doorbell."

"From the time you were old enough to reach our door-bell, you never rang it. You just walked in like everyone else in the family. So what's up?"

Charlie D sighed. "Nothing good. A buddy of mine is part of the crew that went up to Emma Lake. They've been taking shifts at the hospital with Ainsley. You should sit down."

"What is it?" I said, ignoring his invitation to sit.

"Roy Brodnitz died an hour ago." Charlie D put his arm around me. "I wish it hadn't ended this way for him."

"So do I," I said. "Zack should know what's happened. Let me get him."

When Zack and I returned, Charlie D was sitting at the kitchen table. "So what can you tell us?" Zack said.

Charlie shrugged. "Not much. Roy had a second heart attack a couple of hours ago, and it killed him. The doctors are very interested in what caused his total disintegration before he had his first heart attack. Roy had a thorough physical examination for Living Skies's insurance company less than a month ago, and he was in excellent health. They want to do an autopsy, but Ainsley Blair is fighting it."

"She and Roy worked together for thirty years," I said. "He told me she was like a part of him, and he of her. I understand why she's protective."

"But what is she protecting him from?" Zack said. "An autopsy is a fact-finding tool. The doctors simply want to find out what happened that afternoon; I expect the Prince Albert police are curious about that too. I don't get why Ainsley doesn't want answers. People confronted with a sudden and seemingly inexplicable death are always left with a hundred small questions that boil down to one big question: 'How could I have stopped this from happening?' More often than not, the autopsy report shows there was nothing they could have done. They still mourn, but they're at least freed from guilt." Zack's tone was lawyerly; even when something affected him he still stuck to facts.

"Ainsley wouldn't find much comfort in knowing what caused Roy's death," Charlie D said. "He died of a broken heart. The prospect of living without writing killed him."

"Where's that coming from?" I said.

"Roy's own words," Charlie D said. "When I leave here, I'm going to the station and my producer and I are somehow going to edit the three hours of raw, soul-baring material we recorded into an interview that will give our listeners insight into a decent, talented, tortured man who fought the good fight and lost. And I honestly do not know how we're going to do it. If all that mattered was ratings, we could do a quick clean-up of what we have and use as much time as it took to air the gut-wrenching account of a human being's disintegration. It would be a grabber, and it would probably increase the ratings in the U.S. markets we already have and attract more."

"But Roy deserves better than that," Zack said.

"I agree," Charlie D said. "And we can do that too. We can edit out all the blood, pain, sinew and tears and give our listeners a nice sanitized interview to listen to as they go about their daily business."

"Maybe you're overthinking this," I said. "Roy told me once that on a movie set the writer is the eunuch in the harem.

I suspect that's equally true after the production is finished. For an audience, the writer is just a name on the credits. I imagine most of your listeners won't even have heard of Roy."

"That would be true in most cases," Charlie D said. "But Roy Brodnitz made himself the story. Roy's story is classic: his lover dies; he descends into the pit of depression; he indulges in risky behaviours; and just when he's on the point of complete self-destruction, he sees Des Love's painting of the northern lights in a gallery window and something in that painting heals him. He writes *The Happiest Girl*, it's a megahit on Broadway and it's just been made into what promises to be a megahit movie."

"But the story doesn't end there," I said.

"No, and that's where I need a little guidance, Jo. When I'm interviewing someone, I feel this jolt when I know that what they're saying comes from a place that they may not be aware of themselves. It's a rush, and usually I just try to run with it and keep them talking, but from the moment Roy opened up about how he felt when you agreed to collaborate with him on *Sisters and Strangers*, he couldn't stop.

"He was back in the moment, and when he talked about the day he saw *Flying Blue Horses*, and you told him the story behind Sally's painting, and later when you introduced him to Ben Bendure, and the two of you started working together, he was exuberant."

"But the exuberance didn't last," I said.

"No, when he started telling me about Gabe Vickers's death and the aftermath, Roy was overwhelmed by despair. He said he had been relieved when Vickers died because

Vickers had caused Ainsley so much pain, but after Vickers's death, something went dead in him. He couldn't write *Sisters and Strangers* the way it had to be written. He was empty."

Waves of relief, frustration and deep sorrow washed over me. "Since before Christmas, I've believed Roy was angry at me because he thought I'd suggested Ainsley was implicated somehow in Gabe's death. If Roy had told me the truth, we could have worked it out. All that suffering, and now it's too late."

"Don't go there, Jo," Zack said, and his voice was gentle but forceful. "We did our best, You and Taylor and I all tried to get through to Roy, but nothing worked. Taylor was hurt, but Joanne and I were afraid. We had both been with one of my law partners on the day he committed suicide. My partner said he felt the grace had been withdrawn from his life, and he drove his car off the boat dock at the lake where we all have cottages. He'd locked the doors, and there was no way to save him."

I picked up on Zack's parallel. "Charlie D, during that interview did you sense that Roy Brodnitz had reached that point?"

"I did. What's worse, so did Roy. He was despondent, but he kept on talking. It was agony to listen to him. Twice I asked him if he wanted to stop and finish the interview at a later date. He refused. He was obsessed. He kept repeating the words 'Something was taken.' Finally and mercifully, he stopped talking. I walked him out of the studio, and now I have to edit what I have. Any suggestions?"

"You could cut the interview at the point before Roy realizes the gift has been withdrawn," I said.

Charlie D stood. "I could, but as you said yourself, Jo, that's not where the story ends. Roy wrote his own ending to the story that afternoon on the island. And what he did there deserves to be acknowledged too."

After our son-in-law left, Zack looked at me. "So what do you think?"

"There's no easy answer to this one," I said. "Charlie D is a compassionate man, but he's ethical. No matter what he does, he'll feel he made the wrong choice, and he'll suffer. So will Taylor and Vale and Ben when I tell them that Roy's dead. So will we, when we remember the Roy who took such delight in showing us how good it felt to be alive in the city he loved. And I can't even begin to imagine what Ainsley's going through and what's ahead for her."

Zack wheeled over to me. "Time to go outside, look at the forsythia and take some deep breaths."

The news about Roy was cruel, and I was grateful that Vale was with Taylor when I delivered it. Taylor said she and Vale were planning to have an early dinner, then build a bonfire on the beach and watch the sun set. The image of the two young women building a fire together as the sun dipped towards the horizon resonated with me. "I think that's a fitting way to honour Roy's memory," I said.

"I hope so," Taylor said, and her voice was strong. "No matter what happens in the future, Vale and I will both always be grateful to Roy for bringing us together."

* * *

When I called Ben, he was angry, not at Roy but at himself, for not picking up on the fact that Roy was in dangerously deep waters emotionally.

"I might have helped him," he said. "I've been there myself. I had great success in my twenties. When I hit thirty, it was as if the well dried up. I started a dozen projects — all execrable. I thought my life was over. I considered suicide. Instead, I decided to finish my degree and become a high school teacher. I liked teaching. I was content with my life. On my fortieth birthday, I woke up with an idea that ended in an Oscar nomination, and I've been making documentaries ever since. Some failed, some succeeded, but each of them enriched my life. I wish Roy could have had that chance."

"So do I," I said.

When I ended my call with Ben, Zack wheeled in and handed me a martini.

"You are the best," I said. "As Angus would say, I'm feeling stabby."

Zack narrowed his eyes. "I never quite got that — does it mean you feel stabbed or that you feel as if you want to stab?"

"Both," I said, and the sip I took from my martini was a large one.

* * *

Luckily, my glass was still half full when Georgie Shepherd arrived. She didn't waste time on preamble. "I assume you've heard the news about Roy."

"I have, and I've been dealing with the fallout. I haven't had a chance to process everything that's happened."

"Well start processing," she said. "Can I come in? Because I just got off the phone with Ainsley, and you and I have some decisions to make pronto."

I touched her arm. "I'm sorry," I said. "I was taken aback. Come in. Zack's in the kitchen. Shall I call him?"

Georgie eyed my martini enviously. "I could use one of those."

"Make yourself comfortable in the living room, and I'll bring you one."

Zack had just started assembling his new favourite dish, a Cobb salad with chicken, so after I explained the situation and he poured Georgie's martini, I left him to it and joined Georgie in the living room.

When she saw the martini, she beamed and took a large sip. "That hit the spot," she said. "Now there are decisions to be made."

"What kind of decisions?"

"Let me lay out the situation. As tragic as it is, Roy's accident doesn't change the facts: the first day of principal photography is still Monday, June 11, and there are still serious problems with the script."

"But you'll write the script now, won't you?" I said. "That's why you came to Regina."

"Yes, I'll be writing the script, but Ainsley has decided to bring someone in to replace me as executive producer."

"She has a production manager," I said. "Fawn Tootoosis has been part of every decision that's been made since Gabe died."

"And Fawn knows what she's doing," Georgie said. "Twenty-five years of freelance industry experience as a producer, production executive, line producer and production manager, and hundreds of hours producing prime-time TV series and feature-length projects. Fawn is doing a bang-up job for us, and everybody likes working with her."

"So what's the rationale for replacing her?"

"Ainsley says that to complete this project without Roy, she's going to need the support of someone she's known and worked with for years. Buzz Wells fits the bill, and Ainsley wants to get him on board."

"I appreciate Ainsley's need for support," I said, "but bringing someone else in at this stage is an insult to Fawn."

"Agreed, but Ainsley doesn't see it that way. She says she's not firing Fawn; she's giving her an opportunity. Ainsley says working with Buzz Wells will put an international stamp on Fawn's résumé which so far has been largely Canadian."

"If that's the case, what's the problem?"

"The problem is Buzz Wells. He is freaking Rumpelstiltskin." She took another large sip from her drink.

Despite everything, I laughed. "Rumpelstiltskin? Where did that come from?"

"I don't know," Georgie said. "But many people in the

industry seem to believe Buzz has the power to turn straw into gold."

"But you don't want him touching our straw."

"Not much gets by you, does it?" Georgie said. "But you're right. We don't want Buzz's fingerprints on this."

"If Ainsley's directing, and you're writing the script, you'll be able to maintain control."

"I've worked with Buzz before," Georgie said. "He started as a writer and rose through the ranks. Writers' rooms are Darwinian — nature red in tooth and claw — survival of the fittest. But even in that less-than-salubrious atmosphere, Buzz was always a standout.

"I was a writer on a couple of series where he was the showrunner. He always got decent work out of me and the other writers, but only after he'd broken us. I guess I called him Rumpelstiltskin because, like Rumpel, if Buzz doesn't get his way, his face turns red, and he stomps his boot until his opposition's head cracks open."

"Why would Ainsley want him?"

"Because as soon as Buzz heard about Roy, he called and volunteered to take over. Plus, she and Buzz used to be married, and Ainsley knows he'll get the job done."

"Wow. Ainsley's two husbands were Rumpelstiltskin and Gabe Vickers. She's an intelligent, gifted, attractive woman, why would she marry men like that?"

Georgie's laugh was short and derisive. "Riddle me this one, Batman. Why does anybody marry anybody?"

"Point taken," I said. "So what do we do?"

"We need to talk Ainsley down, and I think it can be done. Buzz offered her a life preserver at a time when she was vulnerable. Luckily for us, Buzz can't get here for three weeks, so Fawn and you and I have time to convince Ainsley that we don't need Rumpelstiltskin. Here's what I propose. The production schedule is moving along without a hitch. Fawn just has to keep it moving, and she can do that with one hand tied behind her back. The big problem is the script or lack thereof, but I believe that together, you and I can handle that."

Rattled, I leaned back in my chair. "Georgie, I'm not a scriptwriter. I taught political science. I know how to do research and write academic papers and political speeches. I've written some scripts for a series the producer privately referred to as 'Issues for Dummies' — small nibbles at big questions like the power of the religious right, the challenges to women in politics and the Canadian judicial system, but nothing creative. The division of labour between Roy and me was clear-cut: I told him the history of the Ellards and the Loves and introduced him to people who knew Sally and me, and of course, Taylor was a link. Sally gave birth to her, but I was raising her. Roy felt that understanding how Taylor had come to terms with what was certainly an extraordinary situation would give him insights into our relationships with one another. Roy and I talked, I answered his questions, and when he felt he had what he needed, Roy wrote the script."

"And that's all I'm asking from you, Joanne," Georgie said. "I wish you and I had more time to sort this out, but

I couldn't approach you until Roy said he needed help, and he never did."

"If Roy had just opened up, everything could have been different."

"You think Roy's death was connected with his work?"

I hesitated, and then set down my glass. "I know it was — at least indirectly. This afternoon, Charlie Dowhanuik told me about an interview he did with Roy."

Georgie listened to my account without comment. When I finished, she slapped her forehead with her palm. "Roy never should have signed the contract to write *Sisters and Strangers*. Thanks to Gabe's genius in putting together a production, there was a very tight deadline on the project, and Roy couldn't meet it. He's a romantic — like Keats, Shelley or Whitman. And the conditions have to be exactly right for romantics to spin their shining web. Keats had his nightingale; Shelley, his skylark; and Whitman, his own ecstatic self. When the moment was right, they wrote. Des Love's painting, *Aurora*, gave Roy his moment, and he wrote *The Happiest Girl*. Adapting the play that he had created with such euphoria simply extended the right moment for Roy. Did he ever tell you how long it took him to write that screenplay?"

"No."

"Three weeks," Georgie said. "Exactly the same amount of time it took Edna O'Brien to write *The Country Girls*. That play was so deeply ingrained in Roy that adapting it was a snap."

"But *Sisters and Strangers* was not a snap."

"Far from it. I've known Roy for fourteen years. He always saw himself as an artist. Scriptwriters like me see ourselves as carpenters, using our tools to make something worthy out of the material we've been given. When something goes wrong, we shrug our shoulders and try again, but resilience was never part of Roy's character. When something went wrong for him, he shattered. Which leads us back to the tape. Did Charlie D tell you how he's going to edit it?"

"No. When he left our place, he hadn't made up his mind. I suggested cutting the interview at the point where Roy is exuberant at the prospect of writing *Sisters and Strangers*. Charlie D said he understood my reasoning, but he felt what Roy said about the light going out for him after Gabe's death was part of the story too."

"True, but Joanne, Roy's story doesn't have to end with the light going out." When Georgie continued, her voice had new energy. "If you and I work together we can make *Sisters and Strangers* what Roy believed it could be, and the only name on the writing credit will be Roy's."

"That would mean a great deal to Ainsley," I said. "For that matter, it would mean a great deal to me. But I'm still foggy about what I have to offer."

"Facts, insights, memories, details — you were there, Joanne. All I know about your life and about Des and Sally is what's already in the script or in Roy's notes. It's not enough. Roy told both Ainsley and me that you read every word he wrote, pointed out lines that didn't ring true and suggested alternatives."

"So you'll just need me to do what I was doing with Roy?"

"That's it."

"I can do that."

"If you decide to stretch yourself, feel free to give me a hand with the writing." Georgie raised an eyebrow. "And don't give me that 'shucks, me write?' look. I read your biography of Andy Boychuk."

"That book's been out of print for years," I said. "Where did you even find a copy?"

"The Regina Public Library."

"Georgie, writing the biography of a Saskatchewan politician is very different from writing a six-episode limited TV series."

"They both use sentences," Georgie said curtly. "Can you be at my office tomorrow morning at nine?"

"I'll be there."

CHAPTER FOUR

The Living Skies offices are in the same building as the Saskatchewan Production Studios where Roy and I shared the writers' room. The production studios are within easy walking distance of our house, and the morning was brisk enough to put a spring in my step. I arrived early, in time to pick up notes that I thought might be helpful in my meeting with Georgie.

Sixteen years earlier the Fine Arts building of the old University of Regina campus had been gutted and reconstructed as a movie and TV studio facility. The three sound studios were state of the art, but parts of the building, including the wing of classrooms that included the space now used as the writers' room were left untouched, and they had retained their homely early twentieth-century charm.

Movie equipment is expensive, and security in the sound studios was tight, but because *Aurora*, the Desmond Love painting Roy credited with saving his sanity, now hung in our office, the door was always kept locked. That morning as I walked toward the writers' room, I saw that the door was open — just inches, but enough to quicken my pulse. I continued down the hall, and for a few moments, I stood on the threshold, holding my breath, listening. The only sound I heard was the ticking of the old classroom clock on the wall. "Is anyone here?" I said. When there was no response, I stepped inside.

My eyes travelled immediately to the space where *Aurora* hung. The painting was in its place. I moved further into the room. The blinds were drawn, but there was enough light for me to see that someone was lying on the couch where Roy slept if he worked far into the night. When I moved closer, I recognized the sleeper as Ainsley. She had covered herself in the trench coat Roy kept on the hook by the door in case of a change in the weather. I tiptoed out of the room, closed the door behind me and started down the hall, deeply shaken by my glimpse into Ainsley's solitary pain.

* * *

Gabe Vickers left his mark on our city in many ways, and one of the most striking was the giant, light-filled office he'd had built in what had once been a warehouse at the back of the original Fine Arts building. The space was large, 10,000 square feet, but Vickers had big plans for his production company, and he wanted a showcase. Under the soaring ceilings, every piece of the office's infrastructure was in plain sight: steel beams, trusses, ducts, huge concrete planks — everything painted in primary colours. The space evoked a child's Meccano set and sent a clear message: the tools for creativity are all around us; use them.

Georgie Shepherd's office was glass-walled, and the furnishings, like all the fixtures in Living Skies, were sleek and functional. Georgie was on her phone, but when she saw me, she beckoned me in and indicated that I sit in the chair across from her.

After she finished her call, she groaned. "More bad news if we hadn't had enough," she said. "Ainsley's disappeared. The crew were all staying at the same hotel, and this morning, Ainsley wasn't in her room; she wasn't in the hotel restaurant, and she hadn't checked out. Nobody has a clue where she is."

"I do," I said. "She's down the hall, asleep on the couch in the writers' room."

Georgie rolled her eyes. "You're kidding."

"No. I arrived early, and there were some notes I needed, so I went to the writers' room. The door was open. I stepped inside, saw Ainsley, took the notes and left."

"She didn't hear you?"

I shook my head. "No, she was asleep the whole time."

Georgie picked up her phone. "I'll call Nick and let him know Ainsley's here."

Nick Kovacs was the lighting director on the film. He

and Zack had been poker buddies for years, and Taylor and I were very fond of him and his daughter. Rough-hewn, large-featured and burly, Nick had the slow deliberate step of a man whose life has been spent in hard physical labour. Fate had dealt Nick his share of punishing blows, but Zack said that no matter how tough life got, Nick never took a dive, and he never threw in the towel.

His parents had died within months of each other, leaving Nick, who was in his graduating year of high school, to care for his three younger brothers and keep Kovacs Electric, the family business, afloat. After graduation, Nick took a year off to ensure that the business and his brothers were on solid ground and then earned a diploma in electrical engineering from Saskatchewan Polytechnic. During the years when the province's film industry thrived, Nick worked closely with lighting designers on films and TV shows. It was a first-rate apprenticeship, and after the production companies decamped, Nick continued to learn. Kovacs Electric was now a large and successful company that provided lighting for film, theatre, rock and pop tours, corporate launches and TV and industrial shows. Nick had been the lighting designer for *The Happiest Girl* and was now in charge of lighting *Sisters and Strangers.*

It was impossible for me not to hear Georgie's end of the conversation, and I was struck by the intimacy in her voice and by the fact that she closed off the call by saying, "I really enjoyed our dinner last night. Next time, it's my turn."

After she slipped the phone back in her bag, she gave me a half smile. "So now you know about Nick and me."

"I do," I said. "And I'm happy for you both. Nick's a terrific guy. He and Zack go way back."

"I know — Chloe's told me all about it."

"So you've met Nick's daughter."

"Actually, Chloe brought us together. Nick came into the office one day and saw me scrapbooking." Georgie shot me a warning look. "Don't say a word. Scrapbooking is a great antidote to stress, a commodity that is never in short supply around here. Anyway, it was just before Valentine's Day and Nick said he wanted to get his fourteen-year-old daughter a special Valentine's gift, and he thought she might be interested in what I was doing. I volunteered to help her get started. After work that day, Nick drove me out to the east end to pick up some supplies and then we went to his house to surprise Chloe. Jo, she was so excited. As soon as I took off my boots and jacket, she and I started making Valentines. We stopped to eat and then went right back at it. Nick couldn't stop smiling."

"He's absolutely devoted to Chloe," I said. "And finding activities that work for her is tricky. She's very creative, but she becomes frustrated if she can't get the result she hopes for."

"And with scrapbooking she can choose her own pace," Georgie said. "Before I met Chloe, Nick explained the situation."

When she was seven, Chloe had been in an accident that caused traumatic brain damage, and she still struggled with her limitations.

"But Nick said she thrives on challenges, so he keeps trying new things."

"The demands on Nick are heavy," I said. "Not that he ever complains. Zack says a lot of people think he's sacrificing his life for Chloe, but Nick doesn't see it that way. He sees Chloe as a blessing."

"She's a lovely girl," Georgie said. "And my friendship with her has been a godsend. The only people I knew when I arrived here in February were Roy and Ainsley, and by then, Roy was sinking, and Ainsley was obsessed with keeping him from going down for the third time. The rumours that *Sisters and Strangers* would be postponed indefinitely had started. And once the competition smells fear, you might as well hang up the sign that says, 'Welcome, sharks, it's feeding time.'"

"It's the same in politics," I said. "When the knives come out, it's hard to retain a sunny view of humanity."

"I guess that's why my relationship with Chloe is so important to me," Georgie said. "She makes me remember I'm human. Just watching how proud she is of learning to scrapbook makes me feel good. And she needs me. The school she attends has support for special needs students, but Chloe has all the urges of any fourteen-year-old, and she didn't know who to talk to about them.

"Her teachers at school didn't seem to be an option. She didn't want to talk to Nick because he worries so much about her already, and their housekeeper, Mrs. Szabo, is terrific, but she's well into her seventies and very old school, so Chloe was shy about asking her. Chloe is menstruating, so she understands that, but she has questions about the new feelings in her body, and I try to give her serious answers."

"I'm glad you're there for her."

"So is Nick and so am I, but right now, you and I need to get to work. Let's go to the Courtyard. We can have coffee, and with all the plants around and the light from the sky-lights, life always seems brighter there."

"We could use an infusion of brightness," I said. "But we need privacy and the Courtyard's always crowded."

"Not today. We gave everyone an extra day off for the Easter weekend. I'm trying to store up some good karma with our employees for when we start shooting, and the sev-enteen-hour days start."

Charlie D's text came just as we'd settled in with our cof-fee at one of the glass-topped café tables in the area where the staff of Living Skies ate and visited. I glanced at the text. "The interview airs at eleven," I said. "Charlie D says he did the intro, then played the interview with Roy and cut it just after Roy started to crash. Charlie wrote and delivered the closing himself and he thinks we'll be okay with it."

"Fingers crossed," Georgie said. "Are you going to tell Taylor to listen?"

"Like the rest of us, she and Vale are hurting. They should hear the interview. I'll text her, and then you and I can get started."

For the next hour and a half, Georgie made notes as we talked through the shining threads Roy had started to bring together in episode three, and we floated ideas about how to pick up the strands and continue weaving the narrative to a conclusion. At eleven o'clock, we tuned in to the show, just in time to hear Oliver Jones's cool and carefree "Tippin' Home from Sunday School," the music that introduced the second hour of *Charlie D in the Morning*.

Charlie D's dark honey voice announced that the second half of the show would be devoted to an interview he did a few weeks earlier with Roy Brodnitz, the mercurial and prodigiously gifted writer of the Broadway hit and upcoming film *The Happiest Girl* and of the six-part series *Sisters and Strangers*, the flagship for MediaNation's new dramatic programming. Then he said simply that Roy loved life, and that he had fought the good fight against his demons, but that in the end, his demons won out, and the night before, Roy Brodnitz had died of a massive heart attack.

The interview opened with Charlie D asking Roy about how *The Happiest Girl* came into being.

When Georgie and I heard Roy's gentle and expressive baritone, we looked quickly at each other and then just as hastily averted our eyes.

"If you believe in such things — and given what happened to me — I guess I have to," Roy said, "a year to the day after my husband of fourteen years died, I found the gift that saved me. For twelve months, I'd struggled with the black dog of depression. I've read that depression colonizes us, replacing what we were with more and more of itself until there is nothing left of us to hear the birds sing. There was nothing good ahead of me, and that day, I'd decided the time had come for me to jump off the carousel. I was taking a final walk along West 25th Street in Manhattan, when I glanced at the front window of a small art gallery and saw *Aurora*, the painting that changed my life. The canvas was large,

160 by 130 centimetres, and luminous with the shimmering, pulsating, radiant colours of the northern lights. That afternoon *Aurora* was delivered to my loft in Tribeca. For hours I sat watching the changing afternoon light play on the painting's vibrant bands of colour. Suddenly I realized I was hearing the birds sing again. That's when I sat down at my desk and began writing *The Happiest Girl.*"

For the next forty minutes, Charlie D led Roy through the world of wonders he and Ainsley Blair encountered in the year after *The Happiest Girl* opened. When Roy described his ecstasy the morning he first saw Sally Love's *Flying Blue Horses* and heard the story behind it, Georgie buried her face in her hands, and I swallowed hard.

The interview was almost over when Ainsley Blair appeared at the entrance to the Courtyard. Hair awry, eyes still swollen with sleep, she seemed dazed. "I can't find anybody," and then hearing Roy's voice, she startled. "That's Roy."

Georgie went over and embraced her. "It's a radio interview MediaNation put together."

Ainsley was beyond comprehending. "How could they do an interview? Roy's dead."

"It was taped weeks ago," Georgie said softly.

"Turn it off," Ainsley said. "Please."

When Georgie did as she'd asked, Ainsley became even more agitated. "How did Roy seem in the interview?"

"He seemed fine," Georgie said. "Very upbeat, very excited about *Sisters and Strangers.*"

Ainsley reached out to steady herself on the back of one of the café chairs, and Georgie said, "Why don't you join us?" When Ainsley remained frozen, Georgie guided her gently onto the chair.

"I'll get coffee," I said. I went into the office and poured another cup from the carafe.

After I returned with the coffee, Georgie said, "Ainsley was just telling me that she spent the evening at the hospital filling out forms. She walked along the riverbank near the hospital till it was daylight and then she drove back to Regina in one of the vans the company rented for the trip. I'm trying to convince her to let me take her home, so she can eat something and get some sleep."

Ainsley's eyes widened. "I can't go back to the duplex," she said, and there was an edge of hysteria in her voice. "Roy's things are still in his place on the main floor, waiting for him."

The duplex in which Ainsley and Roy had been living was another example of Gabe Vickers's forethought. He had purchased the attractive two-storey apartment building across the street from the sound studios. He and Ainsley were to occupy the apartment on the second floor, and the space on the main floor would be offered to someone working in a Living Skies production whose stay in the city would be lengthy. Gabe and Ainsley were scheduled to take possession on January 1, but by then Gabe was dead, so Ainsley had moved into the second-floor apartment and Roy was occupying the space on the main floor.

Georgie took out her phone. "Kyle Daly texted me that he and some of the other members of the crew took the early plane from Saskatoon, and he's already at the production studios. I'll text him and ask him to clear out Roy's belongings."

Ainsley seemed numb. She shook her head as if to clear it. "Tell him not to throw anything out or give anything away. I want to be able to go through Roy's things myself and decide." She frowned. "There's so much to decide."

"You don't have to make all the decisions today. And you don't have to make them alone," Georgie said. "Right now, just drink your coffee."

Ainsley tented her fingers and stared at them for a worryingly long time. "Roy faced a hard and cruel struggle," she said. "He did his best."

"He did," I said. "Our family will always be grateful that he was part of our lives. He opened new worlds for us, and he will open new worlds for every person that sees his work. He's leaving a rich legacy, Ainsley."

Ainsley's face was carved with pain. "But he didn't finish *Sisters and Strangers*."

"We'll make certain it's completed," Georgie said. "And Ainsley, the series will be what Roy wanted it to be. I promise." She turned to me. "Jo, I asked Kyle to meet us here, but Ainsley needs to eat something and get some sleep. I'm going to take her to my hotel. Would you mind waiting here for Kyle?"

"Of course not, but he'll need the keys."

"I don't know where Roy's keys are, but I have a copy," Ainsley said, and she began pulling items out of the tooled leather satchel she always carried. As the pile of business and personal care items grew, and the key did not appear, Ainsley was beside herself with frustration. She was known for her ability to remain cool and controlled in the midst of the crises that occur with regularity on film sets, but that morning she was reeling.

Finally, Georgie took the satchel from her and pulled out the keys. "Always the last place you look." Then she helped Ainsley to her feet. "Time for us to go, kiddo," she said. "Jo, I'll give you a call. Kyle won't be long. He's always Johnny-on-the-spot."

Kyle Daly was the production designer for *Sisters and Strangers*. After Roy and I agreed to collaborate, I found myself dealing with people whose titles were grand but meaningless — a phenomenon I was familiar with from political life. When I checked online for descriptions of positions in movie and TV production, I learned that the production designer's responsibility was "to facilitate the artistic director's creative vision for all locations and to produce sets that would give the film its unique visual identity."

Bafflegab. So I closed my laptop and kept my eyes open. It didn't take long to discover that Kyle's job was to identify what needed to be done and make it happen. He ran the ground game, which was exactly what I had done in dozens of political campaigns.

A slight thirty-year-old with dark blond artfully spiky hair, a broad forehead, keen eyes and a pleasing manner, Kyle was liked by everyone including me. He picked up on details that seemed minor but contributed to Roy's vision of bringing viewers into the *Sisters and Strangers* world. When we watched the Ellard/Love home movie together, Kyle noticed that the Ellards used Fiesta dinnerware for everyday meals. He ferreted out a place where he could buy original

Fiesta dinnerware in mint condition and promised me that when the movie was shot, the dishes were mine.

That day when Kyle arrived in the Courtyard, he was obviously distraught, but once again, he was sufficiently in control to have identified a need and taken care of it. "I asked one of our set guys to remove *Aurora* from the writers' room and take it over to Ainsley's. Everyone knows what that painting meant to Roy, and she'll want to keep it close," he said.

"Good thinking," I said. "And here are the keys to Roy's apartment. Do you need the address?"

"No, I've got it, but thanks." Kyle had always struck me as unflappable, but that morning he was agitated. He ran his fingers through his spiky hair several times as if to rid himself of unwelcome thoughts. "I can't believe any of this is happening," he said. "When Ainsley and I came upon Roy, I couldn't take in what I was seeing — I couldn't make myself understand that the frantic, filth-covered man Ainsley was trying to embrace was Roy. We all knew he was having emotional problems, but he was always courteous and articulate — and, of course, he was always immaculate." Kyle's handsome features contorted with grief. "No matter what was going on inside him, he never stopped being Roy Brodnitz."

"It's hard to conceive of something happening that could completely break the man we knew."

Kyle shuddered and walked away without responding.

* * *

My phone had been turned off all morning, and as soon as I got back to the house, I scrolled through the messages. I texted Charlie D telling him how much Georgie, Ainsley and our family appreciated his sensitive edit of the interview. I knew Zack would be in court, so I left a voicemail saying all was well, but that tonight would definitely be a night to forget the world, sit on the deck and catch up on the goings-on of the birds and small animals with whom we shared life on the creek.

When I called Taylor, the sadness in her voice was palpable. She and Vale had listened to Charlie D's interview with Roy, and they had both been grateful that Charlie D had not aired Roy's account of his breakdown. Vale had been in Vancouver filming when Roy's depression returned, but Taylor had been in Regina. As the darkness closed in and Roy distanced himself from us all, Taylor had tried repeatedly to get through to him. Finally, she was forced to accept the fact that Roy was beyond our reach, and all we could do was wait and hope. By the time he died, Taylor had already begun to mourn the loss of the gentle, gracious man who took such pleasure in being her confidante as she embarked on a career in the arts as he had done when he was her age.

But like all of us, Taylor had held out the hope that the Roy who had treated our family with such kindness would return. Now that hope had been dashed. Before I broke the connection, I needed reassurance. "Taylor, I know this has been a terrible blow. Are you sure you're all right?"

"I'm sure," she said. "Lawyers' Bay is always so peaceful, and Vale's here. That quote from Ernest Lindner Charlie D read at the end of the interview really helped. It seemed to express everything we were feeling."

"Georgie and I didn't listen to the end of the show," I said. "Ainsley came in. Hearing Roy's voice upset her, so we turned off the program."

"The quotation is from that book I loaned Roy," Taylor said. "I guess Roy must have mentioned it to Charlie D. It doesn't matter. What Ernest Lindner said about there being no end to anything — there is only change — was exactly the right way for Charlie D to end the interview."

"It was," I agreed. "At the end, I think Roy was searching for answers to questions Ernie had already struggled with."

"Jo, after the interview was over they played k.d. lang singing 'Hallelujah' — all six minutes and sixteen seconds of it. You and Dad should listen to it tonight. It will help." Taylor paused. "Vale and I are coming back to the city Friday morning. Vale says she needs to clear the air with Ainsley before they start work on *Sisters and Strangers*."

"This might not be the right time."

"I pointed that out to Vale, but it's her decision. She says that if she and Ainsley are to do their best work, Ainsley needs to understand that the relationship between Vale and Gabe had nothing to do with emotion, at least not on Vale's part. She's certain that if she'd turned down the 'arrangement' Gabe offered her when she auditioned, she would not have been cast as Ursula, and she knew that Ursula would be her breakthrough role."

"And Vale was prepared to let Gabe use her body that way?"

Taylor's voice was edged with anger. "She knew she could play the role of Ursula, and she knew that if she didn't agree to let Gabe Vickers use her body to perform the only sexual act he was capable of, she wouldn't get the role. Love was not a part of what Gabe did to her; neither was intimacy. The sight of Vale's body aroused him. I know it's disgusting, but don't judge her."

"Taylor, I'm not judging her. Truly, I'm not. Your dad and I are very fond of Vale, and we know how happy she makes you. She's a significant part of your life, and we want to understand her — that's all."

"Then just accept her as she is," Taylor said. "You did that with Dad. I was there in the months before you two got married. Everybody thought you were making a huge mistake. Even Mieka and Pete and Angus were worried, but you loved Dad and that was enough. And being married and being part of a family changed Zack. I'm hoping being with me can change Vale, make her see that she's more than just her talent."

"I hope that too, but Taylor, you can't count on Vale changing."

"I know, that's why I'm just going to do what you did. Accept the person I love the way she is and hope for the best." Taylor paused. "This being an adult isn't all it's cracked up to be," she said, and her wry acceptance of the slings and arrows was so much like Sally's stoic determination to meet life head-on that my throat closed.

* * *

I tried to work on the script, but it was difficult to concentrate, so I drove to Lakeview Fine Foods, and bought fresh asparagus, new potatoes and six of Don's best bone-in pork chops. As I started putting the groceries away, I realized I'd bought dinner for three. I swallowed hard — then froze two of the pork chops.

When Georgie phoned in late afternoon, she sounded tired but decisive. "Turns out Living Skies has a doctor on call. He came over, talked to Ainsley and prescribed something that seems to have done the job. She ate a bowl of soup, showered and she's now fast asleep. The cleaners are coming to Roy's place on Wednesday. As soon as they're finished, I'm moving into the lower floor of the duplex. It was my suggestion. The idea of Ainsley living alone over Roy's empty apartment was just one horror too many."

"How are you doing?" I said.

"I'm sad," she said. "Roy was too young and too good to die, but I'm hanging in. How are you doing?"

"When someone asks how he is, an Irish friend of mine always says, 'Very similar.'"

Georgie chuckled. "Very similar," she said. "I like that. Sometimes 'very similar' is the best we can hope for."

CHAPTER FIVE

Georgie and I both had reasons for deciding against working in the writers' room at the sound studios. Georgie's reason was pragmatic. Although she was now officially working solely as a writer on *Sisters and Strangers*, she had been executive producing for almost two months, and if she was at the production studios, people would be seeking her out with production questions. My reason was personal. For me the writers' room was filled with memories, not only of good times but also of times of confusion, anger and uncertainty. I knew I needed to start afresh in a new space.

On Tuesday, April 3, Georgie and I met in the home office Zack and I had organized over the Christmas holidays. The room had been the previous owners' games room, the showcase for an old and beautiful billiards table that Zack hoped they would leave behind. But the previous owners took their treasure with them, and the former games room became the repository for everything our family couldn't decide what to do with. The room was spacious; it had good natural light, and it was worth reclaiming. I called an online group that connected people with items they no longer needed to people who might use them. Within a single day, the room was bare, and Zack and I set to work.

For sentimental reasons, I had placed Sally Love's old work table in the middle of the room — not as a barrier between Zack's area and mine but as a workspace that was accessible for either or both of us when we needed to spread out. That afternoon, Georgie and I definitely needed space. She'd arrived with her laptop and a satchel that she emptied onto the table, papers and notepads spilling across the surface.

"This is everything Roy wrote for *Sisters and Strangers*, including random scrawls and notes." Georgie picked up one of the daily planner notepads Roy favoured for script-writing. "You heard Roy's voice when he talked about the beginnings of this project. A professor of mine used to say, 'Poetry tries to tell us what cannot be said.' Roy was happiest when he was on the brink of being able to show an audience something that could not be said in words. That's how it was for him when he wrote the first two episodes." Georgie handed me a copy of the script. "So let's start here — with the cold open."

"The teaser before the opening credits," I said.

Georgie slipped on her tortoiseshell reading glasses. "You read the stage directions and Joanne's lines and I'll read Sally."

1. EXT

Mist rising from a lake in cottage
country. A dab of red, pale
through the mist, grows in size and
intensity as the camera moves in
to reveal a red raft upon which two
girls are lounging. We hear their
voices before the camera moves in
close enough for us to see them.

2. EXT. RAFT

SALLY LOVE, 14, perfect tan, wet
blond hair hanging loose, yellow
bikini

JOANNE ELLARD, 15, slightly
sunburned, wet dark hair tied in
a high ponytail, modest two-piece
navy suit.

>   JOANNE
>   Panting with desire, he bent to
>   brush my lips with his . . .

>   SALLY
>   Bruise your lips — brush is lame.

>   JOANNE
>   Okay. Panting with desire, he
>   bruised my lips with his.

That's kind of violent, isn't it?

                    SALLY
He's a boy about to have sex. He's
            out of control.

                   JOANNE
Gasping, he moved his tortured
        body towards mine.

                    SALLY
You still have your bathing suits
            on.

                   JOANNE
He tore off his trunks and then
pulled off the bottom of my bathing
suit. Gasping now, he moved his
    tortured body towards mine.

                    SALLY
            That's good.
        (they're both laughing)

                   JOANNE
    So what do I do next?

                    SALLY
            (exasperated)
You grab his thing and help him
            put it in.

JOANNE

I don't want to touch his thing.

SALLY

Then I'll help him.

JOANNE

Where did you come from? Isn't it
supposed to be just me and the
boy?

SALLY

I'm your best friend. I'm always
there when you need me.

JOANNE

Do you ever think about your
parents having sex?

SALLY

Des and Nina? No! I'm pretty sure
she's frigid.

JOANNE

They would have had to do it once
or you wouldn't exist.

SALLY

Maybe that's why Nina hates me.

JOANNE

She doesn't hate you. Nina wants

you to love her the way I love
her. Give her a chance.

SALLY

You may be school-smart, but you
don't know beans about people.
Anyway, the heck with Nina and
the heck with your witch of a
mother. We don't need them. You
and I are going to lead fantastic
lives. It's like Miss Boucher
tells us at the end of every
Latin class.

JOANNE

"Amor fati, girls. Embrace your
fate!"

Joanne holds out her hand to Sally.
Both girls stand and move hand in
hand to the edge of the raft.

JOANNE and SALLY
(TOGETHER — loud and defiant)
Amor Fati! We embrace our fate!

Sally and Joanne jump off the
raft. The opening credits roll
against the image of the empty red
raft bobbing in the waves.

"Nice scene," I said.

Georgie nodded. "And effective. It does what it has to do: introduce Sally and Joanne, reveal their closeness, give the audience insight into their characters, establish the tone and the style of the series, tease a little and lay the groundwork."

"All that in a little over a page."

"And the way the camera moves in on what appears to be just a pale red splash in the mist with tiny dots of yellow and navy establishes the theme. Nothing is static. Everything is changing. The lives of Joanne and Sally will take shape before the audience's eyes."

As Georgie and I read through episode one together, I found my confidence growing. Roy had not given us a template, but he had given us a solid base on which to stand. Georgie and I were wholly engrossed in making notes when the doorbell rang. I left Georgie to the work and went to answer the door. The visitor was Kyle Daly, and his expression was grave.

"Come in," I said. "Georgie and I are just working on the script. We're about due for a coffee break if you'd like to join us."

"Thanks, but I can't stay," he said. "I'm not finished packing up Roy's things, but there's something I thought you and Georgie should see."

"We're working down the hall," I said. "Follow me."

When she saw Kyle, Georgie half rose. "What's happened now?"

Kyle took a book from his bag and handed it to me. It was the one about Ernest Lindner that we'd given Taylor.

"This was on Roy's desk," he said. "I opened it and saw that it belonged to your daughter."

I looked inside. Every page was dense with multicoloured scribbling: exclamation and question marks, numbers, symbols, stars. Nothing made sense. I passed the book to Georgie. As she leafed through the pages, her intake of breath was audible. "My God. What's this supposed to mean?"

"I have no idea," I said. "It must have meant something to Roy. He put so much pressure on the pens he used that they've ripped through some of the pages."

"I've ordered another copy of the book for your daughter," Kyle said. "The best I could get was 'used,' but the seller lists it as being in good condition."

"Thank you," I said. "Roy was very dear to Taylor. Seeing this would break her heart." I looked again at the defaced pages. "It breaks mine. Roy was such a gentle man. It's hard to imagine him doing this."

"It is," Georgie said. She frowned. "Kyle, you said that book was in Roy's apartment. That means that the 'incident' on the island wasn't the first one he'd had. But Friday when Roy arrived at Emma Lake with the location crew, he was fine, and when he called Joanne around noon, he was perfectly rational."

Kyle was clearly agitated, and he responded quickly. "Maybe he was trying to keep his condition private."

"Roy wouldn't have done that," I said. "We're all assuming he was perfectly normal on Friday morning." I held out the book. "If this was on his desk, he would have seen it, and he would have been horrified at what he'd done and sought help."

Georgie's face was troubled. "Joanne's right. Kyle, the man you and Ainsley describe finding on the island had lost all sense of himself — people don't simply drift in and out of a state like that."

"I guess when drugs are involved, all bets are off," Kyle said.

"So you believe drugs caused the state Roy was in when you and Ainsley found him?"

Kyle's pain at confronting that possibility was palpable. "As Georgie said, rational people don't simply drift in and out of insanity." He started for the exit. "I should let you two get back to work. Joanne, I'll take the book with me. I'll make certain it's destroyed, and I'll get the replacement to you as soon as it arrives."

I tightened my grip on the book. "Thanks but I'm going to hang on to this."

Kyle extended his hand towards me. "But Taylor . . ."

"I'll do the right thing for Taylor," I said. "I promise you that."

When I returned after seeing Kyle out, Georgie shot me a questioning look. "Why did you insist on keeping the book?"

"The idea that Roy would leave the book he had defaced out in plain view doesn't make sense. It's a loose end, and Zack always says, 'Never let go of a loose end until you're certain it leads nowhere.'"

CHAPTER SIX

In the next few days, a semblance of order seemed to assert itself in our lives. Without explanation, Ainsley rejected Fawn Tootoosis's offer to organize a private memorial gathering for Roy's friends and colleagues. Later in the week she sent an email saying that when she could get away she would take Roy's cremains to Lennox, Massachusetts, where he and Lev-Aaron had had their summer home and where they had already purchased a niche in a columbarium.

As planned, Georgie moved into the duplex on College Avenue. She told me that when she'd praised Ainsley for her strength, Ainsley said that for thirty years her greatest fear was losing Roy, and now that she had lost him, she had nothing more to be afraid of.

Normally school holidays gave Zack and me a chance to spend extra time with our granddaughters, but this spring break, the girls were in New York City with their parents, and judging from the torrent of pictures that flowed into my phone, they were having a great adventure. I missed them, but having my days free meant that Georgie and I were able to establish a work pattern.

She arrived at our house at nine o'clock, we worked till noon, had lunch and then resumed work until three o'clock, when Georgie went to the sound studios to meet with Fawn, who had gracefully accepted the prospect of Buzz Wells being brought in as executive producer and carried on working on production details. I used the time to grocery shop, monitor the progress of the bedding plants my grand-daughters and I were growing from seeds, make dinner and read everything I could find online about scriptwriting.

My relationship with Roy had been strictly that of researcher to writer, but Georgie had begun educating me about script-writing. She was a gifted teacher. As we read through the two scripts Roy Brodnitz had completed, Georgie pointed out that each of the episodes was self-contained, and each had its own theme. As a series, *Sisters and Strangers* would be greater than the sum of its parts, but each episode could stand alone.

Georgie showed me how each episode has three story-lines: A, B and C, with A and B being of equal importance and C of less. She took me through each storyline, explaining how a sixty-minute script like ours would have approximately thirty-five beats, or scenes. Georgie said to imagine each scene summarized on notecards. The entire stack of cards would be the plot, but the way we lay them out would be our story arc.

Roy had begun the three strands in episode three, "Mothers and Daughters," and Georgie and I had wrestled with scenes that would lead each story arc to a logical and powerful conclusion. Nothing seemed right, and we were growing increasingly frustrated. When we came back after lunch Thursday, Georgie pulled her tortoiseshell reading glasses from their case, sighed and dropped them on the script we'd spent the morning working on. "Time to concede defeat, rip up what Roy did and start again?"

"Let's give it one more try," I said. "Have you read *The Power and the Glory*?"

"Graham Greene?" Georgie said. "Read it and loved it when I was in college."

"A line in that novel has always stuck with me," I said. "'There is always one moment in childhood when the door opens and lets the future in.' I think the moment that happened in Joanne's life will get our characters where they need to go for this episode."

Georgie raised her arms. "A glimmer of light at the end of the tunnel," she said. "Lay it on me."

"Hold the celebration till you hear me out," I said. "For Joanne, I think the moment comes the first time she realizes that Sally has been telling the truth about her mother — that Nina Love is a manipulative egotist who will go to any lengths to get what she wants."

Suddenly the memory of that moment was there for me in all its ache and concrete details. Without realizing what I was doing, I slipped from the third to the first person. "My need for Nina's love was so desperate that even when I saw the truth, I closed my eyes to it, because I couldn't face a future without Nina. Denying the truth about her became a pattern I repeated until she died. When I finally faced the fact that Nina was a monster, she had killed Des. She had killed Sally, and she had killed Taylor's father, Stuart Lachlan."

Georgie took a deep breath and exhaled slowly. "Jo, if this is going to be too much for you, we can find another way."

"No, Roy promised we would give our audience Sally's and Joanne's lives honestly told, and that's what we're going to do."

"In that case, it appears we have found our lynchpin," Georgie said. "But where does it begin?"

"It's a simple scene," I said. "Nina delighted in al fresco dining, elegant meals served outdoors, especially if there was a guest. I always loved being with Nina, no matter what she was doing, but watching her set perfect tables and serve lovely food was a special joy.

"On this particular day, Izaak Levin, who was a major figure in the New York art scene, was coming for lunch, and Nina had set a round table in a clearing overlooking the lake. Every detail was perfect: the snowy damask cloth had been sewn so that its edges touched the new-mown grass and at every place setting there was a crystal goblet filled with purple pansies, the exact shade of Nina's extraordinary eyes. She'd prepared lobster salad, my favourite, and she'd sent me down to the lake to let Sally and Des know that lunch was being served.

"For Des and Sally, food was simply fuel they needed so they could get back to doing what mattered to them: creating art. They spent hours and hours on the beach working with sand. The structures they built were amazing: massive and fanciful, but always structurally sound. Des not only taught Sally about art, he taught her the principles of engineering — of how to work artfully to bring something about.

"That day, when I arrived on the beach and delivered my message, Des gave Sally what the two of them always referred to as 'The Look.' 'We've been summoned,' he said.

"Sally kept on working. 'I'll come when I'm through here.'

"'Finishing that is going to take a while,' Des said evenly.

"Sally didn't look up. 'You always say, "Give it as long as it takes."'

"Des laughed. 'That *is* what I always say. I'll be back after lunch to help you finish.'

"After Des started up the hill to the cottage alone, I pleaded with Sally. 'Nina spent the entire morning making everything lovely for us.'

"Sally must have heard the quaver in my voice, because suddenly she was furious. 'Jo, how many times does Nina have to send you down here like a little dog to tell Des and me that the perfect lunch is ready, before you realize that she's using you? When are you going to see the truth? She hates me because I can make art; because Des loves me and because you're my friend. She wants to come between me and everything that matters to me, so I'll crawl to her and beg for crumbs.'

"I knew Sally was talking about me. Meek as a beaten dog, I walked back to the cottage. When I told Nina that

Sally would join us when she was finished what she was doing, the look of pain I had seen so often passed across Nina's perfect face, but this time, there was something else. As she picked up the goblet of pansies from Sally's place and dumped the contents on the grass, Nina's violet eyes were fiery with hate. 'Sally tries to ruin everything,' she said. 'But we'll have our lovely lunch, and we'll have Izaak Levin and Des all to ourselves. Trust me, Joanne. We don't need Sally. We'll be fine on our own.'

"I knew at that moment that Sally was right about her mother, but Nina had been the rock in my life for as long as I could remember. If I let go of her, I'd be lost, and so I turned away."

Georgie's face was soft with compassion. "You were very young. Don't judge yourself."

"Too late for that," I said. "Come into the living room. There's a painting of Sally's you should see. She titled it *Perfect Circles*."

Georgie stood silently in front of the painting for a very long time before she spoke. "It's all there, isn't it?" she said finally. "The way the summer light encloses you and Nina as you sit at the tea table absorbed in one another. And the way Sally has placed the circle of herself and Des building that fantastic underwater sea castle in their private world beneath the waves."

"Yes, it's all there. Sally had seen the door open. She knew Nina would never stop hating her, but she didn't flinch. She faced life head-on. When Sally gave that painting to me she told me it was the only painting she ever did of Nina.

She said Nina was so beautiful she could almost forgive her. I used *Perfect Circles* on the mass card for Sally's funeral. Taylor was four at the time. When she saw the painting on the Mass card, she said, 'Is Nina going to kill us all?' I finally had to face the truth, thirty-two years too late."

Georgie and I worked till ten that night. In spite of the shopping I'd done earlier, Zack ordered in pizza, and we joined him for pizza and beer at six o'clock, then went back to it. By noon Friday, we had a first draft of the script for the third episode of Sally and Joanne. It needed work, but we were back on track. Georgie and I were both immensely relieved — not simply because the script was coming together, but because we were fulfilling Roy's vision rather than looking over our shoulders and trying to guess what Roy would have done. Only Roy's name would appear on the final credits, but Georgie and I would know we had done our part.

* * *

Ainsley had been reclusive all week and I was surprised when Taylor called to say Ainsley had agreed to meet Vale on Saturday morning at her duplex. Ainsley's decision meant Vale and Taylor were free all day Friday, and they spent the morning visiting with the crew members they had come to know on the set of *The Happiest Girl*.

Georgie and I had arranged to meet the young women in the Courtyard for a late lunch after they'd made their rounds. Most of Living Skies' staff and the people involved in the series had returned to work by then, so the four of us took our time. We had just started dessert when Danny Kerrigan, a member of Nick Kovacs's lighting crew, came by our table.

Vale leapt up. "Hey, I was looking for you all morning."

Danny's smile started slow but grew to full wattage. "You were? I'm nobody, and you're all over the media now."

"I'm still Vale, the girl you played Snap with between takes. Why don't you join us?"

To be hired on Nick's crew, Danny had to have completed his electrical engineering diploma at Saskatchewan Polytechnic, so he was at least twenty-one, but he had the sweet, bumbling demeanor of a boy in early adolescence. The chairs around the glass-topped café tables in the Courtyard were standard metal bistro chairs and bright red to match the frame of the tables. They were sturdy, but Danny was lanky and in his rush to sit, the chair he chose tipped precariously towards the ficus tree behind him.

Blushing furiously, he righted the chair and began talking to Vale and only to Vale. He wasn't being rude. Clearly, Vale was his sun, his moon, his everything. The rest of us were just distant planets. Danny's words tumbled over one another. "Vale, Nick says your face is a privilege to light. Something about your skin. He says it's as if you have no pores. The light hits you, and you glow. I've watched *Butterflies* at least five times, and I'm going to watch it again tonight. I've seen what Nick means. You're so beautiful."

"That only happens when I'm in front of a camera," Vale said. "It really is the lighting."

Danny was adamant. "No, it's you. You are beautiful, inside and out. And in ten weeks you'll be back here." He lowered his eyes. "I guess your boyfriend will be coming with you."

"I don't have a boyfriend."

"But there are pictures of you with Sebastian Cox in all the magazines."

"They're publicity pictures," Vale said. "Seb and I are about the same age, and we both have movies coming out later this year."

"So he's not your boyfriend."

"Seb is very nice." Vale gave Taylor a mischievous smile. "He's just not my type."

Our daughter dimpled and looked away, but I was relieved that Vale was attempting to keep her relationship with Taylor private. Their life together was just beginning. They needed time to get rooted before they faced public scrutiny, and I was grateful that Vale was doing her best to give them that time.

* * *

Georgie and I were working that afternoon, and there was a movie at the library the young women wanted to see, but Zack and I had a date with our daughter and Vale for an early dinner and a pre-dinner adventure. Vale was returning to Regina at the end of April and filming of *Sisters and Strangers* wouldn't end until October 26. She and Taylor would need a place to live, and Taylor had suggested a property Zack owned that had an interesting history.

A client of Zack's, who went by the single name Cronus, had left Zack an odd collection of real estate in his will. One of the properties was an old building in the warehouse district that housed our favourite steak house, the Sahara Club. On the floor above the restaurant was the apartment where Cronus had lived.

For many reasons, Cronus preferred to keep his private life private, and he'd had an elevator installed that took him and his visitors straight from the back door of the building to his apartment. A cleaning service kept Cronus's place shipshape, but since Cronus's death the only person to occupy the place had been Milo O'Brien, a brilliant, apolitical political operative who loved the game and whose services were invaluable during Zack's campaign for mayor and during his first year in office. When Milo arrived in Regina, I made sure the cleaners had the apartment ready, handed Milo the keys and told him if there was anything he wanted changed to get the work done and send us the bill.

For Milo a house was a place to crash. Real life was lived wherever election cycles took him. When Milo left Regina for a campaign in Florida, he handed me the keys to the apartment. In the year and a half he worked for us, there had been no bills. Milo had changed nothing, so the place Vale, Taylor, Zack and I entered on that mild April evening was exactly as it was when Cronus left it for the last time.

And it was, in a word, gobsmacking.

One wall of the living room was exposed original brick; the other walls were painted cherry red, a perfect complement to the warm brownish red of the brick and to the white oak reclaimed wood floors. A tan brown leather sofa and three matching chairs were arranged in a conversational grouping around a low, ornately carved circular coffee table. Three silver-framed very large black and white photographs of Ava Gardner hung over the fireplace. Mounted on the remaining walls were at least a dozen tanned animal skins that I hoped were faux but suspected were not.

A four-panel lacquered black Japanese room divider painted with images of warriors, and its twin, painted with images of geishas, separated the living room from the dining area — a granite-topped kitchen island with black leather stools — and a compact but well-designed kitchen with granite counters and top-of-the-line appliances.

The walls of the three-piece guest bathroom were the colour of pink quartz and the fixtures were sleekly functional. Zack's intake of breath was audible when we saw the master bathroom. The room was windowless, and as we went in, I touched the switch beside the door and what appeared to be a huge bouquet of tiny crystal lights suspended from the ceiling began to twinkle. All the bath fixtures were free standing, white and sculptural, but the walls were a deep and vibrant red and the sparkle from the crystals seemed to set them afire. The effect was spectacular. The purpose of the master bedroom was apparent: a very large low bed with dark grey satin coverings, a TV that was almost as large as the bed, ruby walls, a mirrored ceiling, muted lighting and an impressive sound system.

The door of the room at the end of the hall was heavy. When I managed to pull it open, I was met by a darkness that seemed absolute. I hit the switch by the door, but the light it provided was minimal. In the gloom, the walls were the colour of dried blood. The room was empty.

No one made a move to go in. "What do you think this room was used for?" Vale's voice was a whisper.

"Cronus was into S&M," I said. "He believed it was an act of ultimate trust — that the deepest commitment lovers could make was to put their lives in one another's hands."

Vale gasped. "Is that how he died?"

"No," Zack said. "Cronus died a hero. He sacrificed his life to save a child he didn't know, and that's a story you need to hear. But I made our reservations for five thirty and it's five twenty-nine. Let's go downstairs and eat."

* * *

Taking a few moments to savour the Sahara Club's beautifully groomed exterior is one of the pleasures of enjoying a meal there. The sidewalk, steps and accessibility ramp are always freshly swept, the large brass knocker on the door always shines and the window boxes are always bursting with the best the season has to offer. That afternoon they were filled with daffodils, the symbol of rebirth and new life.

It was early so the restaurant was almost empty, but the pianist with the slicked back hair, pencil moustache and tuxedo was at his place in front of the baby grand, playing Richard Rodgers's "It Might as Well Be Spring." When the server brought our leather menus, Zack turned to Taylor. "Are you driving us home tonight?"

"If you want me to."

"Your mother and I would appreciate it."

"No problem," Taylor said. "I'm planning to order a virgin Caesar."

"Sounds good to me," Vale said.

Zack smiled at the server. "I believe you heard the young women," he said. "My wife and I will have martinis, extra dry. Taylor, you and Vale choose the appetizers. Jo and I always like your choices." He inched his wheelchair around to face the girls. "So what's your verdict on the apartment?"

Taylor and Vale exchanged a glance. "I think we need more time," Taylor said.

"I'm going to Vancouver in the morning," Vale said. "We don't have a lot of time, T." She turned to Zack and me. "Would it be okay if Taylor and I have another look after we eat?"

"All that red was overwhelming," I said. "A second look will give you a chance to see the place's possibilities."

"That's settled, then," Vale said. "Now, tell me about Cronus."

"That's a tall order," Zack said. "But I'll condense. Cronus was a slumlord charged with murdering his girlfriend, Arden Raeburn. Arden was a respected member of the police force, and public emotion ran high. They were both into rough sex: Arden's body was scratched and bruised and so was Cronus's. The physical evidence against him was suggestive. And Cronus seemed determined to alienate the jury. Despite my suggestion that he purchase a suit off the rack for court appearances, Cronus wore only the best, including a pair of genuine python dress shoes and a wristwatch that he told me cost more than his Porsche."

"Not someone a juror could identify with," Vale said.

"No, but despite everything, I was certain Cronus was innocent, and I could feel the case slipping away from me. I knew his only chance at acquittal was getting the jury to believe that the rock-'em, sock-'em sex between Arden and him was consensual, and the only way to do that was to have him take the stand. I asked Joanne if she'd sit in on a dry run of Cronus delivering his testimony and give us an objective, third-party opinion about the wisdom of letting him testify."

"My opinion was that without coaching Cronus would be a disaster," I said. "But like Zack, I believed he was innocent."

"I remember you two talking to me about that," Taylor said. "About how often you have to be able to get past appearances in order to recognize the truth."

"Luckily for us, one juror was able to do that," Zack said. "She believed Cronus's story, and she would not be dissuaded. It was close, but all that matters is that the puck goes into the net and the red light goes on."

When Vale looked baffled, Taylor gave her a sidelong glance. "Hockey talk," she said. "Also perfect timing — here come our drinks and our appetizers." After one server placed our drink and a small plate in front of each of us; his colleague arranged large platters of smoked salmon, Greek ribs, Tuscan cheese and crudités on the table. Zack proposed a toast to absent friends, and we began sampling.

As was always the case at the Sahara Club, during the first ten minutes after the food arrived, there wasn't much conversation. The restaurant had an excellent chef, and his food merited undivided attention; besides, our family had a rule that when there was food on the table, conversation should be light. The second part of Cronus's story was difficult both to tell and to hear, and Taylor introduced a topic that she knew would give us all a break.

"Vale and I saw Lizzie today," she said. "We drove out to her church."

Lizzie was a teenager who had attached herself to Vale when *The Happiest Girl* was being filmed. She was a waif with no fixed address who appeared to have neither family nor friends. She was obsessed with the need to care for others, and on the streets there were plenty of people who needed care. Every dollar or gift Lizzie received, she gave away. Vale and Taylor did everything they could to keep Lizzie safe and healthy, and she remained close to them and to Zack and me until someone took her to the Church of Bountiful Gifts, a mega-church that owned a large parcel of land just off the highway fourteen kilometres from the city limits. In short order, the church became Lizzie's reason for being. She texted Taylor and Vale that she had been washed free of her sins. She was ready to follow the path of Jesus, and her heart was filled with joy. We were all happy for her.

That night, Taylor's reference to Lizzie captured Zack's attention. "Is she still doing well?" he said.

"She's blooming," Vale said. "She looks great. She's put

on weight, which she certainly needed, she's stopped shaking and biting her nails, and her hair is clean and very pretty."

"So the Church of Bountiful Gifts has been good for her."

"That church is Lizzie's life," Vale said. "They have all kinds of classes and meetings, and Lizzie helps get everything ready and cleans up afterwards. She talks about her Lord and Saviour so often that Taylor and I kept expecting him to join us for coffee."

I laughed. "As long as she's content."

"She is," Taylor said, "and she told us a secret. " Taylor lowered her voice. "Danny Kerrigan has a crush on Vale."

"That was pretty obvious when Danny joined us at the Courtyard today," I said. "But how did Lizzie know?"

"Danny goes to Lizzie's church," Taylor said. "In fact, he was the one who brought Lizzie into the Church of Bountiful Gifts. Lizzie was on set one day waiting for Vale, and she and Danny got talking, and he invited her to a meeting at his church. Danny and Lizzie are in the same young adults group, and the group members really look out for one another. Lizzie knew about the crush because Danny had the flu in January, and Lizzie and another girl from their church took food to his apartment. She said there are pictures of Vale everywhere."

"That's a little creepy, isn't it?" I said.

Vale shrugged. "Not really. *Butterflies* was a big hit with the emos, and they buy a lot of fan magazines."

Zack's brow furrowed. "What are emos?"

"It's a term teens use to describe kids who are too emotional. Emos tend to exaggerate life's problems and take things too seriously. Danny's twenty-two, but he's young for his age."

"Sounds like Danny is about to win the lottery," Zack said. "When shooting starts for *Sisters and Strangers*, he'll get to see you every day."

"The spell will be broken as soon as he and I get back to playing Snap between takes," Vale said. "I'm a loud, mean card player."

"Luckily, Danny and I are able to get past your loud, mean card playing, and adore you," Taylor said, wrapping an arm around her girlfriend.

We continued to chat about mutual acquaintances and future plans as we enjoyed our entrees. We were all too full for dessert, so we ordered ginger tea. When it arrived and was poured, Vale said, "No food on the table, just tea, and Zack, you told me Cronus's story was a story I should hear. I'm leaving tomorrow, so it's either now or a month from now. You said Cronus died a hero. Was he happy at the end?"

Zack shook his head. "That is probably the most unanswerable question anyone has ever asked me. Cronus died an agonizing death. He was strangled, and then his body was beaten to a pulp. But in the twenty-four hours before he died, Cronus found peace; he gave meaning to his life, and he knew — I suspect for the first time — how it felt to truly connect to another human being." He paused. "Has Taylor ever mentioned the Racette-Hunter Community Centre to you, Vale?"

"She took me there before Christmas," Vale said. "The director, Kerry Benjoe, gave us a tour. It's terrific — the gym, the child-care space, the programs for at-risk kids and abused women; the upgrading classes — Kerry said that Racette-Hunter is changing lives in the community."

"And without Cronus, it might never have opened," I said. "We'd planned a big community picnic for the community centre's first day with barbecues, races for the kids, softball — all the usual activities. Everything was going smoothly and then Cronus arrived and told Zack and me there was a rumour that a child would be kidnapped from the celebration."

Zack leaned forward. "I was running for mayor, and the abduction plan was part of the opposition's vicious campaign. If we couldn't keep one child from harm, how could we possibly run a city?"

"The plan had to be short-circuited," I said. "Cronus was the only one who knew enough to abort the plan, but we all realized that would mean putting his life on the line. He had told me many times how grateful he was for my belief in his innocence, so I thought there was a chance I could get through to him. I was always physically uneasy around Cronus, but that day, I stood so close to him that our faces were almost touching, and everything that had separated us fell away. I saw a human being who, like me, was deeply flawed, making a decision that he knew might kill him. I saw the marks life had left on his skin, and he saw the marks life had left on mine. Finally, he said, 'What the hell? We only live once. Might as well make it count. Right, Joanne?' And I said, 'Right.'"

Remembering that moment now, my heart sank.

"Cronus didn't hesitate," Zack said. "He took out his phone and sent the message that would put an end to the abduction plot and might well result in his death. I shook his hand and Jo embraced him. When the hug ended, Cronus said, 'That was nice.'"

"That was the last time we saw him alive," I said. "There was so much I wanted to say to him . . ."

Zack's voice was strong and reassuring. "He didn't need words, Joanne. I saw Cronus's face when he walked away from you. He'd done the right thing, and he was a happy man."

Taylor and Vale both had tears in their eyes when they left to take a second look at Cronus's apartment, and I wasn't surprised that they were back at our table before I had a chance to pour Zack and me a fresh cup of tea.

"We're taking it," Taylor said. She was beaming and so was Vale. "We didn't even make it in. We got to the front door, looked at each other, and we knew Cronus's old apartment was the place for us. It's a great space with a great location, but it was the story that got to us. Cronus was a man who did the right thing when it mattered, and that's a good memory to carry with us as we start our new life together." She took a breath. "So what do you think?"

Zack picked up the dessert menu and handed it to her. "I think this decision calls for desserts all around. Sky's the limit. This has turned out to be a very good evening."

CHAPTER SEVEN

Zack's paraplegia affected every area of his life. There were the everyday frustrations of living in a world that often was not accessible. There were times when he was assaulted by muscle spasms or by pain in his shoulders that had simply been performing too many functions for too long. There were complications that arose because the body's organs and circulatory system were not designed to be locked in a partially paralyzed body. He never complained. He accepted his deeply flawed body as unquestioningly as he accepted his thousand megahertz brain. For him, it was all part of the package.

When we decided to marry, Zack arranged for me to see his doctor, Henry Chan, so I could, in Zack's words, know exactly what I was getting into. I left Henry's office shaken but determined to do whatever it took to make a good life with the man I loved. Zack's wheelchair of choice was manual. That meant that for at least sixteen hours a day, he was literally pushing himself around. He was strong, but by the end of the day his muscles were tight with effort. Nightly massages relaxed the muscles and gave me a chance to check my husband's body for pressure ulcers that if left untreated could kill him. Winter and summer he wore cashmere socks because his circulation was so poor. Exercise was essential so Saturday morning, despite his grumbling, he was headed for the gym.

Taylor and I had plans of our own that Saturday. After we dropped Vale at Ainsley's, we went to take stock of their new apartment. It was painful to think of Taylor no longer spending her nights in the pretty white and Wedgwood blue room down the hall from Zack and me, but our morning of measuring, taking photos and deciding which pieces should find another home and which should stay was filled with laughter and shared memories. I was grateful for our time together, but it didn't change the hard truth that our daughter had come of age and that meant letting go. When the last photo had been snapped and we locked the door, I felt the stab of loss, and I knew it wouldn't be the last.

When we arrived home Vale was waiting in the hall. At breakfast she had been on edge but determined to sit down with Ainsley, face to face, and clear the air before they began working together again. When she saw us, Vale's smile was open, and I felt a wash of relief.

"It was hard for both of us," she said. "But Ainsley and I will be able to focus on the work now and Jo, your story will be in caring hands."

"That's a relief on so many levels," I said.

Vale's voice was low and compelling. "I hope you know how much getting the story right matters to me — not just for you and Taylor but for Sally." When Taylor held out her arms to Vale, I knew it was my cue to leave. Vale had to be at the airport in an hour, and she and Taylor needed time alone.

"I have a couple of errands to run," I said. "And Zack's going to be at the gym all morning. Vale, would it be okay if we said our goodbyes now? You can give me an extra hug to pass along to Zack."

I was sitting in the car trying to figure out how I could kill the next hour and a half when Georgie Shepherd texted asking if there was a time that day when we could get together. I was on my way to meet her in two minutes flat.

At her suggestion we met in the writers' room at the sound studios. I'd just taken off my jacket when Georgie came in. She was carrying a small paper shopping bag with the logo of a snazzy new bistro on Broad Street. She reached into the bag and handed me a steaming drink. "Chai rooibos latte, right?"

"Right," I said. "And a large one costs eight dollars at that place. What's the occasion?"

"Assuaging my guilt for interrupting your Saturday."

"Consider it assuaged." I sipped my latte. "This is good. So what's up?"

"Lots. One advantage of living on the main floor of Ainsley's building is that communication is a snap. I texted you because Ainsley came down to my place and told me that Vale Frazier had visited her. Did you know about that?"

"Only that it happened and that it went well."

"Ainsley said she was glad Vale had taken the first step because they had unfinished business to discuss. Apparently they resolved the issue and had, and I quote, 'an open and rewarding discussion' about Roy's vision for the series."

"Sounds like it's a done deal, so what are we meeting about?"

"We're meeting about you, Jo. Is there a problem between you and Ainsley?"

"There was," I said. "I thought we were past it. Did Ainsley say something?"

"No, but when I said you and I were working as a team now, she was quick to point out that you have no experience writing a television series."

"She's right about that."

"But you're bringing as much to the writing now as I am, and Ainsley should be aware of that. If she has an issue with you, we need to deal with it."

I looked closely at my latte cup. The logo was a latte-art heart, beneath which were the words "the only drink in which creativity can be consumed." I turned my cup to Georgie. "Did you notice this?"

She shook her head and smiled. "Very clever, but I still need to know why Ainsley's uneasy about you."

"I was really hoping this would never come up again," I said. "Ainsley and I clashed about Vale. Apparently, Gabe Vickers felt the only way he could get sexual release was to masturbate in front of a young girl and then shoot his semen onto her body. Vale got the role of Ursula in *The Happiest Girl* because she agreed to let Gabe do that with her."

Georgie's pretty mouth twisted in disgust. "God, that is so sick. How old was Vale when this started?"

"Sixteen. When Taylor and Vale became close, Ainsley was apparently afraid Vale would tell Taylor about her relationship with Gabe. Ainsley came to our house and tried to convince me that Vale couldn't be trusted. She said Vale had problems and I should be careful about believing what she said. I told Ainsley that Vale was Taylor's friend and that Zack and I both liked her and then I showed her to the door."

"Had Vale told Taylor about Gabe?"

"No, she hadn't. She was ashamed. Vale didn't say anything about her relationship with Gabe until she learned that he had assaulted Chloe Kovacs."

Georgie's peaches-and-cream complexion was mottled with anger. "My God. How could Gabe do that to a child like Chloe? She's so innocent."

"You and Ainsley were close," I said. "Was she aware of Gabe's proclivities before she married him?"

The news about Chloe had clearly shaken Georgie, and it took her a few moments to answer. "I'd heard rumours about Gabe, but in our business, there are rumours about everybody. By the time Ainsley married Gabe, I was working in Los Angeles, and she and I had drifted apart. I remember being surprised at the news. I knew what was in the marriage for Gabe. He got the whole package: the option on one of the hottest shows on Broadway, Ainsley Blair as director and Roy as scriptwriter." She paused. "But I was never quite sure what was in it for Ainsley."

"I can shed light on that," I said. "Roy told me Ainsley married Gabe to protect Roy from another breakdown. According to him, a dozen production companies wanted to option the play; none of them was willing to take a chance on a director and a writer who didn't have movie credits. Gabe was the only producer who offered Ainsley and Roy money and key roles in controlling the project."

"So Ainsley married him. And look how well that worked out for her." Georgie's voice was bleak. "Gabe is dead and Roy is dead."

"So much talent lost." I paused. "Georgie, did you ever see Roy and Ainsley dance together?"

"Sadly no," she said. "By the time I knew them, their dancing days were far behind them."

"I saw them perform in Studio One last December at an evening honouring their old teacher. It was set up like a rehearsal hall, and the audience sat so close to the stage, we were almost part of the production. Ainsley planned the entire evening, and it was breathtaking. She and Roy came out to greet the audience and explain what was to follow. They were dressed like a couple in a forties movie musical: Roy was all in white, very breezy, very Fred Astaire. Ainsley was all sparkle — strawberry blond curls sprinkled with glitter, sequins on her pumps, on the bodice of her dress and strewn on her filmy chiffon skirt.

"They danced to 'Begin the Beguine.' Their movements were nonchalant, seemingly effortless, but even I knew the amount of skill required to produce an endless cascade of taps while matching their partner's every movement perfectly. They were so joyful, Georgie, so fully and beautifully alive. Ainsley has lost so much. Let's cut her a little slack about her attitude towards me."

"All right, but we're having a table meeting Monday morning to report on how our part of the pre-production is coming along, and I want you sitting right beside me."

I picked up my cup and drank the last of my latte. "I'll be there."

* * *

The table meeting was being held at the Living Skies office in what was called, accurately if unimaginatively, the Big Room. Georgie was waiting for me inside the building when I arrived. Standing beside her was a broad-shouldered imposing man with obsidian eyes, a mellow brown complexion, a shaved head and a captivating smile. Georgie introduced him as Hal Dupuis, the costume designer for *Sisters and Strangers*, and when Hal's large, strong hand enclosed mine, I felt the warmth of connection.

"You're Ms. Ellard," he said. "Thank you for sharing the home movies Ben Bendure made of your family's life. They've been an inspiration."

"Please call me Joanne," I said. "And it's Joanne Shreve now. I haven't been an Ellard for almost four decades."

He bowed. "I apologize." Hal Dupuis's voice was low and sonorous, and he spoke with the precision of a man who treasured language. "I didn't know about your marriage. We've only been given the films of the years between your birth and your sixteenth birthday."

A frisson of apprehension rippled through me. "I didn't realize those movies had been circulated."

"Then I must apologize again," Hal said. "But please know those home movies have been invaluable not just to me and my colleagues at makeup and wardrobe, but to the production designer, the locations manager, the set construction coordinator, the music producer, the food stylist — everybody!"

I was overwhelmed. Suddenly it seemed that, like Alice, I'd stumbled headfirst into the rabbit hole. "There's a food stylist?"

Hal Dupuis's hearty laugh seemed to come from somewhere deep within. "Oh yes," he said. "And he has had far too much fun learning how to make candied violets the way Nina Love did." Hal cupped my elbow in one of his large hands. "Let's go in and meet everyone. Once you see the ways in which we've used what you've given us perhaps you'll forgive us for being intrusive."

There were perhaps twenty-five people at the meeting. Except for Nick Kovacs, who greeted me with a hug, and Ainsley, Georgie and Fawn Tootoosis, I knew no one, but as Hal guided me around, making the introductions, everyone was cordial and commented on how helpful Ben Bendure's home movies had been to their preparations.

Ainsley was at the head of the table, and when she spotted us, she gestured to the three empty places to her right and Georgie, Hal and I settled in.

"I should have told you about the movies being circulated," Georgie said.

"Don't worry about it," I said. "They've obviously served a purpose."

Georgie tented her fingers and looked at them thoughtfully. "There's something else. Because of the movies, everyone at this table feels intimately connected with your family and Sally's — but for us you're all characters to be dressed or lighted or moved in and out of a scene. No one will be intentionally insensitive, but . . ."

Ainsley cut her off. "I'll handle it, Georgie." She was very pale and the circles beneath her eyes seemed to have darkened with every sleepless night. Ainsley was forty-four, Roy's age. The night they danced so blissfully to "Begin the Beguine," it seemed they were two people whom age would never touch. But they had been mortal after all. Now, five months later, Roy was dead, and Ainsley was suddenly old. As soon as she turned to face the group, the chatter stopped and the room became quiet. "Before we begin," she said. "I'd like to welcome Joanne Ellard Shreve to the table and ask everyone to remember that the characters we're dealing with were people Joanne knew and loved. I know you will show them and Joanne the respect they deserve." She turned to the series' producer. "Now, Fawn will get us started."

I had only met Fawn Tootoosis on a few occasions, but each time I'd been impressed by her quiet intelligence and her composure. She'd spent years in the film industry and had also learned the importance of watching and listening from the elders on Poundmaker Cree Nation, near Cut

Knife, Saskatchewan. Gabe Vickers's sudden death had rocked the lives of everyone in his orbit; it had also raised serious questions about the fate of his company, Living Skies Productions, and about the future of the company's major project, *Sisters and Strangers*, but whatever else he was, Gabe Vickers was a dynamic executive producer, and he left what would turn out to be his final project in great shape. The financing for *Sisters and Strangers* was in place; two of the principal actors had been signed, and negotiations with Gabe's first choices for the other five principal roles were in final stages. The heads of all the departments had been chosen and the series' director and writer were already at work.

Everything was where it had to be, but time was not on the side of *Sisters and Strangers*. Rosamond Burke would be eighty-one when shooting was scheduled to begin. She was in good health but as Rosamond herself pointed out, twelve-hour working days could be taxing for an actor who was no longer an ingénue. At eighteen, Vale was still able to pass as Sally at fourteen, a girl on the cusp of becoming a woman. That delicate balance was critical in the early episodes of the series, but if the project were delayed, Vale would almost certainly outgrow the part.

Fawn looked around the room and said, "We are all —" but then heads turned as Kyle Daly burst into the room, apologized for being late, looked desperately around the table for a vacant chair and then having located one, collapsed into it. Fawn gave him a forgiving "we've all been there" smile and waited until he settled in before she spoke.

Fawn's long-fingered hands were graceful and expressive,

as essential to communicating her thoughts as her words. As she began again, she held out her hands, palms up in a gesture of inclusion. "We are all missing Roy today," she said. "This past week has been difficult for us, and we are still reeling. But ready or not, we must move on. Roy once told me that when he was hurting, his work took him out of himself. Remembering Roy's words, let's get to work and hope for the best.

"This is primarily a creative meeting — so this is the time for me to step back, listen and take notes. I have met with you individually, and each of you has identified your department's needs and flagged possible bumps in the road. I'll be meeting regularly with heads of departments, but if you discover you need special equipment, run into an unexpected expense or face a problem with time, please let me know asap.

"I'll end by saying what I always say: no path is without obstacles. They are as frustrating as they are inevitable. But often the way you overcome the obstacle opens a new creative path, so hang in there. Try the options, talk them out, and if nothing works, remember we're all in this together. Everyone working on this project has the same goal. We all want to make something incredible. We are co-creators. We've got you covered. You are safe." Fawn turned to Ainsley. "Ready to say a few words?"

When Ainsley shook her head, Georgie shot her a worried look and then picked up the cue. "Fawn's right about no path being without obstacles," Georgie said. "At first, Roy's death seemed to be an obstacle that was insurmountable, but now we know that he left us the blueprint and the tools to find our way without him. The scripts for the first two episodes are locked, and you've all read them. You know that Roy has already created the landscapes — physical and emotional — for the series and that in *Sisters and Strangers*, he had given us complex, nuanced characters with beating hearts. There are points of real drama in these scripts, times when major events happen, but mostly what we are doing is inviting the audience into our characters' lives, showing in detail the moments that shaped the women Sally Love and Joanne Ellard became: sisters who were strangers for much of their lives, but who were joined with a bond that even death couldn't sever.

"Together, Joanne and I have completed the episode that Roy began but never finished. The writing needs to be polished, but we've found our path and we know where we're going. Stay tuned."

Hal Dupuis leaned towards me and whispered, "That is such a relief. We've all been on tenterhooks." He slid a drawing out of his art portfolio, laid it face down on the table and stood to address the gathering. "I've only begun, but I already know that dressing the women in this series will be a joy," he said. "All those stunning outfits of the early sixties. And of course, Nina Love was a goddess — in her own mind, and" — he looked towards me — "and, of course, to you, Joanne."

I was dumbfounded. Until that morning, I hadn't known Hal Dupuis existed, and yet he knew about the darkest love I'd ever experienced.

When he saw my expression, Hal looked crestfallen. "And I've blundered again," he said. "Let me try to explain. We were all given what Roy Brodnitz had written. The scripts and his notes. Roy's writing is sublime, but I couldn't grasp the complexity of Nina Love's character from words on a page. I needed more. When I saw Nina in Ben Bendure's movies, I began to understand her — her love for beauty, her narcissism, her obsessive need for control and her charm as she manipulated those around her. In the presentation folders in front of you, you'll find a drawing of the gown Nina will wear the first time she appears onscreen."

Hal bent, turned over the drawing that had been face down on the table and slid it towards me. "I think you'll recognize it," he said quietly.

The drawing took my breath away. In every detail, it was the dress Nina had worn at the first grown-up dinner party I'd ever attended. That evening, our island seemed enchanted. The lake was calm; the moon, full; the night, starry; and fairy lights had been strung through the branches of the willows. The air smelled of nicotiana, expensive perfumes and cigarette smoke. The men were all handsome, and the women were all lovely, but none was lovelier than Nina in a dress whose clean lines showcased her graceful arms, her elegant neck and her exquisite heart-shaped face. She had worn her dark hair in a chignon that night, and when she leaned forward to chat with her guests, her pearl and diamond drop earrings glowed as they touched her cheeks.

"A sample of the material we're using for the dress is attached to your drawings."

The piece of vibrant blue silk Hal Dupuis gave me was larger than the swatches of material stapled to the drawings.

Nina had taught me how to tell true silk from fake. She said that when you held true silk, it would lay across your hand as naturally as a second skin. As I looked at the graceful drape of the silk in my hand, I swallowed hard, remembering.

Beside me, Hal relaxed as appreciative nods and murmurs of approbation met his design. "Every time I start a new project, I remember Helen Mirren saying she wept the first time she had a costume fitting for *The Queen* and saw the clothes and shoes she would have to wear to play Elizabeth II. Mirren said, 'I can't play anyone who'd wear those clothes.' Then she began researching and she understood that the Queen dresses as she does because she's uninterested in clothes and she doesn't care what she looks like as long as it's the right thing for the right moment. When Mirren began donning the clothes that the Costume Department made for her she was thrilled about how the clothes, all lined with incredibly expensive silk, felt, and about how she felt when she wore them. Mirren said that only when she put on the clothing of the Queen did she begin to understand what it was like to be the Queen.

"I believe that when the actor playing Nina Love puts on this dress, she'll understand what it was like to be a woman with the beauty, power and ruthlessness to twist the lives of others until they gave her what she wanted." He paused. "That's it for me. I have a score of other designs but they're not in their final form."

Hal took his seat and turned to me. "Did I pass the test?"

"Yes," I said. "You passed the test. Wherever did you find Prussian blue silk?"

Hal's expression was rueful. "Online," he said. "These days, the world is our oyster. Now tell me how did you come to know the name of that particular shade."

"Nina told me," I said. "The dye is made from cyanide salts, but it isn't toxic because it's bound to something else."

"Iron," Hal said. "It's a tight bond that renders the cyanide harmless."

"Unlike Nina," I said.

The communal show and tell continued. The locations manager, Edie Gunn, a deeply tanned, athletic woman with a steel-grey Dutch bob and a no-nonsense attitude, asked us to turn on our tablets. She'd posted photos of Ernest Lindner's cabin and of the virgin forest that surrounded it. At Kyle Daly's request, she too, had taken a number of photos of forest undergrowth, fallen branches, lichen and tree bark. Edie said Kyle believed the photos would help determine the design style for sets, locations, graphics and even camera angles. "I didn't see the point of it, myself," Edie added, "but I'm a team player."

The distance between Regina and Emma Lake was 415 kilometres, but Edie said the lake surrounding the island was as pristine and undeveloped as an Ontario lake in the early 1960s would have been, and she felt the authenticity was worth the expense. She suggested that the production company shoot exteriors in Northern Saskatchewan for three weeks in summer and two weeks in autumn and have the cabins' interiors built at the production studios. Edie Gunn had other news. The MacKenzie Art Gallery in Regina had given the go-ahead to film there for a few days between exhibitions, however Sally Love's notorious fresco *Erotobiography* would have to be re-created on set. The MacKenzie had been polite but firm in refusing to have a fresco of the sexual parts of the one hundred individuals with whom Sally Love had been intimate painted directly on one of its gallery walls.

Everyone chatted quietly as they checked out their tablets, but Ainsley, who had not opened hers, remained silent. The reports continued. Nick Kovacs discussed Roy's desire to use as much natural light as possible in shooting and said that when Ainsley was ready they would go through the locked scripts together, marking scenes where the use of natural light would be feasible.

Sketches of sets were passed around and discussion broke out about whether music would be used to foster a mood, evoke the era or as a Greek chorus with lyrics commenting on the story. The room hummed with the energy of professionals beginning a new venture together, but Ainsley remained expressionless, isolated by grief.

After the last person in the circle had reported, Fawn thanked everyone and turned to Ainsley. "Anything you'd like to say before we go our separate ways?"

Ainsley picked up her satchel. "I have nothing," she said, and she left the room, her bleak statement hanging in the air like a pall.

Hal Dupuis was a heavy man with a face made for smiling, but as he watched Ainsley leave, his features had a bloodhound droop. "That poor soul," he said. "This was a misery for her, but Joanne, your morning mustn't end on a sad note."

"It's okay," I said hastily.

"Today was your first meeting with the people who are going to bring your story to life. It's always a special moment, and it should be celebrated," Hal said. "Roy told me once that when he was writing, he always needed a talisman, an object that connected him with the story he was telling." Hal handed me the swatch of Prussian blue silk. "Take this. Souvenir of your first table meeting. I was watching your face when you saw my design for Nina's dress — I suspect there might be unfinished business there. Having this piece of Prussian blue silk close might help you finish it."

* * *

Georgie and I left the Big Room together. We had planned to buy sandwiches at a deli, take them to my place and get back to work, but at the meeting, Georgie's anxiety about Ainsley was apparent, and I wasn't surprised when she cancelled lunch. "Jo, I'm sorry. I know you and I have work to do, but I can't leave Ainsley alone — not the way she is now."

"It's only been a week," I said. "Everything in that meeting was a reminder of the man who wasn't in the room."

Georgie's sigh was deep. "And of the woman who wasn't in the room, Ainsley Blair — there in body, but not in spirit. She has to decide whether she's in or out. She can't stay in limbo, pouring salt in her own wounds and sucking the spirit out of the production. I know she's grieving, but if we're going to finish on time and on budget, Ainsley needs to be actively involved with every person at the table today. Decisions have to be made. Gabe's forethought and Fawn's determination kept us afloat through Roy's breakdown, but if Ainsley doesn't provide leadership, we'll lose momentum, and we can't afford that."

"Do you think it's time to talk to Ainsley about bringing in another director — just on an interim basis until Ainsley finds her feet?"

"I see the logic," Georgie said. "But that's the last door I want to open. The minute I raise the possibility of bringing someone else in, Ainsley will call Buzz Wells."

"He's not a director."

"That won't matter to Ainsley. Buzz will dig up someone who's available, but he'll insist on coming along to executive produce. You and I have promised Ainsley that *Sisters and Strangers* will be driven by Roy's vision. If Buzz Wells gets anywhere near this project, his tiny footprints will be all over it."

"In that case we won't let him get near it. Georgie, you do know that if there's anything I can do to ease the situation, I'll do it."

"I know, and I'm grateful. You have my back, and so does Nick. Speaking of . . ." Georgie reached into her bag and took out an envelope. "I almost forgot to give you this. It's an invitation to Nick's birthday dinner on Friday. Nick told me he'd already invited you and Zack, but Chloe made a special invitation." Georgie raised a warning finger. "No steaming open the envelope. Chloe wants you and Zack to open it together."

* * *

When Kyle Daly caught up with me on the steps outside of the production studios, I was daydreaming about the possibility that Georgie, Nick and Chloe might share a future. Kyle's voice caught me by surprise. "I was afraid I'd missed you," he said.

"Well, you're in luck," I said. "What can I do for you?"

"Advise me," he said. "Joanne, I don't know Taylor well, but I have an idea that could involve her. *Sisters and Strangers* is about artists, and we're going to need paintings. We never use real art: the insurance is out of sight, and on a movie set the only things handled with kid gloves are the actors. Taylor is a serious artist. I've seen her work and it's incredible. I also know how much her paintings sell for — our offer for her work would be generous for set decoration but not even in the ballpark for Taylor's original paintings.

"That's the negative," Kyle continued. "Here's the positive. This series is about Taylor's family, and I thought she might like to be involved. Plus Vale's role is so significant, and Taylor could give Vale insight into her character's process when she makes art. Do you think Taylor will be insulted if I approach her about this?"

"No, she may have other plans, but she won't be insulted. I'll give you Taylor's number, and you can get in touch."

Kyle's eyes were searching. "But what do you think of the idea?"

"I think it's terrific," I said. "I know Sally would want her daughter to be a part of our story. I want that too." I held up my hand. "See? Fingers crossed."

The tension drained from Kyle's face. "Thanks." He held up his hand. "I've got my fingers crossed too."

CHAPTER EIGHT

After I left the production studios, I shopped for dinner, picked up Zack's dry cleaning and bought a dozen red and yellow tulips to brighten the dinner table. When I arrived home Taylor and Kyle were sitting at the kitchen table with tea and their tablets.

Taylor jumped up to help me put away groceries and Kyle joined her. "So, what's the verdict?" I said.

Kyle grinned. "We got our wish, Joanne. Taylor said yes."

"I'm going to make the art for the series," Taylor said, "and Kyle is going to help me decorate the apartment while Vale is away."

"Fair exchange," I said.

"We think it is," Kyle said. "I'm in need of distraction, and Taylor told me that she and Vale want to move into their new place as soon as Vale arrives back in Regina."

"Nineteen days," I said. "Not much margin for error."

"We have a terrific crew," Kyle said. "They'll get the job done, Joanne. The Art Department has a meeting in half an hour. Taylor's going to sit in. We'll explain what we need, Taylor will explain what she needs, and then she and I will grab a quick bite and check out the apartment."

* * *

I always enjoyed our daughter's company, but after the three of us said our goodbyes, and I heard the door close behind Kyle and Taylor, I heaved a sigh of relief. The table meeting had taken its toll on me. Collaborating with Roy, and now with Georgie, as we wove together the strands of my life had evoked some painful memories, but the writing experience had the intimacy of a private talk with a friend.

That morning as Hal Dupuis's colleagues perused the design and fabric for Nina's gown, and a woman from Hair and Makeup asked me for the names of Nina's favourite perfume (Joy), lipstick (Rouge Dior) and mascara (none, her lashes were naturally long, black and full) and I saw sketches of my bedroom in the cottage on MacLeod Lake and of the bench under the tree overlooking the water where my father and Des smoked their pipes, I felt as if I were witnessing my own autopsy. The people at the table were strangers and watching them dispassionately lay out shards of the past that had formed me, filled me with something very close to panic.

I needed an afternoon of peace and diversion, and I knew exactly how to create it. When it comes to the *New Yorker*,

I am a hoarder. I have three shelves filled with back issues in our garage, and with a five-minute search, I can always find exactly what I need. That afternoon when I discovered that the July 3, 2017, issue featured an article titled "Hemingway, the Sensualist," I knew Lady Luck was sitting on my shoulder. After I arranged the tulips in a Mexican pottery vase, I made a plate of toast and a pot of tea and took my tray and magazine to the chair by the window where I could see the forsythia. By the time I'd finished my tea and toast, I was once again a woman at peace with herself. I celebrated by taking a long nap and when I awakened, I put a chicken in the oven, snapped green beans, scrubbed carrots, peeled potatoes and set the table.

Zack and I had started reading in bed before we turned out the lights. There was not much stillness in my husband's life. He still routinely worked at least ten hours a day, and trial law is high stress. In an ideal world we would take long walks and make love more, but we did not live in an ideal world. For the time being, reading in bed before we turned out the lights would have to do. I'd just put the *New Yorker* with the Hemingway article on Zack's nightstand when Ben Bendure called. The weakness was gone from his voice, and he sounded almost like his old self.

"I'm not even going to ask how you are," I said. "It's so good to hear that rich, rumbling bass again."

"It's good for me to hear my voice too," Ben said. "Laryngitis is cruel and unusual punishment for a garrulous, opinionated old man."

"None of those adjectives applies to you," I said. "I've missed you, Ben. Email isn't the same."

"Agreed. Do you have time for a real talk?"

"I do," I said, kicking off my shoes and settling cross-legged on the bed.

"Good, because you, Roy Brodnitz and the fate of *Sisters and Strangers* have been much on my mind."

"Anything specific that you want to know?" I asked.

"Everything," Ben said. "Tell me everything."

And I did. I started with my ambivalence about the table meeting that morning: my excitement about the passion, intelligence and energy of the people in the room, but my almost atavistic fear that what those strangers were taking from my life might diminish me.

"Many cultures have believed that the camera can steal the soul," Ben said. "We dismiss their beliefs as primitive, but I've often thought they were onto something. When I leave my camera rolling in the face of someone's unspeakable loss, I am stealing something from them. I justify my action by saying I'm simply showing a truth about the human condition."

"Does that rationale work for you?"

"No, because I know that the real reason I keep the camera rolling is because I want to make a great documentary. My need to leave my mark matters more to me than my subjects' right to keep their inner lives private. That's unpalatable, but it's the truth."

"Ben, there's another truth. You're an artist. *The Poison Apple* exposes a wickedness that we need to understand.

Snow White, the Evil Queen and the mirror that tells the truth will always be part of the human story. But there is hope because people like Sally defeat the Evil Queen by living passionate, fearless lives."

There was a pause on his end. "Joanne, Sally wasn't the only one who defeated the Evil Queen. You raised Sally's daughter to be a young woman who knows the truth about her mother and her grandmother and who understands and accepts herself. That's no small accomplishment."

I felt a rush of relief. "Ben, you have no idea how much those words mean to me. I overthink everything, and I can't afford to get so mired in the existential swamp that I can't help solve the practical problems facing *Sisters and Strangers.*"

"Is there anything I can do to help?" Ben said. "I was fond of young Roy, and of course I've known you forever."

"Maybe it would help if you let me just talk it out," I said.

Ben was sanguine. "Sometimes that does clarify a situation."

"Here's hoping," I said. "I guess the most pressing problem is Ainsley Blair. Everyone understands that she's grieving, but after the meeting this morning Georgie Shepherd took me aside and told me that the production can't go ahead without Ainsley being actively involved as director. She's just not there. I suggested hiring someone on an interim basis, but Georgie is afraid that would open the door to Ainsley hiring her ex-husband, a man named Buzz Wells."

Ben seldom raised his voice, but when he heard Buzz Wells's name, he bellowed, "Not him — not ever! I had no idea Ainsley Blair had been married to that man. He's

feckless and ruthless, and he has a serious gambling problem. Stay away from him, Joanne, and keep him away from
the production. I don't know Ainsley Blair but I've seen and
admired her work, and I've heard nothing but praise for her
as a director. She doesn't need Buzz Wells. When is the first
day of principal production?"

"June 11."

"Judging from what I've heard about Ainsley's commitment to her colleagues, I would bet my bottom dollar
that when she walks onto the set that morning, she will be
prepared."

"I hope you're right," I said. "There's so much riding on
this series."

Ben's voice was gentle now. "Try not to lose your perspective, Joanne. That's an occupational hazard of this business.
When I had my first success, I was riding high — too high.
My father worked on the line at the Viceroy Rubber plant,
and I guess he'd had enough of my crowing. He told me
Harry Enfield, the man who worked next to him on the line,
saw one of the first movies I ever made and he didn't think
it amounted to much. According to my father, Harry said it
was 'just a bunch of shifting pictures.'"

I laughed. "I'll hold onto that thought," I said. "Ben, I'm
very glad you're there. I'll keep you in the loop."

As soon as I broke the connection, I realized I hadn't
told Ben about the book on Ernest Lindner's life and work
that Taylor had loaned Roy. The memory of Roy's wan-
ton destruction of a book devoted to the career of an artist
he revered broke my heart, and I knew learning about the

incident would be painful for my old friend. When we'd ended our phone call, Ben and I were both in good spirits. He deserved a respite from the sorrow that enveloped us all since Roy's death, and I decided news of the defaced book could wait.

I called Georgie and left a message. I passed along Ben's "shifting pictures" story and told her that Ben was confident that Ainsley was a professional who would be prepared when she walked onto the set on June 11. Georgie got back to me before the hour was out, and she too, was optimistic. "There's been a breakthrough," she said. "I've tried a dozen approaches with Ainsley, and nothing worked. I might as well have been talking to a catcher's mitt, but when I told her what Ben Bendure said about her professionalism, she listened. Tonight, she and I are going to set up a schedule for her to meet with department heads. Fingers crossed, Jo, but tell Ben Bendure if this works, I'll treat him to an afternoon watching the shifting pictures of his choosing and I'll throw in a super-sized popcorn with extra butter."

* * *

For the next three days, Ainsley met with the department heads as scheduled. By all accounts the discussions were mutually beneficial, and Georgie and I were able to get back to our writing. It seemed that Ben was well on his way to claiming his super-sized movie snacks, but on the morning of Friday, the 13th, the first hints of a troubling undertow appeared.

Esme and Pantera and I were late starting our run. Rain had been predicted, but by sunrise, the rain had held off, so at six fifteen we set off. There was a chill in the air, and the wind was shaking the branches of the native bushes that had been planted on the creek banks as flood protection. It was not a pleasant morning to be outdoors, so except for a few hardy souls, the dogs and I had the bike trail to ourselves. I had stopped to retie a shoelace, when my phone vibrated.

The caller was Charlie D, and he knew my priorities. "Everybody's fine," he said. "Madeleine and Lena are having the time of their lives, and Mieka has discovered her inner Uptown Girl."

"In that case, I'll let my pulse know it can stop racing," I said.

"Don't send out that message just yet," he said. "I'm calling about *Sisters and Strangers.* I've been hearing rumours. I haven't passed anything along, because we live in the age of disinformation, and I needed to make certain I knew the facts. I still don't have the whole picture but what I know is coming from a credible source, and we can't ignore it."

The first drop of rain hit me. The sky was now leaden, and Pantera, who despite her tough bullmastiff exterior loved a warm fire on a chilly day, shot me a baleful gaze. I stroked his head, mouthed the word "sorry" and returned my focus to Charlie D. "I'm on the bike path with the dogs and it's starting to rain," I said. "Can I call you when I get home?"

"I have an interview waiting in studio," he said. "How close to home are you?"

"At least fifteen minutes away," I said. I pulled up the hood of my windbreaker. "You might as well go for it."

"Okay. Julian Chase, the head of MediaNation's entertainment division, has been asking me questions about the series."

"Why would he have questions about a series that's still in pre-production?"

"Because of Roy's death. Jo, some people, including Julian, don't believe Roy's massive heart attack was just a tragic twist of fate."

Charlie D's words were a body blow. I'd come to a bench that overlooked a favoured nesting place for the creek's ducks, and I sank onto it. Baffled, Pantera and Esme looked up at me. The rain was steady now, and we did not normally stop in a rainstorm, but I needed time to take in what I'd just heard. Finally, I said, "I thought we all agreed Roy died of a broken heart because he'd lost his ability to write. I know we discussed the possibility that Roy had tried a hallucinogen, but Roy is dead. Whatever he did in those last hours is irrelevant."

"Not to everyone," Charlie D said tightly. "Someone working on *Sisters and Strangers* believes that Roy either didn't understand the potential danger of what he was ingesting or didn't realize that someone had tampered with the water bottle he was carrying."

I was shivering. "How did you find that out?"

"Anonymous tip. But this person knew things that are not public knowledge."

"Like the fact that some of us suspected hallucinogens had induced Roy's frenzy that afternoon," I said. "But why would anyone want to kill Roy?"

"Here's where the narrative gets murky," Charlie D said. "There are two stories, but they agree on one point: the intent never was to kill Roy Brodnitz. In our anonymous tipster's account, the hallucinogens came from someone working on *Sisters and Strangers* who gave the drug to Roy believing it would rescue Roy from the creative block that was crippling him."

"And the second account?"

"It's almost the same, except in this case, Roy didn't knowingly take the LSD. Someone wanted *Sisters and Strangers* to tank, and for that to happen, they needed Roy out of the picture. Both stories agree on another salient point. Roy's death came about by accident: whoever got the drug to him did not foresee the result the hallucinogen would have. What happened was the result of a miscalculation."

The rain had quickly stopped, but I didn't move from the bench. "I'm not following this."

"That's because there are huge pieces missing from the puzzle," Charlie D said. "But today Julian Chase told me something that you need to know. Julian believes that what happened to Roy was payback for whatever Gabe Vickers did to undercut the company that produced the six-part series the network was prepared to green-light until Gabe Vickers shoved it out of the way."

"So someone from a rival production company is behind what happened to Roy on the island," I said, stroking the dogs' backs with a calmness I didn't feel.

"That's the theory," Charlie D said. "And apparently, when Mr. or Ms. X learned that despite Roy's death, pre-production on *Sisters and Strangers* continues to move along, they did not accept defeat. They are putting out the word that *Sisters and Strangers* is already on shaky ground and that another stroke of bad luck could finish it."

"That could be construed as simply a statement of fact," I said.

"It could," Charlie D said. "I guess it depends on tone and context. Julian Chase is working on the identity of the person behind the words. Whatever the case, there's no disputing the fact that someone working on *Sisters and Strangers* is communicating regularly with Mr. or Ms. X." He paused. "Jo, I have a bad feeling about this. Tread softly."

* * *

When Pantera, Esme and I got home, Zack was dressed for court, but the coffee was on and there was a stack of towels on a chair by the kitchen door. I removed my windbreaker, gave my hair a desultory towelling and then started drying Esme.

Zack wheeled over. "What's wrong?" he asked.

"I need a minute," I said, and I continued rubbing Esme's curly black coat. Zack picked up a towel and despite his beautiful Harry Rosen suit, started drying Pantera, all one hundred and thirty pounds of him. When both dogs gave their final shake, I filled their food bowls and sat down at the kitchen table.

Zack poured me a cup of coffee and moved close. "I take it something happened out there."

"Not out there," I said. "But there is trouble, and it's closer to home."

As a trial lawyer, my husband had learned to be an active listener, soaking up information without comment or question until the person speaking is through. As I related what Charlie D told me, Zack's dark eyes never left my face. When I was through, he sighed. "Well, fuck. I hate situations where there's not enough information to involve the cops, but too much to ignore."

Hearing him say it made me realize the significance of Charlie D's information even more. "An impasse."

"Right," Zack said. "We'll have to count on Julian Chase and Charlie D to ferret out what they can in New York, but we can handle this end. Georgie Shepherd is still nominally the executive producer of *Sisters and Strangers*, isn't she?"

When I nodded, Zack said, "That's a break. If she checked the CVs of everybody who's working on pre-production, we could eliminate the people on the *Sisters and Strangers* payroll who never worked in the U.S. That's a start, and once we hear the name of the other production company we can see if any of the crew working on *Sisters and Strangers* have been connected with them. Let me know Georgie's feelings about looking at the CVs. She may have privacy concerns, but right now, anybody who works in the Living Skies offices has access to those files, so convincing Georgie that this is a case where the end justifies the means shouldn't be difficult."

"She'll be here at nine o'clock to start work, I'll talk to her then," I said. "My immediate concern is that you have dog hair on your suit. I'll get the clothes brush."

Zack moved his chair towards me. "I'll be in court," he said. "My robe will cover the dog hair. What I need is a kiss for luck and make it a good one, because I think I'm already screwed, blued and tattooed on this case."

* * *

When Georgie arrived, she seemed more relaxed than she had been since Roy's death. She and the dogs exchanged their usual exuberant and mutually affectionate greetings, and after she refused coffee, we went straight to the home office. Georgie settled in, pulled out her laptop, turned it on and said, "Anything new on the horizon?"

"As a matter of fact there is," I said.

Georgie scowled when I told her about Charlie D's phone call. "A traitor in our midst and an enemy at the gates," she said. "It's possible that the rumours swirling around MediaNation are just the product of someone's overheated imagination, but I guess that's too much to hope for. We have to tackle this head-on. I have no problem with checking the CVs. Zack's right that the privacy concern is negligible. We're not opening up the entire employee file, just a résumé that's wholly work-related.

"I agree it's unlikely that a Canadian whose entire experience in the industry is in Canada would be funnelling information about *Sisters and Strangers* to an American production company, but it's not impossible," Georgie said. She narrowed her eyes. "Incidentally, how come nobody knows the name of our rival production company? Surely there's a record of its name and officers somewhere."

"From what Charlie D says, MediaNation is hot on the trail, but so far nothing definite." I picked up my phone. After I texted Zack, telling him Georgie would go through the CVs, I said, "Well that's taken care of. Time to go to work?"

"Yes, because I have to leave early. Chloe and I are getting our hair styled this afternoon. She's so excited about Nick's party tonight. She's been poring over her teen magazines deciding on just the right look."

"Mieka was crazy about those magazines," I said. "Taylor not so much, but Mieka had a subscription to *Seventeen* for years. Is it still around?"

"Yep. Going strong, and it's Chloe's favourite. She loves to look at the ads with me and guess what the girls in the pictures are doing. I'm sure they're doing exactly what they were doing when Mieka was reading *Seventeen* — going to school or dances or rock concerts or to the beach with their friends." A shadow passed over Georgie's face. "Once in a while, Chloe asks me when she'll be doing all those things. It's a hard question to answer, but I do my best."

* * *

Georgie and I made ourselves sandwiches and worked through lunch. When she was ready to leave, I walked her to the door. "That was a productive morning," I said.

"It was. Now we can play hooky without feeling guilty." She hesitated. "Joanne, I know Zack and Charlie D are aware that someone out there does not wish us well, but I don't think we should mention it to anyone else."

"I understand," I said. "Loose lips sink ships, and our ship is already in uncertain waters."

* * *

Our family's gift to Nick was a pair of cashmere-lined leather driving gloves, like the pair Zack owned and Nick claimed to lust after. I'd just tied the bow on the present when the doorbell rang. The caller waiting on the porch was Kyle Daly. I'd seen him the day before, and he'd been fine, but he was now sporting a black eye that looked painful.

"Come inside, and I'll get you some ice for that," I said.

Kyle followed me to the kitchen and sat at the table. I took a package of frozen peas from the freezer, cracked it on the side of the table to move the peas around so the bag would be more flexible, wrapped the bag in a clean tea towel and handed it to Kyle. "Try to keep it on the area around your eye, not on the eye itself," I said. "So what happened?"

He tried a smile. "Would you believe I walked into a door?"

"Try again," I said.

He winced. "Joanne, I wasn't going to come to you with this, and then I realized it was probably something you should know. Danny Kerrigan and I were in a fight."

"Danny — that gangly boy who has a crush on Vale?"

Kyle nodded. "Yeah, and that crush is the problem. I was talking to one of Nick's guys, Bernie Farron, about the best lighting for the room at the end of the hall in Taylor and Vale's new place. Bernie called Danny over to join the discussion, and when I explained the exchange of services our department had arranged with Taylor, I mentioned that Taylor and Vale would be sharing the apartment. Danny said something like 'It'll be nice for Vale to have a roommate.'

"Bernie's kind of a wise guy so of course he couldn't leave that alone. He said, 'Duh — they're not roommates, dude, they're in a relationship.' When Danny just stood there looking confused, Bernie said, 'You are aware that there are chicks who are into other chicks, aren't you?' Danny still didn't seem to get it, so I tried to clarify. I said, 'Vale and Taylor are a couple — they're in love.'"

"And Danny was hurt," I said.

Kyle adjusted the pack of peas on his eye and winced. "Danny's reaction went well beyond hurt," he said. "He went nuts. He called me a liar and told me to take back what I said because what I was saying meant Vale was a sinner who would burn in hell, and she wasn't a sinner, she was perfect. I tried to explain that there was nothing wrong with two women loving each other, but Danny wouldn't listen. Finally, he hauled off, hit me in the eye and ran out of the room crying."

Suddenly I was overcome with weariness. "I'm so sorry," I said. "For Danny, for you and for Taylor and Vale. I was hoping they'd be spared this, but I guess not."

"Nobody I know gives same-sex relationships a second thought," Kyle said. "These days it's a non-issue."

"Apparently it's not a non-issue for Danny," I said. "He seems like a nice guy, but that church he and Lizzie belong to might have a pretty narrow interpretation of Biblical teachings."

"It does. The first day we worked together, he gave me some pamphlets and invited me to come to a meeting at the Church of Bountiful Gifts. I tried to be gentle when I turned him down, and he seemed to take it well. He said he'd pray for me, and the subject hasn't come up again."

"It sounds as if his heart's in the right place," I said. "I just wish he could understand how destructive that kind of intolerance can be. A friend of mine who waited until he was forty to come out said that he'd wasted years translating his life into something other people would accept. My friend is a gentle person, but he was bitter about the years he'd lost."

Kyle looked miserable. "I shouldn't have said anything."

"No, you did the right thing," I said. "But if Taylor asks about your eye, stick with the door story. I'll talk to her later."

CHAPTER NINE

On the invitation Chloe had made for Nick's birthday dinner, she had printed the time the party would begin in turquoise ink — a clear indication that a six p.m. arrival was non-negotiable. So at the stroke of six, Taylor, Zack and I were on the porch of Nick's childhood two-storey brick house on Winnipeg Street. Despite the fact that Zack had, by his own assessment, been "squashed like a cockroach" in the judge's ruling, he was in fine fettle, relieved to have done his best in an impossible case and lived to litigate another day. Taylor had spent a blissful afternoon in her studio studying Sally's technique in *Flying Blue Horses* and considering how best to replicate the painting for the series. My day had been complex, but when Chloe and Georgie greeted us at the door wearing airy pastel dresses that whispered of spring, and Chloe twirled to show us how her silky raven hair had been styled in a French braid, the clouds parted.

Except for Taylor and me, the guests at the dinner were all members of the poker group that had met most Wednesday evenings for over twenty years. The group's domestic lives were checkered. Vince Treadgold's first wife had committed suicide, and his second had taunted Vince with her infidelities. Henry Chan and his wife had recently separated, and Nick's marriage had ended cruelly; Zack and I had been the lucky ones, meeting in mid-life and entering into a marriage that sustained and enriched us both.

Together, Nick, Vince, Henry and Zack had celebrated joys and weathered sorrows. As they greeted one another in a home that, I suspect, looked much as it had during the years when Nick and his brothers were growing up, the four men had the easy camaraderie of veterans who knew the secrets of one another's lives and hearts. They knew that Nick's life centred on the girl moving carefully around the living room in her petal pink polished cotton dress, offering her family's guests platters of Hungarian appetizers — korozott, paprika hummus and Hungarian cheese puffs — and reminding us in a kind but firm voice, not to eat too much because there was way more food coming.

After we selected our appetizers, and Chloe moved on, Zack drew my attention to Georgie and Nick sitting on the couch across the room from us, hand in hand, following Chloe's progress with private smiles and watchful eyes. "They look right together, don't they?" Zack said. "Wouldn't it be great if . . ."

I placed my finger on his lips. "Don't say the words or you'll jinx it, but yes, it would be great if . . ."

As Zsofia Szabo, who had been the live-in housekeeper for the Kovacs family since Nick could remember, led the eight of us into the dining room, I was struck by how powerfully the room conveyed the lives of the three generations that had taken their meals together around the heavy oak table. The walls, like the walls of the living room, were hung with pictures of the Holy Family and the Kovacs family, juxtaposed in a way that suggested a close and easy relationship between the family's faith and its everyday life.

As Zsofia stood at the head of the table, gesturing us to our places, she said Nick had requested a meal that was nothing special, just an ordinary family dinner for an evening with friends. When Zsofia added that the tablecloth, bright with embroidered birds and flowers, was over eighty years old and brought out only on family birthdays, there was a collective intake of breath. Sensing that her comment had made us uneasy, Zsofia patted the air in a calming gesture. "Please relax. In this home, guests are family. This cloth has seen many birthdays, including those of Nicholas and his brothers. It has survived more spills than could be counted on all the fingers and toes in this room, and it is still flawless. No stain has ever been stubborn enough to defeat me. Enjoy your dinner. A spill is a spill, but a dinner with loved ones is a blessing. Nicholas and Chloe will tell you about the meal."

Father and daughter rose and took turns explaining the significance to the Kovacs family of the dishes being served: paprika-spiced cauliflower soup, chicken paprikash,

Hungarian cucumber salad, rolls with cracklings and prune jam, Hungarian-style stuffed cabbage. There were a few slips, but father and daughter finished strong, and when Nick said dessert would be plum cake, and Chloe chimed in that there would also be a real birthday cake from Dairy Queen, our applause was enthusiastic.

The meal was far from ordinary, but Nick's wish for a happy evening with friends was fulfilled. The Kovacs hadn't stuck to the male/female seating arrangement. Nick sat at one end of the table, Georgie at the other. I was seated between Nick and Vince Treadgold; Zack was between Vince and Georgie. On the other side of the table, Taylor was seated between Nick and Chloe, and Henry was between Chloe and Georgie. Ms. Manners might not have approved, but it worked for us.

Vince was a long-time member of AA, so that night he was drinking soda water with a slice of lime. When Nick poured me a glass of Malbec, Vince raised his glass to Nick. "Thank you for seating Joanne and me together. It's been too long since she and I had a chance to talk."

"I was thinking that very thing," I said. "So fill me in. What's going on in your life these days?"

"Except for work, absolutely nothing," Vince said. "I'm still in that huge house on Albert Street where Lauren and I lived. I no longer have the salukis. I sent them to live with my daughter, Celeste, in Ottawa. I'm at the hospital from five in the morning till after eight at night. The yard is fenced, but my housekeeper was living in mortal terror that Dalila and Darius would somehow get out and take off. Not an unreasonable fear — salukis are hunters. They'll run after anything that moves and they can travel at sixty-nine kilometres an hour. I miss them, Joanne. I really do, but keeping them without companionship or running space wasn't fair to them or to my housekeeper. So I'm rattling around in that mausoleum knowing that if I'm going to have a life, I have to make changes, but I don't lift a finger."

Vince had the cool watchful eyes of a sentry, but his crooked smile revealed a surprising vulnerability. "The first course hasn't been served yet," he said. "It's not too late for you to ask someone at the table to trade places. You deserve to sit next to someone more scintillating than a lugubrious bone doctor."

I touched his arm. "I'm exactly where I want to be," I said. "I'm sure you've considered all the obvious changes you can make: sell the house on Albert Street, get a dog that can't run sixty-nine kilometres an hour and cut back on your patient load."

"I have," he said. "Maybe the reason I haven't done any thing is because I know that living in a smaller place with a slower dog and reduced hours won't be enough. It will just be more of the same."

"Maybe it's time for some radical thinking," I said. "When you were a kid what did you want to be when you grew up?"

Vince shrugged. "My father was an orthopedic surgeon. He died when he was thirty-eight. That pretty well decided it for me."

"You told me once that when a parent dies young, children often feel the touch of the scythe on their own necks," I said. "Did you become a surgeon to replace your father?"

"To be honest, I never gave it any thought," he said. "I did well at school and it seemed logical for me to simply follow my father's footsteps and become an OS." Vince's brow furrowed in concentration. "But before that . . ." Suddenly his eyes widened in surprise. "I wanted to be a farmer," he said. "A farmer who raised animals — not to kill them, just to breed them and learn."

"Is that a life that still appeals to you?"

"I don't know. I'd have to think about it."

"Fair enough, but let me point out that even the prospect of spending your life raising animals made your face light up."

Vince's laugh was open and robust, and Zack turned his chair to face us. "What's going on here?" he said.

"Joanne is changing my life," Vince said. "Now if you'll give us some privacy, she'll be able to finish the job."

As we savoured Zsofia Szabo's amazing meal, the talk around the table was inclusive and general. Henry Chan was curious about how a TV series came into being, and Georgie and Nick were eager to explain the process. When Nick mentioned that the company would be shooting on Lindner Island, Henry's interest was piqued. "Kismet," he said. "We — or I guess it's just me now — anyway, I have a cottage on Anglin Lake, half an hour away from where you'll be. It's a big place, and I probably won't come up this year. Nick, you, Georgie, Chloe and any guests you wish to bring along are welcome to use it."

Taylor raised her hand. "Please put Vale and me on the list. She'll be working, and I've always wanted to see Ernest Lindner's island."

"Consider yourselves on the list," Nick said. His look took in Chloe and Georgie. "So just like that we have a cottage and our first guests. I wish all of life was that easy."

Chloe had been quietly eating, listening and laughing when everyone else laughed. She did not take part in the conversation, but her pleasure in being part of the circle in which the conversation took place seemed to be enough for her and for Nick.

The only interruption in the party came when Nick's phone rang just as Zsofia Szabo and Chloe were clearing away the dishes from the main course. After a quick look at his phone, Nick said he had to take the call and excused himself. When he returned to the table, he said, "Just a work problem. Nothing serious," and the party resumed its easy conviviality. At the appropriate time, the lights were dimmed, and Zsofia and Chloe brought in the two cakes, both with flickering candles, and we sang "Happy Birthday." When Chloe put the Dairy Queen cake in front of Nick she whispered, "Don't forget to make a wish, Daddy."

"I won't forget." Nick held out his arm. "Now come help me blow out the candles, and since there are two cakes with candles, you can make a wish too."

When Chloe blew out her candles she said, "I wished for a sleepover." She turned to her father. "You can have a different wish. You and Georgie have sleepovers all the time."

Nick blushed and cleared his throat. "Okay, everybody. Time to put in your cake orders: plum, DQ or both?"

After the dessert plates and coffee things were cleared away, we trooped into the living room; Nick opened his gifts and we said our goodbyes. Before we started for our cars, Vince took me aside. "When everybody was singing 'Happy Birthday' to Nick, I looked at Nick's face and I realized he doesn't want anything more from life than what he has. I envied him, Joanne. I don't know where to start with this whole farm idea, but I'll figure it out."

"When Peter and our daughter-in-law were married, he took over her family farm. He has a breeding program of heritage poultry — turkeys, ducks, geese and chickens — and they have goats, sheep, cows and four riding horses. Their farm is seventy-five kilometres south of the city. If you're interested, I'll give you his contact information."

"I am interested. Let me sleep on it, but I may just follow through with your son," Vince said. He leaned forward and kissed my cheek. "Thanks. I'm excited about this."

Taylor was driving us home, so I was sitting in the back seat. As soon as we snapped our seat belts, Zack half turned towards me. "Okay, what's going on with you and Vince?"

"You heard the man," I said. "I'm changing his life."

After I related my conversation with Vince, Zack said, "You have no idea how glad I am to hear that. I've been worried about Vince ever since his marriage to Lauren blew up — actually even before that. I tried to get through to him. So did Nick and Henry, but Vince is a very private guy. I don't know how you got him to open up to you. I'm just glad he did."

"So am I," I said.

"Do you think he really is serious about this farm idea?"

"I don't know," I said. "But I hope so."

"So do I," Zack said. "Vince hasn't had much happiness in his life. He's been a good friend to me and a lot of other people. It would be nice if he finally had a shot at the brass ring."

* * *

Taylor might have been an eighteen-year-old woman in a committed relationship, but she still liked to have Zack and me come to her room to say good night. And we still liked to be there.

That night our daughter had an announcement. "Don't count on me being home tomorrow night," she said. "Chloe asked me if I could come to her house for a sleepover, and I told her I'd be delighted."

"Good news all around," Zack said. "And this is Friday the thirteenth. So much for superstition. We made it through."

I glanced at the pretty Wedgwood wall clock my older children and I had given Taylor for her first birthday as a member of our family. It was ten thirty-five. Remembering what the anonymous informant had told MediaNation about the role hallucinogens had played in Roy Brodnitz's breakdown and death, I shivered. We weren't safe yet.

* * *

The clients of trial lawyers keep irregular hours, so when Zack's phone rang after we'd both fallen asleep, I was annoyed but not concerned. Zack kept his voice low, and I didn't strain to hear what he said. When he broke the connection, he moved towards me and touched my shoulder. "That was Nick," he said. "He's at Georgie's. There's a fire at the production studios."

"Is it bad?" Georgie and Ainsley's apartments were across the street from the studios.

"Too soon to tell, but I think it may be. At this moment, Nick and Georgie are standing at her living room window watching the fire and feeling helpless."

"Is Ainsley with them?"

"Nick didn't say. All he said was that he thought I might want to be there because our firm represents Living Skies, so we have a vested interest in *Sisters and Strangers*."

"I'm coming with you," I said. "I have a vested interested in *Sisters and Strangers* too."

* * *

Both Georgie's apartment and the production studios were on College Avenue. Anticipating that College would be blocked off for emergency vehicles, I took a route that would get us to the alley behind Georgie's building, and Zack called ahead and arranged for her to meet us there. When we left our house, the night was pretty: mild, clear and starry, but as soon as we parked behind Georgie's and opened the car doors, a thick, acrid smoke enveloped us, and Zack had to fight to breathe as he hurried to snap together his wheelchair. Georgie was waiting by the door for us, and it was a relief to step inside the apartment and inhale. Georgie was clearly exhausted and worried.

Zack moved his chair close to her. "How's it going?"

She shrugged. "Come see for yourself." We followed Georgie into the living room. The blinds on the window overlooking College Avenue had been pulled up, and Nick was standing in front of the window, watching firefighters battle a wall of flames that appeared to be at least twenty metres high.

Zack wheeled over to him. "Are they getting it under control?"

"Everybody's doing the right thing," Nick said. "We called 911 as soon as Georgie saw smoke coming out of the building. The trucks were here within minutes, and the firefighters hit the ground running, but the fire moved so fast. The flames were like a wave that just kept gathering force and pressing on."

"I hope no one was hurt," I said.

"The ambulances arrived at the same time as the fire trucks, and none of them has moved," Nick said. "That has to be a good sign."

"It is," I said. "Where's Ainsley?"

"Upstairs in her apartment," Georgie said. "She told me there was nothing she could do about the fire, and she needed to figure out the next steps for the production if the worst happens." Her smile was wry. "She's probably spending her time more wisely than we are."

"I agree," Zack said. "We need to do what Ainsley is doing — figure out our next steps if the worst happens, although I suspect Ainsley's 'worst' is different from mine."

"Arson," Nick said grimly. "Arson would be the worst."

"For many reasons," Zack said. "But the most immediate

is financial. Replacing what's destroyed will be costly. Until the insurers are convinced the fire was accidental, they drag their feet about paying out, and Jo tells me this production is on a tight schedule. If arson is a possibility, identifying the culprit fast is to our advantage. The police will be asking questions about whether we know of anyone who had a motive for doing this, so we'll need answers."

"I can't get the phone call that came during the party out of my mind," Nick said. "The call was from Bernie Farron, a member of our lighting crew. He'd had a nasty encounter with a coworker yesterday morning, and the other guy didn't show up for work in the afternoon. Bernie's been trying to get in touch with him to apologize but no luck. The other guy, Danny Kerrigan, is a grown man, and normally this wouldn't be a cause for concern. But Danny has worked for me since he graduated from the Polytechnic. He's Mister Reliable — never late, never takes a sick day, always ready to work overtime or on weekends if I need him."

Earlier, when I looked at the hands on Taylor's wall clock and realized we had not yet emerged unscathed from Friday the 13th, I'd felt a twinge of unease, but Zack had been confident that all was well, so I'd dismissed my doubts. When Nick said that Danny Kerrigan had dropped out of sight, my twinge of unease escalated into full-blown alarm, and my imagination ran amok. In Georgie's words, the *Sisters and Strangers* production was suddenly dealing with "a traitor in our midst and an enemy at the gates." For Danny Kerrigan the concepts of right and wrong were clearly defined. If he learned that Roy's fatal heart attack had been induced by a hallucinogen that someone dropped into his water bottle, Danny would feel morally obligated to report what he knew to his employer, MediaNation. If the person who had dropped the drug into Roy's water bottle had discovered that Danny knew the truth about Roy's death, Danny would have been in danger.

As I watched the firefighters' futile efforts to battle the wall of flames, my thoughts were as out of control as the fire. My husband's sane and sensible observation drew me back to the situation at hand — he was right that if Danny was as reliable as Nick believed him to be, he would have made certain someone knew how he could be reached. Once again, I was a woman standing behind a window, watching from a safe distance as an inferno raged.

Nick turned from the window to Zack. "You're right," he said. "But we can't seem to discover who Danny confided in. Bernie says he texted and phoned Danny repeatedly — no response. Finally he was concerned enough to go to Danny's apartment. Danny wasn't there, but a member of Danny's church group was there and she was worried too. Apparently, there was a farewell party for the leader of their young adults' group last evening, and Danny was supposed to present the gift and make the speech. He never showed up. I checked my phone just before you came. There were three more texts from Bernie — the last came just after midnight, and Danny was still not responding to his calls or texts. Bernie said they fought over a comment he made about Vale. He didn't elaborate and I didn't ask, but whatever it was, Bernie thinks he might have pushed Danny over the edge."

"He may be right," I said. "Kyle Daly came to our place this afternoon."

Both men turned to me, surprised.

"He told me about the fight," I admitted. "It erupted when Kyle mentioned that Vale and Taylor would be sharing an apartment. Danny assumed they'd be roommates, and Bernie mocked him for being naïve. Danny couldn't seem to grasp what Bernie was getting at, and Kyle tried to help by explaining that Vale and Taylor were a couple and they were in love. Apparently, Danny lost it. He called Kyle a liar, and said if Vale lay with a woman, she'd be a sinner who'd burn in hell, and she wasn't a sinner, she was perfect. Then he punched Kyle in the eye and ran off crying."

I could see from the set of Zack's lips that he was furious, but years in a courtroom had taught him to keep his focus. "So Danny has some deeply entrenched religious beliefs and he's infatuated with Vale. Why would he want to burn down the production studios?"

"Who knows?" I said. "Danny's a fanatic, and fanatics have no difficulty justifying their extremism by saying they're serving their god. Leviticus 20 is obviously a central tenet of the teachings of the Church of Bountiful Blessings. Danny could have believed that burning down the production studios was a small price to pay for saving Vale from eternal damnation."

"What is Leviticus 20?" Georgie asked. "I must have skipped Mass the day we covered that one."

"You didn't miss anything," I said. "That passage has caused a lot of pain. 'If a man lies with a male as with a woman, both of them have committed an abomination, they shall surely be put to death: their blood is upon them.'"

"So Danny torches the place where he works to keep the girl he worships from committing an abomination?" Georgie said. "That seems like a stretch to me."

"Maybe," Zack said. "But I think Danny Kerrigan's worth keeping an eye on." He squinted at the site of the fire. "Is it just wishful thinking on my part, or does it seem that they've got the fire under control?"

Georgie moved closer to the window. "I think you're right," she said. "The flames aren't burning as intensely as they were a few minutes ago, and the fire doesn't seem to be pressing forward the way it was."

"It does look as if the worst is over," Nick said.

Zack and I exchanged a glance. We knew the worst might have been over at the site of the fire, but *Sisters and Strangers* was still facing deeply troubling uncertainties. Zack shifted his wheelchair so he could face Nick. "There are some developments we need to talk about," he said. "Joanne and Georgie are already aware of some of this, Nick, but the information has come our way in pieces, and I think the time has come to stitch it together."

"Our son-in-law Charlie D has been very interested in how quickly the financing for *Sisters and Strangers* came together. He's heard disturbing rumours about Roy's death, and now there's a fire. Charlie D has come up with a fairly compelling argument that someone, in all likelihood someone connected with the series that Gabe Vickers elbowed aside to get the green light for *Sisters and Strangers*, is determined to make *Sisters and Strangers* tank."

"Payback," Nick said.

"Yeah," Zack said, "but payback that got out of hand. Charlie D and his boss at MediaNation's New York office picked up on a rumour that Roy Brodnitz's 'incident' was not an accident of fate, but a deliberate attempt to get him out of the picture. They also heard that when the person behind what happened to Roy learned that *Sisters and Strangers* continued to move forward despite Roy's death, they made it known they would attack on another front."

"The fire," Nick said. "That theory does have weight, and it raises an ugly possibility. If the person behind this has inside information on the day-to-day workings of our production, one of our colleagues is not only feeding information to someone who wants us to fail but may be carrying out orders to ensure that we do."

"That prospect makes me sick," Georgie said. "I'm checking our employees' CVs for people who worked with American production companies during the months when the series we knocked out of the way was being filmed, and Charlie D's boss in New York is trying to track down the name of the production company that lost out to Living Skies for the green light. Anyway, the hunt is on."

"Anybody have anything else?" Nick said. When none of us spoke up, Nick shrugged. "Then I guess we call it a day."

"Try and get some sleep," Zack said. "Tomorrow's going to be gruelling. As soon as the fire department says it's safe, the police and Fire and Protective Services will go through the site: measuring, taking pictures and samples — doing whatever they need to do. When they give you the okay, it will be Living Skies' turn to go through with your insurer and describe what's been destroyed and take more pictures. I recommend strongly that whoever goes with the insurance agent takes along a lawyer. Ainsley owns the majority of stock in Living Skies, so she would be the logical person to go through the inspection, but as executive producer, Georgie, you might be able to take that duty off her hands. My firm Falconer Shreve represents Living Skies, so call us when you're ready and someone from the firm will be there."

CHAPTER TEN

Saturday morning, Zack and I slept in till nine o'clock — an unheard-of indulgence for us both. When we didn't start our walk at the usual time, Pantera and Esme gave me a fourteen-minute grace period and then began nosing me, licking my face and whining. I got up, let them run around the backyard for ten minutes, fed them and went back to bed. A saw-off, but like me, the dogs were old enough to know that half a loaf is better than none. There was a Saturday morning yoga class Taylor liked, and she'd already left by the time Zack and I went into the kitchen to make breakfast. After he started the coffee, Zack turned to me. "So what's the protocol here? Do we contact Georgie and Nick or wait for them to contact us?"

"Wait for them," I said. "They were probably awake most of the night, but I think you should be on call for whenever they need you. I know we'd planned to pick Mieka, Charlie D and the girls up at the airport at noon, but Taylor and I can take her car and the station wagon — plenty of room for Mieka and Charlie's family and their luggage."

"I hate missing the girls' triumphant return from the big city," Zack said. "But Nick's always been there for me."

"That's settled then," I said. When Zack's phone rang, he checked caller ID and mouthed Nick's name.

I went to the fridge and took out juice, poured us both a glass, handed one to Zack and started slicing bread and cracking eggs.

When Zack's call ended, he wheeled over to me. "Anything I can do?"

"Nope, scrambled eggs and toast is a one-person operation. So what did Nick have to say?"

"He said that it could have been worse. The fire's out. There's still a lot of smoke and smouldering. Fire protection services doesn't want anybody on-site yet. They still have safety concerns. The real damage seems to have been limited to the area where the cameras and lighting equipment are stored. Replacing them will be expensive, but they can be replaced. There's smoke damage, but the three sound stages are intact, as are the Courtyard and the Living Skies offices." Zack had been watching my face as he relayed the latest news. "So what do you think?"

"I think that was a very considerate fire — just enough damage to cost money and eat up time, but not a total wipeout."

Zack raised his eyebrows. "That's what I think too," he said. "Let's eat."

After we'd both showered and dressed for the day, Zack left for Georgie's, and I went out to the backyard to see if any tulips were peeking through. When I came around the house to check the flower beds in front, Lizzie Ewing was standing on our front porch.

I called out to her, and she jumped. "I'm sorry," I said. "I didn't mean to scare you."

Lizzie looked down at her feet, her black hair hiding her face slightly. "I need to talk to Taylor."

"She's at yoga, and she and some of the people in her class are going out for coffee afterwards, so she won't be home till around noon. Lizzie, I haven't seen you in ages. Let me make us some tea, and we can get caught up."

Lizzie was still staring down at her feet.

I went to her. "I really would like to hear about your new life."

She started to cry. "You and Zack were so nice to me."

I put my arm around her shoulders. "What's happened?" Lizzie shook her head numbly, but when I opened the front door and led her down the hall to the kitchen, she followed. She was still sobbing as I pulled out a chair for her. "Sit down," I said. "I'll get you a glass of water and some tissues."

The water and the chance to take deep breaths and mop her eyes seemed to calm Lizzie. Vale and Taylor had commented on how well she looked, and as I sat opposite her, it was apparent Lizzie was healthy and well-cared for. Then I noticed something else. Lizzie smelled of smoke. When the silence between us lengthened, it occured to me that perhaps she was upset because of the fire.

"Were you over at the productions studios?" I said.

She tensed. "Did somebody see me there?"

"No." I touched the sleeve of the pretty daisy-splashed cotton shirt she was wearing. "Smoke has a way of clinging to clothes. Lizzie. I'm not suggesting you did anything wrong. It's human nature to be curious."

"That wasn't why I went there."

"Then why were you there?" Whenever I'd been with her before, Lizzie's eyes had been heavily made up: lashes clotted with mascara and eyelids ringed with liner. Now she was fresh-faced and her eyes were guileless.

"I needed to find out if . . ." She paused and then finished hurriedly. "I needed to find out if anybody got hurt."

"Did you think Danny Kerrigan might have been somewhere close to the fire?"

My intent had been to prolong our conversation, but my words hit a vulnerability, and Lizzie was out of her chair and halfway across the room before I got to my feet. "There's somewhere I have to be," she said.

"Just stay for a minute . . . please?" I said. "It's important. Lizzie, I know Danny disappeared last night, and you were looking for him. I also know that he ran off because he found out that Vale and Taylor were more than just friends."

"What they do is a sin." Lizzie sat back down. "If they don't stop, they will burn in hell."

"Did you come here this morning to tell Taylor to stop being with Vale?"

Lizzie's words tumbled over one another. "Danny came to Bountiful Gifts yesterday looking for Pastor Kirk. Danny was the one who led me to the path of righteousness. I owe him everything. When he told me about Taylor and Vale, he was crying. He said it was up to us to save them." She stopped to take in a ragged breath. "I would do anything to save Vale and Taylor. They cared about me when nobody else did. Vale gave me food and money, and she let me stay at her place when it was cold, and when I was afraid to talk to the police the night Mr. Vickers died, Taylor asked you and her dad to help me. And she gave me her beautiful red coat — do you remember that coat?"

"I do," I said. "Taylor loved it, and after she outgrew the red coat, it made her happy to see you wearing it."

Lizzie's eyes darted desperately around the room, searching for deliverance or rescue. When neither was forthcoming, she leapt again to her feet. "I have to leave."

"Just give me one more minute," I said. "Please, just look at me." Lizzie slowly met my gaze. "Do you think Vale and Taylor are good people?" I said. When she nodded, I continued. "They're kind. They don't hurt people, and they helped you. Do you really think that because they love each other, they'll go to hell?"

"Pastor Kirk says . . ."

"Let's keep Pastor Kirk out of it for a minute," I said. "Lizzie, I know belonging to your church has been a wonderful thing for you. Your church has given you a good life, and all of us are very happy about that. But churches are made up of people, and people make mistakes. I know that people in your church believe that by loving each other Vale and Taylor are committing a sin. Some people in my own church believe that too. But when I look at how happy Vale and Taylor make each other, I don't see sin. I just see love. I'm not asking you not to believe what Pastor Kirk tells you. I'm just telling you not to worry about Taylor and Vale because like you and me and Danny and Pastor Kirk, they are God's children, and they'll be fine."

She tried a smile. "I feel better."

"So do I," I said. "Lizzie, do you think you could pass along what I said to Danny? It might make him feel better too."

"I'll pray about it," she said, "but first I have to pray that I find Danny."

I went to the front door with Lizzie and watched as she walked down our front path. When she reached the sidewalk, she turned and waved to me, the way my kids and grandkids had waved when they were little. The gesture touched me, and I found myself hoping Lizzie's prayer to find Danny would be answered, and that when she found him, Danny would be able to tell her that he'd been nowhere near the fire the night before.

* * *

Not surprisingly when I drove to the airport to meet Taylor and pick up Mieka, Charlie D and their family, my younger daughter was still very much on my mind. I spotted Taylor in the terminal before she saw me, and for a few moments, I had the odd sensation of observing her from the perspective of a stranger.

She was striding towards the arrivals area unhurriedly but deliberately. Taylor had inherited Sally's long-limbed beauty and her father's brown eyes, dark hair and chiselled features. She was a striking young woman, and more than a few heads turned as she walked by. When she noticed me, Taylor's face brightened. "Hey, there you are."

Her smile was broad and open, and Lizzie's words about my daughter and Vale being consigned to hell because of their love hit me with the force of a slap. I reached out to Taylor and drew her close. Her hair smelled of rosemary and mint. "Everything okay?" she said. "That's a very warm welcome for a daughter you tucked in last night."

"Just thinking how lucky we are to have you," I said.

"That goes both ways," Taylor said, and then she glanced over my shoulder. "And look — here comes our clan!"

After a round of hugs and excitement, we claimed the Dowhanuik-Kilbourn luggage and headed for the parking lot. When everything was unloaded at Mieka and Charlie's and the bags were carried upstairs, Taylor ordered pizza for all, and Madeleine and Lena began texting friends to announce they were home.

"If nobody minds, I'm taking off," I said. "There was a fire last night at the production studio. No one was hurt, but Zack's with Georgie Shepherd and Nick Kovacs dealing with the aftermath, and I want to be at home if they need me."

"No problem," Mieka said. She glanced at her husband. "Charlie has been the soul of discretion, but I'm aware there are complications with *Sisters and Strangers*. Mum, if it gets ugly, promise you'll back off. You're the only mimi the grandkids have." She tried to lighten the mood. "Besides you haven't seen the fourteen hours of New York videos the girls made."

"I promise I won't take any chances," I said. "And we're all getting together at Pete and Maisie's tomorrow afternoon. There'll be plenty of time for me to get into that New York state of mind then."

Mieka and I hugged each other goodbye, but when I moved towards Charlie D, he said, "Let me walk you out. We need to talk about that fire, and there's other news."

When we got to my car, I said, "I can't tell you much about the fire beyond what I told you in the text I sent last night. All we know so far is that it started sometime around midnight, and it appears that the firefighters got it under control relatively soon. What's the other news?"

Instinctively, Charle D and I both kept our voices low. "Julian Chase uncovered some facts about the company that produced the series Gabe knocked out of the way to get the network to green-light *Sisters and Strangers*. It's called Aunt Nancy Productions."

"Anansi," I said. "That's clever: Anansi the Spider, the spirit of all stories."

Charlie smiled. "You misheard. Not Anansi, the spirit of all stories — Aunt Nancy as in an aunt named Nancy."

I laughed. "Not as inspired as 'Anansi,' but solid and reassuring. No matter what, Aunt Nancy will always be there with milk and cookies."

Charlie D raised an eyebrow. "Not quite," he said. "Aunt Nancy's had her ups and downs of late. A year and a half ago, the owner decided to retire. The company's reputation was sound, and it sold quickly. Work on the six-part series — which incidentally was called *At the Algonquin* — was going well, and Julian says the change in ownership shouldn't have mattered. The script was locked, the actors and director had been hired, the pilot was being shot and the network was prepared to sign on as the streaming service."

"Then Gabe brought *Sisters and Strangers* to the network and they decided to go with it rather than the other series."

"That's what we thought," Charlie said. "But that wasn't the way it happened. When Gabe approached the network, Aunt Nancy had already pulled *At the Algonquin* because of 'creative differences.'"

"Is that usual?"

"No. Not at that stage. *At the Algonquin* appeared to be home free, but I guess something happened, and Aunt Nancy decided to pull the plug before the network did."

"And Aunt Nancy's announcement about 'creative differences' was just a way to save face."

Charlie D shrugged. "Apparently. But whatever the circumstances, Aunt Nancy was decimated. The rent on its offices has been paid until the end of the year, but it's now just a shell company — no employees, no customers, no products, no services."

"But the company still exists," I said. "And someone out there does not wish *Sisters and Strangers* well. It's hard not to suspect a connection."

Charlie D's hazel eyes were troubled. "It is. First the rumours about what happened to Roy Brodnitz on that island and now the fire. When I told Julian about the fire, he said he'd worked in MediaNation's entertainment division for ten years and his Spidey Sense tells him this is going to be a big story. Anyway, we agreed that he'll keep digging for answers in New York, and I'll do the same in Regina."

"Why do I suddenly feel a chill?"

"Probably for the same reason Julian and I both did when I told him about the fire," Charlie D said. "Something bad is happening. Jo, promise me you'll take Micka's words to heart. If the situation starts getting weird, back off."

"Okay, but only if you'll make the promise too," I said. "Your mum and I waited thirty-four years for you and Mieka to find each other, and we've always counted on a happy ending."

* * *

On Sunday, when Zack and I arrived at the Kovacs' to pick up Taylor, she and Chloe met us at the door. Taylor had brought her a paint-by-numbers set, and Chloe was fizzing with excitement about the picture they'd painted together. "Wait till you see it," she said. "The girl in our painting has black hair like me and a cat like Taylor's." Chloe turned to our daughter. "I forget the kind of cat."

"It's a tortoiseshell," Taylor said. "And our painting is already hanging in its place of honour over the mantle."

I kicked off my boots, and Zack and I followed the girls

into the living room, where Nick and Georgie were waiting by the fireplace. Nick was wearing the cashmere pullover Georgie had given him for his birthday, cornflower blue "to match Nick's eyes" Georgie had said. After we'd admired the art, Taylor and Chloe went upstairs to get Taylor's overnight bag, and Zack wheeled closer to Nick. "Anything new on the fire?"

Nick shook his head. "Nothing concrete, but Fire Protection Services is interested in the fact that the damage was so contained."

Zack's tone was even. "Jo said it was 'a very considerate fire.'"

Nick frowned. "Fire Protection Services share Jo's opinion. They say the limits of the fire were almost 'surgically precise,' but there's no evidence of arson, so for the time being, we're in limbo."

No evidence of arson. It seemed that Danny Kerrigan was off the hook. I felt my nerves unknot. The teachings of the Church of Bountiful Gifts were cruel and punitive, but Kyle Daly had told me Danny's heart was in the right place, so there was hope that Danny might find his own answers. Relieved, I turned my attention back to Nick's explanation of the next steps the company could take in the aftermath of the fire.

"Living Skies has a good credit rating and a promising financial future," he said, "so I'm going to meet the director of photography this afternoon. We'll write up our wish lists, and Ainsley can handle it from there."

"Isn't she planning to take Roy's ashes to Massachusetts sometime this week?" I said.

"She's leaving for New York tomorrow morning," Georgie said. "She and some friends are driving to a columbarium near Lennox to place Roy's ashes in the niche with Lev-Aaron's. Ainsley and her friends are going to stay at Roy and Lev-Aaron's summer place until Thursday, and she's flying back here on Friday."

"Ainsley has a tough week ahead of her," I said. "But the production studios are intact, so we should be grateful for small mercies."

At that point, Taylor and Chloe returned, and Nick's face softened. "Not to mention being grateful for blessings like these two." He smiled his transforming smile.

"An exit line if I ever heard one," Zack said. "Time to hit the road."

As they stood together in the doorway, seeing us off, Nick with his arm around Georgie's shoulder and Chloe in front, close to them both, they were a handsome trio and a happy one. "Nick looks ten years younger," Zack said. "He told me once that every morning he hopes this will be the day when he'll find a way to forgive himself for ruining Chloe's life."

"The person who blew the red light and T-boned Nick's car is the one who should be seeking forgiveness," I said.

"But Nick was the one who undid Chloe's seat belt when she complained it was too tight," Zack said. "They were almost home, so Nick figured she was safe."

It was a sobering observation, and the three of us were silent, absorbed in our own thoughts until we passed the city limits and reached the prairie. Zack's car window was partially open, and when the air drifting in became fragrant with the scent of moisture and warming earth, Zack inhaled deeply. "Spring," he said, and his tone was blissful.

"Not yet," I said. "Kurt Vonnegut says that for people who live in climates like ours, Spring is May and June. Summer is July and August. Autumn is September and October, and then comes the season he calls 'Locking.' Vonnegut says that November and December aren't winter. They're Locking. January and February are winter, and then come March and April, the Unlocking months when the earth warms and opens and new life begins."

Zack reached over and rubbed my leg. "I like that warming and opening part."

Taylor coughed theatrically. "You do realize that I can hear you, don't you?"

* * *

Maisie Crawford and her twin sister, Lee, had grown up on a farm seventy-five kilometres south of Regina. The girls had always done everything together, but when they enrolled at the University of Saskatchewan their paths diverged. Maisie entered the College of Law, and Lee began work towards a Ph.D. in Animal and Poultry Science. After she was called to the bar, Maisie stayed in the city, but Lee returned to the farm to continue the breeding programs begun by the guardian who had raised them. When shortly after Peter and Maisie's wedding, Lee died, the newlyweds moved into the farm to continue her life's work. The decision had been made in haste and grief, and two years later, I suspected that neither Peter nor Maisie was certain that their choice had been the right one.

Maisie was pregnant with their twin boys when she and Peter married, so the first order of business was to convert a farmhouse that had been built before World War I and was solid and well maintained into a home that could serve the needs of a young family and a doting grandfather who was paraplegic. Change was necessary. A new wing was added on the main floor and except for the parlour where Maisie and Lee had done their homework and practised piano forty-five minutes a day, every room in the house was extensively renovated. The result was a home that was bright, warm, welcoming and child- and wheelchair-friendly.

Taking up Lee's work was a perfect fit for our son, and he reveled in the fact that except for chores, his work was flexible enough to accommodate raising two little boys. But the fit was not perfect for Maisie. She was a gifted trial lawyer, but the demands of criminal law are punishing. Maisie and Peter were deeply in love, and Maisie loved their sons. But she was most fully alive during the hours when she was preparing a case or in court, and she was frank about feeling restless and unfulfilled as a stay-at-home mother. Falconer Shreve had an excellent on-site child-care facility and so far Peter and Maisie had managed to balance their commitments, but their respective careers were growing, and so were their sons.

My late husband's mother was a wise and realistic woman who told me that a mother-in-law's role is to keep her lips closed and her arms open. That was my policy too, but I had noticed the strain that had begun marking Maisie's face and Peter's, and I was counting the days till June 11, when *Strangers and Sisters* would begin shooting and I would be free to lend a hand with the boys. Until then, an afternoon in the country with our kids, their kids, newborn animals, chicks, poults and a field of crocuses was just what I needed. When we pulled into the driveway to the Crawford-Kilbourn farm, it appeared that Vince Treadgold had decided that an afternoon in the country was exactly what he needed too.

"What the hell?" Zack pointed towards the red Mercedes parked beside Charlie D and Mieka's Volvo, his eyes wide in disbelief. "Do you see what I see?" he said. "That's Vince's Mercedes. Your little chat at Nick's party must have convinced him to trade it in for a tractor."

When Peter came out to greet us, Vince was with him. Both wore rubber boots, blue jeans and sweatshirts. Peter's said "World's Best Dad," Vince's bore the name of a pharmaceutical company. Both men looked as surprised, delighted and apprehensive as two people who had agreed to pool their resources to fund a start-up after meeting twelve hours earlier at the croupier's table of a casino.

Zack grinned. "I'll bite. So what's going on?"

Vince and Pete exchanged a quick look, and Pete began. "In broad strokes, Vince called me yesterday morning, said that he'd told Mum he was interested in farming, but he had no idea where to start, and she'd given him my contact info.

He asked if there was a time when he could see our operation and I told him to come ahead."

"Pete was kind enough to let me follow him around all day. He even let me lend a hand. It was the best day I'd had in a very long time," Vince said. "We had dinner with Maisie and the boys and after Colin and Charlie were settled for the night, Pete and I went upstairs to his office. I told him that I wanted to work towards having an operation like his and asked him where I should start. And we came up with some answers."

"Which we can talk about after lunch," Pete said. "Right now, I'll just say Vince and I have a plan that should work and we're both pretty excited about it."

Vince went over to Zack and clapped him on the back. "In the thirty years we've known each other, this is the first time I've ever seen you at a loss for words," he said. "That alone may have been worth changing my life for."

* * *

That afternoon at the Crawford-Kilbourn farm was filled with memorable moments. Lena, for reasons known only to Lena, had decided to make certain that Vince felt included in the gathering. To that end, she sat beside him at lunch, told him that her favourite part of her trip to New York City was seeing the SpongeBob SquarePants musical at the Palace Theatre, and asked if he'd seen it yet. When Vince confessed that he hadn't seen the musical, and in fact, didn't know who SpongeBob SquarePants was, Lena pulled her chair closer.

As she began describing the life of the happy-go-lucky sponge who lives in a pineapple in a community known as Bikini Bottom on the ocean floor, Vince looked confused, so Lena piled on the details. She told Vince about Mr. Krabs, SpongeBob's boss at the Krusty Krab, a single father who is devoted to his adopted sperm whale daughter Pearl but is sometimes mean to SpongeBob, telling him he's just a simple sponge who somehow doesn't seem to absorb very much. When that didn't do the trick, Lena persevered, telling Vince about Sandy Cheeks, the clever karate-trained squirrel in an astronaut suit who is SpongeBob's friend. Vince was still confused. But when Lena described SpongeBob's starfish sidekick, who asks questions like "Is mayonnaise an instrument?" Vince laughed, and Lena clapped her hands in triumph. "I knew you'd get it," she said.

There were other nice moments, Zack as always stationing himself between the twins at lunch so he could encourage them to try the lentil soup by taking spoonfuls himself and smacking his lips. It always worked, and that day, Colin and Charlie cleaned their bowls. After lunch, the twins in matching red rubber boots, followed the men out to the barnyard to do chores, while the womenfolk snapped photos to send to the boys' Uncle Angus in Calgary.

Every year when we went to see the first crocuses, I told our children and later, our granddaughters, the story of Demeter and Persephone. This was the first year Charlie and Colin were old enough to join us on the climb up the hill, and Madeleine asked if she could be the one to tell the story of the daughter who went to the underworld to comfort the spirits of the dead and of the mother who missed her daughter so much she decided that nothing would ever grow again.

The ground was damp, so we'd brought blankets for the kids to sit on. After Taylor set out the blankets, she, Madeleine, Lena, the twins and, at his request, Charlie D, sat in a circle and Madeleine began. When she reached the part of the story where Demeter said she was so lonely she wanted to die, Madeleine's face was grave and Charlie and Colin looked anxious.

Madeleine picked up on the boys' uncertainty and rushed to the happy ending. "But guess what? When Demeter thought she would never be happy again, a ring of crocuses pushed their way through the dirt." Madeleine pointed to the crocuses on the ground in front of them. "The flowers Demeter saw were just like these, and guess what else? They were whispering to her. Taylor, Lena and I will show you how to put your ear close to the ground so you can hear what the crocuses say." When everyone was in position, Madeleine whispered, "Can you hear them? They're saying, 'She's coming. She's coming. Persephone is coming.'"

Colin nodded. He was hearing the message of the crocuses, but Charlie was dubious. He was a resolute child, and he kept grinding the side of his head into the ground. If he didn't hear the crocuses, at least he'd been given permission to burrow in the mud.

Madeleine held out her arms. "Demeter was so happy she began to dance, and she made a cape out of white crocuses to give to her daughter when she returned."

It was an idyllic ending to an idyllic afternoon, but the afternoon wasn't over. The twins discovered that flattening out on a hill was fun and rolling around until they found a mud puddle was even more fun. As we trooped home, the boys were very dirty, very happy and very weary. When we reached the porch, Maisie and I stripped the twins down and, despite their protests, led them to the showers.

I took Charlie into the boys' bathroom and Maisie took Colin into hers. None of my children had curly hair, and I was impressed by the tenacity with which Charlie's beautiful copper curls gripped mud. He was eel-slippery, and by the time his curls were squeaky clean, I was soaked to the skin. When Maisie and Colin arrived in the nursery, she held out a robe for me. "I'll put your wet clothes in the dryer. I wish we were the same size, but since we're not, dry and warm is the best we can manage."

"Dry and warm is fine," I said. We helped Charlie and Colin into pyjamas and then, as was their pre-nap ritual, we carried them around their pretty lemon-yellow bedroom looking at the paintings Taylor had made of the heritage birds Maisie's late sister, Lee, had cherished and Peter was now breeding. The stately beauty of the birds and the poetry of their names evoked another time: pink-billed Aylesbury ducks, Blue Andalusians, Ridley Bronze turkeys, Swedish Flower hens and scarlet-combed Langhams. The litany of the names lulled the boys, and by the time we tucked Colin and Charlie into their big boy beds, they were both half asleep.

"Mission accomplished," I said.

"It's always easier when it's one-on-one," Maisie said.

"Now with Vince Treadgold around, that ratio will be come up more often. I was at Falconer Shreve yesterday, but Pete said the twins had a great time tagging along with Dr. Vince, as they call him. Charlie, Colin and Dr. Vince will be able to learn about farming together."

"So you think Vince is here to stay?"

A shadow passed over Maisie's face. "Nobody is ever here to stay." She walked towards the wall where a portrait of her twin sister hung. Maisie had asked Taylor to paint it from a photograph taken of Lee when she was seven. Lee was lying in a field, looking up at the sky. Her copper curls were tousled; there was a smudge of dirt on her nose, and her smile revealed two gaps where her baby teeth were missing. The photo was of a girl in love with life, and Taylor had been reluctant to undertake the task because she wasn't certain she could give Maisie what she needed, but Maisie had been reassuring. Taylor worked for almost a month on the piece. We all agreed that the finished work captured Lee's spirit, but it was over a year before Maisie was able to take the painting home.

That afternoon, Maisie gazed at the painting for several minutes before she turned to face me. She was teary, and she wiped her eyes with the back of her hand. "I'm sorry, Jo. Every so often I just lose it." I put my arm around her and she lay her head on my shoulder; it was an action we had both become familiar with after Lee's death. Finally, Maisie straightened and looked into my face. "The life I'm living is the life Lee wanted. The farm, the comfortable house, the loving husband, the beautiful kids. Not a day goes by when I'm not overwhelmed by the knowledge that I am living the life my sister longed for and never experienced. And what's worse, I'm not grateful. I want more. What's the matter with me?"

"There's nothing the matter with you. You're strong, you're smart, you have a huge capacity for love, and in the two years since you and Peter were married, you've faced an onslaught of changes that would have flattened most of us: Lee's death. The twins' birth. Renovating this house. Moving here from the city. Becoming an equity partner at Falconer Shreve and handling at least a half-dozen complex criminal cases — two of them high profile. And look in the mirror — you're still standing."

Maisie's laugh was sardonic. "Barely," she said. "I'm starting to wobble."

"You're exhausted," I said. "I can help with that. You and Peter never had a honeymoon. I'll be finished with *Sisters and Strangers* by June 11. Zack and I can take the twins, and you and Pete can go north to Jan Lake and have the honeymoon you planned. But that's almost two months away. Short term, why don't we arrange for a four-day weekend. We can come out here and stay with the twins. Zack loves the farm, and with Bobby Stevens's help, Vince, Zack and I can handle the chores while you and Pete do something crazy like go to New York."

Maisie tried a smile. "And see *The SpongeBob Musical*?"

"I hear it's transcendent."

"Pete and I might not be ready for transcendent yet," Maisie said. "But the prospect of being alone together for a weekend at Lawyers' Bay is very tempting."

"The keys to the cottage are in my purse," I said. "I'll give them to you before we leave. And Maisie, I'm not taking the keys back until you and Pete have used them at least once."

CHAPTER ELEVEN

Our first stop when we got back to the city was dropping Taylor off at the apartment over the Sahara Club. She and Kyle Daly were meeting there to check the progress his crew had made. The apartment was off-limits to the rest of us until the renovations were complete and Taylor could show Vale their first home together. Taylor's emotions had always been too close to the surface to hide, and when she and Kyle came back in the early evening, she was bubbling, and Kyle looked pleased. The barter of professional services was clearly a success.

"I take it from your faces that the apartment is shaping up," Zack said.

"Kyle and his crew are working miracles," Taylor said. "It's a beautiful space, and it's starting to look like home — a very spiffy home — but still a place where Vale and I will be able to kick back and just be together."

"Our guys are doing a great job," Kyle said. He held up a DVD of *Frida*, the biopic of the relationship between Frida Kahlo and Diego Rivera, the acclaimed husband-and-wife Mexican artists and activists. "This is Taylor's and my homework for the set decoration part of the bargain. Ainsley thought the ways in which Julie Taymor, the director of *Frida*, used images to communicate characters' mood and the narrative's messages to an audience might generate some ideas for us. Given your involvement with *Sisters and Strangers*, we thought if you didn't have other plans, you might be up for a movie night."

I had seen *Frida* when it was released. The film covered a period in the history of Mexico that seethed with unrest, and it was engrossing and visually stunning. People lived large, and Taymor had focused on passions, political and sexual, that flamed hot and dangerous and often ended in violence. It was a terrific movie by any standard, but I understood why Ainsley believed the film would be of special interest to Kyle and Taylor.

When she was eighteen, Kahlo had been severely injured in a trolley crash that shattered her back and punctured her body with a steel rod. She lived in constant pain, and Taymor had shown how the extravagant colours of Kahlo's imagination enabled her to create art that allowed her to rise above her suffering.

Zack and I had no plans for the evening, so after Taylor made popcorn, we settled back with our drinks of choice and watched *Frida*. When the end credits ran, and I flicked on the lights, Zack stretched his arms and inhaled.

"That certainly packed a punch," he said. He turned his chair to face me. "How do you think we would have fared if we'd followed Frida and Diego's lead and promised to be 'not faithful but loyal'?"

"About as well as Frida and Diego did," I said. "But despite all the affairs, the battles, the divorce and the remarriage, their relationship lasted nineteen years. They were fated to be together."

Zack held out his arms to me. "Just like us."

"Right." I leaned in for a hug. "Two colossal talents and two colossal egos — just like us."

Taylor and Kyle had both been struck by the way in which Taymor blended Frida's experiences with images that revealed how the experience changed her life. Two images of the trolley accident stood out for all of us. In the first, a bluebird Kahlo is holding flies from her hand at the moment of impact; in the second, a container of gold flakes another passenger is holding spills over Kahlo's bleeding body. When Kyle said he'd read that both images were rooted in incidents that occurred at the time of Kahlo's accident, Taylor's excitement was palpable. "That's why the images are so powerful," she said. "They're proof of the ways magic touches our lives."

The film had quickened my pulse too. I had always been attracted to Frida Kahlo's art with its blend of realism and magic. I had never connected Kahlo's work with Sally's, but

Sally's painting *Flying Blue Horses* provided an example worth exploring.

To me, the parallels between the lives of Frida Kahlo and Sally Love were striking. Both women had many lovers, male and female; both lived dramatic, tempestuous lives, scarred by pain: Kahlo's was physical; Sally's was emotional. Sally never recovered from losing Des and believed until she died that the father she adored had committed suicide and tried to kill Nina and her. Both Kahlo and Sally found a way to channel their pain into art that was heartbreakingly intimate but resonated because the emotions their work evoked were universal. The connection between the two artists was another layer in understanding how Sally's art revealed her, and that night as I slid into bed, I thought of Emily Dickinson's poem "I Dwell in Possibility" and smiled.

* * *

The next morning after Zack left for Falconer Shreve and Taylor went out to her studio, I took my laptop to the kitchen, poured myself a second cup of coffee and looked up Frida Kahlo's *Henry Ford Hospital, 1932.* In the painting Kahlo lies naked on a bed, her body and face twisted in agony. She has suffered a miscarriage and the sheet beneath her is soaked in blood. Six images float in the space around her, one is the image of a male fetus, the son she and Diego longed for. The juxtaposition of reality and fantasy makes the work difficult to look at but impossible to forget, and my mind turned to a painting of Sally's that, despite my best efforts, had also left an indelible mark.

When Ben Bendure asked what Taylor and I wanted from Izaak Levin's collection of art using Sally as a subject, we made our choices, and I suggested that Ben select his favourites and that he send the rest to our mutual friend, the art dealer Darrell Bell with the request that the self-portrait Sally had given Izaak Levin as a birthday gift be kept from public scrutiny. Sally had painted the piece I wanted kept private when Izaak told her that artists admitted to the American Academy in New York were required to give the academy a self-portrait, and that, as his student in his "Academy of One," Sally should follow the tradition.

She was fourteen years old and he was forty, but they were already lovers. As her teacher, her agent and, periodically, her sexual partner, Izaak was part of Sally's life until they died within minutes of one another at a banquet in Sally's honour. When we were both in early middle age, Sally gave me a pithy description of her first years with Izaak Levin. "I painted and we went to galleries and we fucked, and that was my school of the arts."

Izaak himself had shown me the self-portrait, and what it revealed about Sally's assessment of herself at fourteen enraged and sickened me. It would have been easy to dismiss the picture because, at first glance, it seemed so stereotypical: a '50s magazine ad for a soft drink or suntan lotion. A pretty girl wearing a halter top and shorts hugged one knee and extended the other leg along the hood of a yellow convertible — a glamorous pose, sex with a ponytail. But

Sally had used colour to create light in an odd and disturbing way. The car glowed magically surreal — it was a car to take you anywhere — and the hot pink stucco of the motel behind the girl panted with lurid life. Sally herself was a cut-out, a conventional calendar girl without life or dimension, an object in someone else's world of highways and clandestine sex.

Like Frida Kahlo, Sally had used the extravagant colours of her imagination to create art that allowed her to rise above her suffering. I had hoped that Taylor would never see her mother's self-portrait. Now I knew that in order to do their best work, both Taylor and Vale, who had been cast as the young Sally Love, needed to see the painting.

Ben Bendure picked up on the first ring, and thrillingly, his musical bass was once again strong and filled with life.

"You sound terrific," I said.

"I surprised myself and my doctor by healing quickly," he said. "My doctor is within hailing distance of my age herself, so she's a cheerleader for all her octogenarian patients."

"Good for her, good for you and good for me, because I need you, Ben."

"Anything specific or just in general?"

"Both," I said. "But let's take care of the specific first."

When I told Ben about the connection I'd made between Frida Kahlo's work and Sally's, he was intrigued, and we had a ten-minute conversation about art and life, two subjects of which we never tired. Ben agreed that the self-portrait belonged with us, and he volunteered to call Darrell Bell and have him deliver the work the next time he came to Regina.

"Now that's settled," Ben said. As always when it was time to move on, Ben was brisk. "Tell me about this arrangement Taylor and Kyle Daly made to trade services. That kind of barter was common among people working in the arts when we were young and broke. So much has changed. It's cheering to realize that artists still believe in fair exchange."

"Kyle and Taylor certainly do," I said. "Kyle's a talented art director who needs someone who can replicate brilliant original paintings, and Taylor's a gifted artist who needs someone to create the perfect apartment for her and Vale."

Ben chuckled. "I gather your daughter and Vale Frazier have already decided on a future together."

"They have," I said. "It's the first real romantic relationship for both of them, and they're making thoughtful decisions about what comes next. Taylor says she and Vale will have demanding careers, so they want to use the months when Vale will be working on *Sisters and Strangers* here in Saskatchewan to build a firm foundation."

"You and Zack have raised a wise child," Ben said. "Taylor and Vale have extraordinary gifts. I've been a fan of Taylor's work since I met her, and it's been a privilege watching her art deepen and grow more daring as she finds her way. Vale is going to be intriguing to follow too. While I was recuperating, I watched the movie *Butterflies* twice just to see her performance. That young woman is the real deal."

"So you believe Vale is a good choice for the role of Sally."

"Better than good — inspired. Vale has that aura Sally had of radiating light cut through with sudden flashes of darkness." He paused. "Vale has not had an easy life, has she?"

"No," I said. "She hasn't, but she is absolutely without self-pity. A friend once told me that the priest who prepared her for confirmation said, 'Take what you want from life. Take what you want, but pay for it.' The first time Vale spent the evening with Zack and me, I thought of those words. Vale has paid in hard coin for her success."

"Sally did too," Ben said, and I could hear the ache in his voice.

"Ben, when you're feeling ready to travel, why don't you come to Regina?" I said. "I've always wished we lived closer to each other, but I'm grateful we're within easy driving distance. Anyway, all of us miss you, and you and Georgie Shepherd still haven't met. Georgie and I are working on the script together, and we could use your insights."

"That's a tempting offer. I promise I'll give it serious consideration."

"Please do," I said. "Because *Sisters and Strangers* needs you, and I need you."

* * *

The last time Ainsley paid me an unannounced visit had ended badly. She and I had made some progress since the day a year and a half earlier when she attempted to convince me that Vale Frazier's version of her relationship with Gabe was not to be trusted, but there was still a chill between us. That morning when I opened the door and saw Ainsley dressed for travel in a turtleneck, longline cardigan and leggings, her face pale and drawn, my heart went out to her.

The pain of carrying Roy's ashes to their final resting place in the columbarium near the summer home he and his late husband shared was incalculable, and nothing I could say or do would lessen it.

When I invited Ainsley to come inside, she gestured to the taxi waiting on the street. "I'm on my way to the airport, but I wanted to leave something with you." She reached into a soft pink leather tote, took out a large mailing envelope and handed it to me. "A few people are coming from New York for a farewell gathering, and I put together a memoir of Roy. I wanted you, Taylor and Zack to have a copy, and there's a rough cut of *The Happiest Girl* in the envelope too. The narrative flow between scenes is choppy, the score is incomplete and some of the visual and sound effects need tinkering, but there's enough there to give you an idea of the final product." Her voice broke. "It's going to be brilliant, Joanne — everything Roy wanted for it and more."

"I know it will be," I said. "And Ainsley, everyone working on *Sisters and Strangers* is determined to make the series what Roy believed it could be. Kyle and Taylor brought your DVD of *Frida* over to watch with Zack and me last night and seeing how Kahlo used the elements of magic realism in her work opened a vein of possibilities for Georgie and me to explore."

Ainsley's smile was faint. "Roy felt magic realism was the way into the heart of *Sisters and Strangers* too," she said. "At lunch the day he died, Roy was telling me about a book dealing with the work of an artist friend of yours, Joanne. Taylor had loaned it to him, and he was captivated by it.

Roy said he'd forgotten to bring the book with him, but he'd give it to me as soon as we returned home. Those were the last coherent words he spoke to me. After that, he and Kyle Daly walked into the woods, and the next time I saw Roy he was . . ." Her eyes narrowed as she searched for the words. "He was no longer Roy," she said finally. "He was a stranger — a crazed stranger with dirt under his fingernails from digging in the ground like an animal." Ainsley took a step towards me. "Do you think I'll ever get over this?"

Then she turned and walked towards the cab without waiting for an answer. And that was lucky, because I didn't have one.

After I closed the door, I took the envelope containing the memoir and the DVD into the family room and left it, unopened, on the mantle. Later, Zack, Taylor and I could read the memoir, watch the rough cut of *The Happiest Girl* and mourn the friend we had lost and the work he might have done had he lived. But Ainsley's account of her final conversation with Roy raised a question that was too vexing to be recollected in tranquility.

Everyone with whom Roy interacted the day he died believed he had turned a corner and was once again on solid ground. Nothing indicated that his mental state was so precarious that within hours his mind would explode. But it had. And the only concrete proof that Roy was in deep emotional trouble was his promise to bring a book he had violently defaced to Ainsley as soon as they were back in the city.

I still didn't know where this loose end led. I had hidden the book in my sewing basket, a relic of the '70s that for decades I had opened only to hide Christmas stocking stuffers. I went to the mudroom and took down the wicker basket. Nestled in the psychedelic-orange and harvest-gold swirls of the polyester lining, the book appeared unremarkable, but when I opened it, I was stunned by what it revealed about Roy's state of mind as he destroyed what he believed was the key to recovering his ability to write. I was thumbing through the pages searching for some sort of pattern when my phone rang.

Ben Bendure was on the line, and he had welcome news. Taylor's art dealer and our friend, Darrell Bell, was driving to Regina on Thursday. The prospect of delivering Sally's self-portrait to our house and having a visit with Taylor, whom he had represented since she was fourteen years old, had been impossible for Darrell to resist. If I was agreeable, Ben was going to tag along, so he could meet Georgie and the three of us could talk about *Sisters and Strangers.*

Georgie and I had fallen into the habit of having a cup of tea and exchanging news before we began our workday. As we sat at the kitchen table waiting for the tea to steep, Georgie stretched lazily. "This is always such a nice part of the day. And we have one less thing to worry about. Nick just called to say that Danny Kerrigan is back at work."

"Did Danny offer any explanation for where he'd been since Friday?"

"No, and Nick didn't press him. Nick said Danny seemed fine, and when Kyle came by to talk to Nick, Danny apologized."

"That's a good sign."

Georgie frowned. "I'm not sure it is. Nick said Danny's apology was not exactly fulsome. Danny said he was sorry for hurting Kyle, but that Pastor Kirk told him he had done the wrong deed for the right reason."

I cringed. "If Pastor Kirk's path and mine ever cross, I'm ninety-nine percent certain I'll do the wrong deed for the right reason too."

"I'll be in your corner, holding your towel and spit bucket."

"I'll count on that," I said. "And now, to paraphrase John Cleese, time for something completely different." After I explained how seeing Julie Taymor's use of magic realism in *Frida* had made me think about the potential that magic realism had for taking an audience to the heart of *Sisters and Strangers,* I turned on my laptop and opened Kahlo's *Henry Ford Hospital, 1932.*

Georgie stared at the screen for a long time. "My God. That poor woman," she said. "Did Sally ever paint anything that revealing?"

"She did," I said, "it's a self-portrait she made at the age of fourteen after — well, you know what her life had become by the time she was fourteen."

Georgie looked away. "I do," she said. "Ben Bendure's footage of Sally after Nina sent her to live with Izaak Levin in New York is searing — that child was dead inside."

"And her self-portrait reveals that," I said. "As soon as I saw *Frida*, I knew we needed Sally's self-portrait, and very soon it will be here with us. Darrell Bell's been hanging onto it since Izaak died and he and Ben are coming here on Thursday. So you two will finally meet."

"Good news all around," Georgie said. "I've watched *The Poison Apple* more times than I can count. I'm a Ben Bendure groupie — it'll be a thrill to meet him. And Sally's self-portrait will be invaluable to Vale Frazier's preparation for her role as Sally." Georgie lifted her teacup to me. "Well done."

"Ainsley came by this morning on her way to the airport. She brought the memoir she'd written about Roy and a rough cut of *The Happiest Girl*. Have you seen it?"

"Last night. Nick and Chloe and I watched it together. Chloe loved it, and I was blown away. That movie absolutely shimmers. I'd lost sight of how good both Roy and Ainsley were, and I'd never seen Vale. She's astounding. Watching the scenes between her and Rosamond Burke made the hairs on the back of my neck stand on end. Rosamond was generous about allowing Vale her moments, and Vale was graceful about accepting them. Nick said Ainsley created an atmosphere on *The Happiest Girl* set that brought out the best in everyone." Georgie shook her head. "We lost so much with Roy's death. If Ainsley is too mired in grief to do her best work on *Sisters and Strangers,* that loss will be compounded."

"Finding out the truth about Roy's death might help."

Georgie tensed. "You don't think we know the truth?"

"I don't know," I said. "I've always had questions, and then Ainsley said something that set me off again." I told Georgie about Roy promising to give Taylor's book to Ainsley as soon as they got back to Regina.

"That is curious," Georgie said. "And worrying. If Roy blocked the memory of what he did, he was in worse shape than we thought. But that will have to be a problem for another time. Right now we should get to work. I have to leave early — doctor's appointment."

"Everything okay?"

"Just a menstrual problem."

"I am so glad all that is behind me."

"My body may be moving in that direction too," Georgie said. "My period has always been irregular, but it's really gone wacky since I came to Regina."

"Stress can throw everything out of sync."

"True, but I'm forty-four. I checked with Dr. Google, and apparently that's early for menopause but within the normal range. No big deal. Now, I have an idea about how we can use that self-portrait of Sally's as a bridge between the scene where Sally escapes from the hospital and runs through the rain to beg Izaak not to force her to go back to Nina and the scenes of Sally in New York. I thought an establishing shot of New York City, a couple of quick scenes — no dialogue: Sally at a smart hair salon getting her hair cut; Sally, very chic, at an art opening with Izaak; Sally in bed having a cigarette, looking down on Izaak beside her, obviously post-coital, sound asleep. Then the scene with Sally painting the self portrait for admittance to the Academy of One. And while we watch Sally's portrait take shape, there's a voice-over from Rosamond Burke telling how Sally described her life with Izaak. 'We painted, and we went to galleries and we fucked, and that was my school of the arts.'"

"That's good."

"It's not bad," Georgie said. "And then what?"

Georgie and I had one writing rule: the best line in the room wins, and that day we came out even. The pathos of Sally's situation was undeniable, but we were determined to show that Sally had not been defeated by the hand she'd been dealt. As an adult, Sally told me she saw her relationship with Izaak as a fair exchange: she got what she needed from him, and he got what he needed from her. It was difficult for anyone, including me, to see Sally's relationship with Izaak as anything other than that of victim and predator, but Sally had not allowed herself to be a victim. She bore scars, but she lived life on her own terms. She made the art she wanted to make, she loved and was loved, and she lived fully. Georgie and I decided we could show that through intercutting scenes of Sally's often tumultuous growth in her relationships with Izaak and other lovers and the increasing boldness and assurance of her work.

We had lunch at the work table, and we were both surprised when Georgie's phone beeped and it was time for her to leave for her doctor's appointment. We had worked through a knotty problem, and we knew where we were headed. We were optimistic, and when we parted, we exchanged a brief hug and Georgie promised to call and let me know what the doctor said.

* * *

Two hours later when there was no phone call, I felt the first stirrings of unease. The offices of ob-gyns are notorious for running late, and the specialist Georgie was seeing had a stellar reputation, but as the minutes ticked by, my mind began running through the myriad of gynecological complications women's bodies are prey to, and I grew increasingly anxious.

When my phone rang and Georgie asked if she could see me, I didn't hesitate. "Of course. Just . . . are you okay?"

"I'm standing on your doorstep, and instead of knocking like any normal human being, I called you on my phone. Obviously, I'm not playing with a full deck."

"The door's not locked," I said. "Come in."

I ran up the hall to meet her, and when I saw Georgie's face, I feared the worst. She appeared dazed. I took her hand. "Come and sit down. Can I get you anything. Water? Tea? Something stronger?"

Her head shake was vigorous. "Nothing stronger," she said. "Jo, I'm not having an early menopause; I'm having a late-life baby. My due date is November 7." She grinned. "I walked into that office thinking I was about to say 'goodbye to all that,' and now I have a due date. How the heck did that happen?"

"I'm pretty sure you're the one with the best line on that one."

"You're right." Georgie squeezed her eyes shut in concentration. When she opened them again, her face relaxed into a smile. "Valentine's Day," she said. She shook her head. "No clichés spared for Nick and me. It was our first time, and we barely knew each other. It just felt right. After that, we were always careful."

"It only takes once."

Georgie rolled her eyes. "And another cliché enters the ring," she said. "But pile it on. We acted like teenagers. We had it coming." She looked away. "Jo, how do you think Nick's going to react to this?"

"He'll be elated," I said. "So will Chloe. When Chloe was passing around the appetizers at Nick's party, Zack commented that the three of you looked right together, and that it would be great if . . ."

"If what?"

"I wouldn't let Zack finish his sentence," I said. "I was afraid that if he said the words, he'd jinx your happy ending. Luckily, motile sperm cells are not superstitious."

Georgie's lips curved into a smile. "You're happy about this aren't you?"

"As long as you are . . ."

"I am," Georgie said. "When I left the doctor's office, I went straight to Groovy Mama on 13th and looked at baby things. Who knew babies needed so much?"

"The staff at Groovy Mama are great about suggesting what's necessary. Did you tell them you were pregnant?"

Georgie's expression was rueful. "Nope, unlike motile sperm cells, I am superstitious."

"When are you going to tell Nick?"

"As soon as I leave here. I'll be able to catch him at the production studios. But I think we should wait till after the three-month mark to tell Chloe, and I'm only at nine weeks. Dr. Nawaz wants to see me again then, and she said she might want to take an ultrasound. I told her about Chloe and she said that in addition to showing if the fetus is developing as it should, an ultrasound could help Chloe understand how the baby is coming into being."

"Dr. Nawaz sounds very caring."

"She is," Georgie said. "The baby and I are in good hands, Jo."

CHAPTER TWELVE

That afternoon, Taylor called to say she and Kyle had finished ordering all the furnishings needed for the apartment, and they were celebrating by bringing a feast from Peking House to our place for dinner. After we had eaten our fill, and Esme had polished off the extra order of moo goo gai pan, Kyle, a non-dog owner, had left on the counter, the four of us settled in the family room and watched *The Happiest Girl*.

Zack had not been present for any of the production's filming; I had watched isolated scenes; Taylor had been on set most days; Kyle had been working in the U.S. and had no connection with the shoot. We came to the rough cut from very different perspectives, but like Georgie, we were all blown away by what we saw.

Rosamond Burke and Vale Frazier are the only actors I'd ever known, and I wondered if my personal relationship with them would make it difficult for me to suspend disbelief as I watched the movie. I had no grounds for concern. There are few human characters in the film, and only two are significant. The bond between Ursula, the anthropologist who has given her life to studying the relationship between humans and the polar bears of Churchill, and her granddaughter Ursula, who shares both her grandmother's name and her passion for the bears, is palpable. The film begins on the longest night of the year. Eight weeks earlier, the grandmother ventured onto the tundra and never returned. She is presumed dead, but Ursula refuses to believe that her grandmother would leave her without a message. On this, the winter solstice, the bear Callisto appears at the grandmother's cabin, and Ursula knows that Callisto has come to take her to her grandmother.

When Rosamond, in her role as the Grandmother, began to speak — "Winter is the time for story telling in the northern hemisphere" — the screen was black, but as her thrilling voice continued, the aurora borealis began its dance across the sky and the screen pulsed with undulating bands of colour: luminous white, yellow-green, indigo, violet, and finally a deep, vibrant red.

The grandmother narrates the Inuit myth that the northern lights are torches held in the hands of spirits seeking the souls of those who have just died to lead them over the abyss at the edge of the world into the spirit world, and the camera moves in on Vale Frazier as Ursula. She is alone on the tundra as she has been on the five nights since she and her mother arrived from Winnipeg to pack up the grandmother's belongings so the cabin can be sold.

The camera continued to move toward Ursula until the screen was filled with a close-up of her face. In person, Vale was an attractive young woman — auburn hair, blue-green eyes, flawless skin — worthy of a second glance but not mesmerizing. Onscreen, Vale seemed to emanate light, and her eyes had depths that drew the audience in, but it was her expression that held my attention.

Everything Ursula was feeling was in Vale's face: disbelief, grief, anger and terror at the possibility that what everyone was telling her was true, that the link between her and the grandmother who connected her to everything she cared about had been irreparably broken. Without saying a word, Vale made the audience feel the emotions that were tearing Ursula apart. I'd watched an interview in which the host asked Vale if she drew on memories of her own life to generate emotion. Vale seemed faintly amused at the question, but her answer was polite. "No," she said, "when I'm playing a role, the only experiences I can draw on are the character's. I have to find the place where she was happy or hurt or whatever and pull my emotion from that."

There was something else about Vale's performance. When she was with us, I always sensed there was a part of Vale that remained closed off, but onscreen Vale was completely open to everything going on around her. Vale's Ursula was fully present in the moment, and she was never more present than she was in the flashbacks to the summers she spent on the tundra with her grandmother. As I watched Rosamond and Vale together — listening, responding, offering, receiving, reaching out, embracing — I knew I was witnessing an actor nearing the end of her career welcoming an actor just beginning.

At the movie's end, Ursula finds her grandmother in the ancient cave of the bear-people where she has come to die among the bones of her ancestors. Ursula promises her grandmother she will continue her work with the polar bears, and the grandmother gives Ursula the tan camera bag that holds her prized Nikon. For a time they stand apart, facing each other, fixing their last moment together in memory.

Finally the grandmother speaks. "Now, it's time for you to leave. The aurora borealis is putting on a real show tonight, Ursula. Don't miss it. Look up at that big sky. All the stories are there."

Ursula is obviously warmed by the memory. "My favourite was the one about the northern lights being the spirits of children waiting to be born playing ball in the heavens until their turn comes. You and I used to make up names for every child and we gave each of them a story." Ursula's voice breaks. "Nana, I can't go on without you."

"But you won't be without me, Ursula. An elder once told me that their language has no sense of time. In the old language, the past, present and future happen all at once. That's how it will be for us, I will still be happening through you. You and I will always be in each other's present tense."

We were silent as the end credits ran, and Zack was slow to flick on the lights. Even then, the four of us remained still, reluctant to leave Ursula's world. Kyle was the first to break the spell. He stood abruptly, mumbled, "I'm sorry. I have to get out of here," and bolted for the door.

Taylor was quick to follow. When she caught Kyle's arm, he half turned. "Are you all right?" she said.

Without responding, Kyle lowered his head and strode towards the front door. Taylor followed him. "My car is in the driveway," she said. "I'll see what's going on with Kyle. I won't be long."

"What do you suppose that's all about?" Zack said.

"The movie was intense," I said. "I'm sure Kyle connected the grandmother's death with Roy's. Don't forget he and Ainsley are the ones who discovered Roy that night. When Ainsley dropped off the rough cut, she talked briefly about how *The Happiest Girl* would be everything Roy wanted for it and more; then, almost immediately, she was drawn back to that day on the island, and she began describing how Roy looked when they located him in the forest. Zack, it wasn't a recollection for her. She was there, facing the man who for thirty years had been the centre of her life, and he was digging on the ground like an animal. Her last words to me were, 'Do you think I'll ever get over that?'

"Kyle experienced that moment too," I continued. "I know his relationship with Roy wasn't especially close, but when Kyle came back from Saskatoon the morning after Roy died, he relived the moment when they discovered Roy. Kyle said he couldn't take in what he was seeing because despite his inner turmoil, Roy was always Roy: courteous, articulate and immaculate. Watching *The Happiest Girl* must have made Kyle wonder if he would ever get over what he saw that night on the island."

"If that's the case, Kyle should get help immediately,"

Zack said. "I've had clients who suffer from PTSD, and it devastated their lives."

"We should talk to Taylor about that," I said. "She's obviously fond of Kyle, and I think if she suggests Kyle might need professional help, he'll listen to her."

"I don't know about you, but I'm ready to hit the sack," Zack said. "That movie packed a wallop."

"It did," I said. "Between us, you and I just about emptied that box of tissues. Ainsley told me that the rough cut still needs work, but it's already amazing. I kept wishing Roy could see it. And Zack, I was wishing Gabe Vickers could have seen it too."

Zack nodded. "The first time we met, Gabe said *The Happiest Girl* would put Regina on the map as a place to make movies. He said his movie was going to be a blockbuster, a perfect family movie — and he was right. When production companies realize it's possible to make first-rate movies and TV series here, the Saskatchewan Production Studios will be humming, creating good jobs and changing many lives for the better."

"Including Vale's," I said. "Rosamond is brilliant, but Vale wasn't overshadowed. I couldn't take my eyes off her. She's headed for a very big future."

"And a challenging one," Zack said. "And our daughter will be part of it. People will have opinions about her relationship with Vale."

"I mentioned that to Taylor once, and she reminded me that people had opinions about our relationship, but you and I loved each other too much to let go."

"Thank God for that."

"I do," I said. "First thing every morning, last thing every night."

"Do you think Taylor and Vale will be able to weather the storm?"

"They're aware there will be difficult times ahead," I said. "That's why they're determined to start their life together in Regina where they won't be in the spotlight. They've thought this out. They believe living here will give them a chance to forge a link strong enough to withstand what's ahead."

Zack sighed. "I'm not ready for this," he said. "Wasn't it just yesterday that Taylor was making me check the garage for spiders before she'd come out to get in the car?"

* * *

Zack and I were in bed reading when Taylor returned home. The door was ajar so she came in and perched on the edge of the bed.

"I thought I'd better check in," she said. "I knew you'd be worried."

Zack peered at Taylor over his glasses. "Is Kyle all right?"

"He says he will be, but he wouldn't let me stay with him. Apparently, he's been having what Kyle calls 'post-traumatic stress episodes' about the day he came upon Roy in the woods on the island. He had one tonight when the movie ended."

"That's what your dad and I thought happened," I said. "We think Kyle might need professional help."

"I suggested that," Taylor said. "Because Kyle is really suffering. He says he can see Roy, and it's terrible because he knows it's too late, but he can't stop it — it's already gone too far."

"That doesn't make sense to me," I said. "Did Kyle explain what he meant by not being able to stop it because it had already gone too far?"

"No. And I asked him about it. Kyle said there was no point talking because nothing he said now could change what happened. Then he thanked me for making sure he got home safely and asked me to apologize to you both." Taylor took a deep breath. "So that's what I did, and now I think I should have stayed."

"Don't second-guess yourself," Zack said. "You did what you could. But you might sleep better if you texted Kyle and told him you've left your phone on in case he wants to talk later."

Taylor smiled. "That's exactly what I did, Dad."

Zack held out his arms to her. "Good. Knowing that will make us all sleep better."

CHAPTER THIRTEEN

The previous fall, Zack and I had planted seventy Red Dynasty tulip bulbs in the bed outside the kitchen window. When the dogs and I returned from our run the morning after we watched the rough cut, the first of the tulips was blooming. Zack was at Falconer Shreve for a partners' meeting, so I sent him a photo along with a note saying Charlie D had called saying he had news about Aunt Nancy and he was coming over as soon as his show was over.

After I'd showered and dressed for the day, Taylor and I sat down to breakfast together.

I poured us each a glass of juice. "Any word from Kyle?"

"Just a text this morning thanking me again, apologizing to you and Dad again and asking if I wanted to join him at their unit's production meeting this morning."

"Are you going?"

"I wouldn't normally," Taylor said. "I have work of my own I should get back to, but I'll be more focused if I know Kyle's okay."

"You're fond of him, aren't you?"

"I am. He's bright, he's creative and he's fun to be with. Wait till you see what we're doing with that apartment. It's going to be perfect — not just to look at, but to live in. Anyway, I owe Kyle big time, and I'm one of the few people who is close to him, so I'm going to make sure he gets this PTSD or whatever it is under control."

"Keep us posted," I said. "We like Kyle too."

Taylor sipped her juice. "We never got around to talking about the movie last night."

"After you left, your dad and I talked about it," I said. "*The Happiest Girl* is breathtaking. Vale is going to be able to write her own ticket. You two have a bright future ahead."

Taylor leaned closer. "You don't look very happy about that future."

"We are happy," I said. "We're just concerned about your private life becoming public."

"Vale and I have discussed that."

"And . . ."

"I told Vale what you've always told me. We can't control what people say, but we can control how we react to what they say." My daughter's smile was wry. "Once in a while, I actually do pay attention to your wise words, Jo." As quickly as it came, Taylor's smile vanished. "Vale and I know not everyone is going to be accepting of us. All we can do is love each other and hope for the best." Taylor covered my hand with her own. "That's what you and Dad did, and it worked for you."

* * *

When Georgie Shepherd arrived at nine, her mile-wide smile said it all. I held out my arms to her. "Are congratulations in order?"

"You bet they are," Georgie said. "Nick and I are getting married. As soon as I told him about the baby, he proposed. I said yes, we told Chloe that we were going to be a family and just like that" Georgie snapped her fingers — "there's going to be a wedding."

"The kettle's on," I said. "Let's have a cup of tea and talk details."

Georgie was too buoyant to wait for the tea to be poured. "It's going to be very small," she said. "Just Zack and you as witnesses — if you agree. We haven't known each other long, but I thought with Zack and Nick's years of friendship, you might be willing. Ainsley is the only alternative, and given everything she's been through, asking her would be cruel. And Chloe's going to be my bridesmaid. Anyway, just the five of us in the wedding party — if you say yes."

"I say yes."

Georgie rubbed her hands together. "Winner, winner, chicken dinner."

I laughed. "Where did that come from?"

"Believe it or not, from one of the nuns who taught me at Holy Cross. Anyway, there'll be the five of us in the wedding party and Mrs. Szabo, Taylor, Henry Chan and Vince Treadgold. Nick's brothers are far flung and they all have large families. There are friends I could invite, but out-of-town guests who've never met Nick or Chloe would be a complication we don't need. We want this wedding to be small and soon. Nick called his brothers, and they've agreed that a big Kovacs family reunion here in the summer would be perfect, and I can invite friends then."

"So 'small and soon' is our byword," I said. "That certainly simplifies things."

"Nick and I want a Catholic wedding," Georgie said. "He and Chloe have been going to Mass at Campion College at the university."

"That's a lovely space," I said. "Bright, airy, contemporary. And very welcoming."

"Chloe likes it, and Nick says Father Sami is very good about explaining things to her. We have an appointment to see him right after lunch. Father told Nick the chapel is free at three o'clock on May 5 — Cinquo de Mayo — so that's when it's happening."

"You and Nick seem to have everything well in hand," I said. "All that's left to decide is what to wear and what to eat. So shall we take our tea down to the office and get to work?"

* * *

In truth, Georgie and I didn't get much work done. We both had our laptops, and the secrets for creating the perfect, intimate, elegant wedding were only a click away. When she left for her meeting with Nick and Father Sami, I walked her to the door. We were both still bubbling with plans and possibilities. "I am so happy for you all," I said.

Georgie's eyes were brimming. "This feels so right," she said. "Nick says we were meant to be together, and I believe that too."

* * *

Charlie D in the Morning ended at noon so after Georgie left, I made a plate of tuna salad sandwiches and a pitcher of iced tea and sat down to wait for Charlie D.

He arrived at 12:10, and when he saw the sandwiches, he rubbed his hands together gleefully. "I'm ravenous, and tuna salad — my favourite. Do you still make it with curry?"

"I do," I said. "And there's more tuna salad in the fridge, so eat hearty."

My son-in-law and I ate in companionable silence, but after we'd polished off the platter of sandwiches, I said, "So what's the skinny on Aunt Sally?"

"Where to start?" Charlie D said. "It involves a man named Buzz Wells."

"I've heard his name," I said. "I've also heard that he's trouble."

"There are two schools of thought on that," Charlie D said. "Wells is said to be overbearing, but he also performs miracles on moribund scripts, so whatever problems he creates evaporate the second the box office opens."

"He spins straw into gold."

Charlie D laughed. "I'm sure that's Buzz's take. But he doesn't sign on for a project unless he's relatively certain he can triumph. And his skills go beyond scriptwriting. He's apparently a genius at coordinating writing with directing and editing."

"Executive producer skills."

"Look at you," Charlie D said. "The ink isn't dry on your union card, and you've already nailed the job descriptions. My father always says you're a smart broad."

"And I always stand a little taller when he says that. So what's the connection between Buzz Wells and Gabe Vickers?"

"This is where the story gets tangled. Remember me saying that *Sisters and Strangers* got the green light from the network by knocking another six-part series out of the lineup?"

"It's been on my mind ever since. You said Gabe Vickers used dark magic to make the other series disappear."

"It turns out there was no dark magic. Vickers just engaged in some down-and-dirty deals with some very questionable people. Apparently, Buzz Wells is the new owner of Aunt Nancy . . ."

My breath caught. "Aunt Nancy," I said, "and you and I were wondering . . ."

"Yes, exactly, and he was executive producer of the six-part series. Wells has a serious gambling habit, and Gabe found out that Wells was in way over his head with the kind of people who don't take it kindly when other people renege on financial commitments. So Gabe approached Wells's creditors and convinced them to put pressure on Buzz Wells to come through with the money he owed and invest that money in a hot new project another production company was set to produce."

I could feel goosebumps rising on my arms. "And that new project was *Sisters and Strangers.*

"What did the people who Buzz owed money to get in return?"

"Shares in Living Skies Production Company. It was an easy sell for Gabe. Everyone connected with *The Happiest Girl* knew it would be a huge hit and Gabe had commitments to the new project from Rosamund Burke, Vale Frazier, Ainsley Blair and Georgie Shepherd."

"So the squeeze was on."

"Exactly. As executive producer, Wells had access to the development fund for the series, and he drained the coffers to pay his gambling debts."

"And his creditors purchased stock in Living Skies Productions, and Gabe Vickers used that money to finance *Sisters and Strangers.*"

"It gave Vickers enough capital to approach potential backers and put together the rest of the financing. Meanwhile, back at the ranch, Buzz Wells was telling his investors that their production was stalled by creative differences and would have to be delayed."

"The original backers are still expecting Wells's series will be produced?" I said. "That explains why Aunt Nancy is still paying the rent on their offices. Wow! Buzz Wells is certainly gutsy, but how long can he delay the inevitable?"

"Rich people go on extended winter holidays, and Buzz

was able to keep up the pretense that all was well till the middle of February. That's when he came up with the 'creative differences' scenario. Of course, the clock is ticking on that one."

"I'll bet it is," I said. "Charlie D, does that mean trouble for us?"

"It could, but let's jump off that bridge when we come to it."

* * *

In mid-afternoon, Georgie called. The music had gone out of her voice, and her tone was grave. "Joanne, I've been deliberating about whether to even bring this us up. It may mean nothing, but in case it signals a problem, I think you should know that Ainsley called me twenty minutes ago. She and her friends were ready to set out for the drive to Lennox with Roy's ashes. Ainsley says Buzz Wells met her when her plane arrived at JFK, and he's been by her side ever since. According to her, he's taking care of everything and she is beyond grateful because she is running on empty."

* * *

I believe in synchronicity, but by definition, "synchronicity" demands that events that appear related because they occur simultaneously must have no discernible causal connection. Within the space of a few hours, I had learned that Buzz Wells was in desperate need of cash; that he had turned up at the side of his grief-stricken ex-wife, a woman who had access to the considerable assets of Living Skies Productions; and that he was making himself indispensable. For me, the causal connection between those events was written in flaming letters in the sky. I called Charlie D. When I passed along Georgie's news, he uttered his favourite expletive and suggested we sit tight and let events unfold before we acted, so I went back to the office and opened my laptop.

But instead of opening the script we'd been working on, I typed the words "Buzz Wells, Producer," in the web search space and hit the link for Buzz's official site. The headshot on his page was of an attractive man with a tan, a silvery crewcut, a pleasant if practised smile and shrewd, observant grey eyes. I was trying to deduce the character of the man behind the photo when my phone rang. It was long distance from an area code I didn't recognize. When I picked up, a voice, male and assured, asked to speak to Joanne Shreve.

"I'm Joanne," I said.

"This is Buzz Wells," the man said. I looked again at the photo on my laptop screen and shuddered at the powers of technology. "I'm a friend of Ainsley Blair's," he said, "and I need to get in touch with Georgie Shepherd. She's not answering her phone and her assistant told me, she often works with you."

"She does," I said. "But Georgie is taking a personal day, so she's off the grid." To that point, Buzz's smooth baritone had been warm and inviting, a charmer's voice, but when he spoke again, there was a definite edge. "Surely, you're able to get in touch with her."

"I am," I said. "Is this an emergency?"

"Ainsley collapsed at the columbarium service."

My impulse was to be cooperative, but Georgie was planning her wedding, and I was determined to keep Buzz Wells away from her. "Has Ainsley been hospitalized?"

As the silence between us lengthened, I knew that wherever he was, Buzz's fury was building and like Rumpelstiltskin, his tiny foot was itching to pound the earth in rage. "It's a simple question," I said. "Is Ainsley in the hospital?"

"She's being cared for by friends."

"So she's in no danger," I said. "When I see Georgie, I'll have her call Ainsley."

"Have her call me." Buzz's voice was coldly furious. "I'm taking charge until Ainsley recovers, and I need to hear from Georgie Shepherd asap."

"Why?"

Buzz didn't answer, but I did hear a definite sputter before he ended the call.

* * *

Buzz Wells's headshot was still on my screen when Fawn Tootoosis called. Nominally, Georgie Shepherd was still the executive producer of *Sisters and Strangers*, but day to day, Fawn's cool head and steady hand had been steering the project since Gabe Vickers's death.

Fawn was uncharacteristically agitated. "Joanne, I may have put you in the middle of a difficult situation, and the least I can do is provide context."

"If the situation involves Buzz Wells, I'm already involved," I said. "He just hung up on me."

Fawn sighed. "I am so sorry, Joanne. When Mr. Wells called, he demanded to speak to the executive producer; since Georgie wasn't here, the receptionist put him through to me. He told me he needed to speak to Georgie personally about an urgent matter and that her phone was going straight to voicemail. I knew Georgie turned off her phone when the two of you were working, but Mr. Wells was so insistent that I gave him your number."

"No harm done," I said. "But Georgie's not here. She had errands to run, and I've heard enough about Buzz Wells to know that, as Georgie's friend, I should keep him away from her today."

"That was probably wise," Fawn said. "Joanne, Buzz Wells's call might just be the tip of the iceberg. Would it be possible for you to come here so we can talk face to face? Hal Dupuis was with me when Mr. Wells called. He just shared some very unsettling information and, given the terms of your contract about *Sisters and Strangers*, I think you should hear what Hal has to say."

"I'll be at your office in ten minutes."

"No, not here," Fawn said. "This should be kept confidential. I have the keys to the writers' room. Let's meet there."

* * *

When the Fine Arts building of the old University of Regina was gutted and reconstructed as a movie and

TV studio facility, most of the classrooms remained untouched. Juxtaposed with the crayon bright, hard-edged brutalism of the renovations, the old classrooms with their blackboards, oak furnishings and segment head windows evoked a gentler age, and I had been pleased to learn that the room in which Roy Brodnitz and I would be working was one of the old classrooms. My memories of the buoyant beginnings of our collaboration had been shining, but the dark weeks of confusion, anger and fear after Gabe's death had all but obliterated them, and that afternoon as I walked down the shadowy halls to the writers' room, I was apprehensive.

Fawn and Hal were already seated at the old oak table when I came in. Hal rose, came over and took my hand. "After our time together at the all-departments' gathering, I'd hoped we'd meet again soon," he said. "And here we are. I wish the circumstances were more salubrious."

My encounter with Buzz Wells had jangled my nerves, and Hal's slow and melodious voice was soothing. "Whatever the situation, it's a pleasure to see you again," I said.

"I hope you'll still feel that way after I've explained my role in all this," Hal said. After Fawn and I exchanged muted greetings, Hal pulled out a chair for me, made certain I was comfortable and then, without preamble, he began. His first question blindsided me. "How much do you know about the financing behind *Sisters and Strangers*?" he said.

"Until today, I knew nothing, but my son-in-law, Charlie D, who hosts *Charlie D in the Morning*, has been curious about how quickly the entire project came together, and this morning, he told me he'd learned where Gabe Vickers got the seed money to finance the series."

Fawn and I were sitting across from each other with Hal between us at the head of the table. As I delivered my précis of Charlie D's report, I watched their reaction. Hal's eyes were downcast and his shoulders slumped. Clearly nothing I said was news to him. But my words were having an impact on Fawn. She and Hal were friends, and the looks she cast him as I spoke were anxious. When I finished, Fawn tented her long expressive fingers. "So Gabe robbed Peter to pay Paul."

Hal nodded. "I haven't heard that expression since I was a child," he said. "But that's exactly what happened, and I made it possible."

Fawn touched Hal's arm. "I don't believe that," she said. "Hal, you're a fine person."

"Thank you, but what I did was wrong. At the time, it seemed like justice. Gabe Vickers did me a great kindness once, and Buzz Wells harmed someone I love. I was given a chance to redress the balance, and I took it." He fell silent, seemingly gathering his thoughts. Under the overhead light, Hal's shaved head gleamed, brown-gold as a tiger eye. Finally, he stood and began to pace and to talk.

"Last December, Gabe Vickers called and told me he needed to move on the series quickly. Gabe's principal concern was the actor he wanted to feature in the series, Vale Frazier. He believed the part he had in mind for her would be her breakout role, but the character she would play was in her early to mid-teens, and Vale was already eighteen. Time was of the essence. Gabe had put together a strong cast and crew package to take to potential investors, but he needed seed money, and he needed it fast."

"And he came to you for money?" I said.

Hal's laugh rumbled from somewhere deep inside. "If I'd had it, I would have given it to him gladly. Thanks to Gabe I earn a very comfortable living, but I didn't have the kind of money he needed."

"Hal, I don't mean to pry," I said. "I'm just trying to get the full picture here. You said Gabe Vickers did you a great kindness. I never saw that side of him."

"It was there." Hal returned to his place at the table. "I didn't learn about the darkness in Gabe until I came to Saskatchewan. Since then, like you, Joanne, I've been trying to reconcile the person who saved me with the person who committed such unimaginable acts."

Fawn's expression was strained. "How did Gabe Vickers save you?"

"When no other producer would touch me with a ten-foot pole, Gabe hired me," Hal said. "I was twenty-three when I had my first big success on Broadway. It was a heady time. I was a wunderkind, the golden boy that everybody wanted.

"But as the poet said, 'Fame is fickle food/upon a shifting plate.' I was hired as costume designer for an expensive, ambitious, elaborate show, and the morning after the show opened, I was finished. The reviews were excoriating, and my costumes were singled out as emblematic of everything that killed the production: its pretensions, its excesses, its absurd aping of other designers' work. And just like that, my phone stopped ringing. The silence lasted for over a year."

"You've never told me about this," Fawn said.

"It was a painful memory," Hal said. "But then Gabe called and hired me for a small off-Broadway show he was producing. The play was set in 1919, the year after the Armistice was signed, and centred on Adelaide, a nineteen-year-old nursing volunteer at a rehabilitation hospital, and two of her patients: a young soldier who'd been blinded, and one who'd been crippled. The only set was the sunroom of the rehabilitation facility. The budget line for costume design was in the low four figures, but I was determined to honour Gabe's faith in me, and I produced the historically accurate, unexceptional wardrobe that the script demanded. There was one bright spot. When the two young soldiers see that Adelaide is becoming mired in the pain and hopelessness of her work, they chip in and ask her to buy a dress that will make her happy.

"She chooses a deeply vibrant red dress with a full chiffon skirt and when she dons it to show the young soldiers, she twirls and says, 'This dress makes me feel as if I'm dancing in a field of poppies.' The show takes its title from that line, and the playbills and advertising for *Dancing in Poppies* featured a striking photograph of Adelaide in a field of poppies with her skirt swirling gracefully around her. That photograph restored my reputation, and my phone began to ring again."

"That's a lovely story," I said. "I understand why you wanted to help Gabe. How did the opportunity come about?"

"That story is far from lovely," Hal said. "And I'm ashamed of my role in it. My sister, Stella Delacroix, is a writer. Six years ago she wrote a pilot for a television show called *Broders' Annex*. It was based on the neighbourhood Stella and

I grew up in — Black, working class, aspiring. Buzz Wells was hired to executive produce, and he signed himself on as show-runner. Stella's a strong woman, and she's not easily cowed, but from the beginning, she felt that Wells was determined to break her. He ignored her ideas, demeaned her and shunned her. My sister stuck it out to the end of the first season. Then she quit. The show ran five seasons. The situations and plot lines changed, but for all that time, the characters and relationships Stella created for the pilot were the heart of the series."

"Clearly that was a violation of intellectual property laws," Fawn said.

"I'm sure it was," Hal said. "But that kind of case is in the courts forever, and Stella wanted to close the door on Buzz Wells."

Fawn's hands were clenched into fists. "Is your sister still writing?"

"She is," Hal said. "For one of those teenage werewolf shows. The show's doing well, and Stella's happy enough. To be honest I think she's been over what Buzz Wells did to her for quite a while. But I'm her big brother . . ."

Fawn's smile was understanding. "And you weren't over it."

Her warmth seemed to raise Hal's spirits. "No, I wasn't, and over the years, I've kept an eye on what Wells was up to. His gambling problem was well-known and before Christmas I heard that he was heavily in debt and his creditors were breathing down his neck. I knew Wells was producing a new series, and when Gabe told me he needed start-up money for his new project, I asked around about the status of Wells's series. Wells was vulnerable. I described the situation to Gabe, and he took it from there."

"By convincing Buzz Wells's creditors to put pressure on him."

Hal nodded. "And you know the rest. In return for the money Wells's creditors handed over for *Sisters and Strangers*, Gabe gave them shares in Living Skies Productions. He wasn't worried about buying the shares back. He knew *The Happiest Girl* would be a hit, and when the money rolled in, he could buy back the shares, and no one would be the wiser."

"But Buzz's timetable wasn't as flexible as Gabe's," Fawn said.

"And here's the kicker," Hal said. "The people who invested in Buzz Wells's series are still expecting it to go ahead. *The Happiest Girl* won't be bringing in money until the end of the year. Buzz needs money now."

"And Ainsley Blair owns a good chunk of Living Skies and has access to the development money for *Sisters and Strangers*," I said.

Hal looked stricken. "Joanne, I hope you know that I never anticipated this outcome."

"I know that," I said. "And I'm grateful we had this talk. Forewarned is forearmed, but I wish I knew what we're armed against. Until Buzz Wells makes his move, all we can do is speculate. If Buzz arrives in Regina with Ainsley, we still don't have anything. He'll be a paragon, the model ex-husband rushing to the side of his former wife in her time of need. And the cherry on the cheesecake — Buzz Wells has the professional skills to be of real use to his ex."

"So we watch, wait and feel helpless," Fawn said.

"We're not helpless," I said. "Fawn, you've seen my option contract. Any time we have proof that Buzz Wells and Ainsley are acting against the best interests of the production, I can have the contract nullified. But that's a game of chicken I don't think any of us want to play. If I kill the project, Living Skies and the Saskatchewan film industry will take a huge hit in lost revenue and jobs, Roy's final project will go down in smoke and, selfishly, a story that matters to me will never be told. We have to do everything possible to keep the situation from reaching that point."

CHAPTER FOURTEEN

Shortly before noon on Thursday, Darrell Bell's silver Ford passenger van pulled up in front of our house. Georgie and I had been working on the script all morning, and we went together to greet Darrell and Ben Bendure.

To use one of Ben's favourite expressions, he appeared to be "in the pink." His snowy beard was neatly trimmed, his complexion was ruddy and his eyes were bright. He was wearing his favourite outfit: a long pocketed khaki vest, an Oxford cloth shirt, roomy slacks and walking boots, soft with wear. His ivory handled cane was clearly a necessity, but as we walked to the house after the introductions, Ben was nimble.

It was a soft spring day, far too lovely to eat inside, and Taylor and I had set the picnic table for lunch. I poured everyone a glass of iced tea and led the way to the patio. Taylor was working in her studio at the edge of our property.

She was fond of Ben, and Darrell had been her mentor, confessor and art dealer since she sold her first painting. As soon as she heard their voices, she came flying across the lawn, arms outstretched, but before she reached in for the hug, she checked her t-shirt and jeans. "You're safe," she said. "No wet paint. Hug tight."

Georgie had volunteered to bring lunch. When I said I didn't realize she cooked, Georgie raised an eyebrow. "I don't," she said. "But craft services does, and they not only deliver, they pick up the dirty dishes."

Zack had a client meeting, so there were just the five of us at the table, but it would have been difficult to find a more congenial group. True to her word, Georgie was a Ben Bendure groupie, and her perceptive comments and questions about *The Poison Apple* had him glowing. Ben had queries too, and his interest in how we dealt with the complexities of the relationships between the Ellard family and the Loves opened some new possibilities for Georgie and me.

In addition to being a successful gallery owner, Darrell was a gifted landscape artist whose ability to capture the light and the wind of the big prairie space had earned him a reputation that went far beyond Saskatchewan's borders. There would be sixty candles on his next birthday cake, but tall, husky and affable, Darrell always seemed like a prairie boy to me, and at lunch as he and Taylor chatted about the art she was creating for *Sisters and Strangers*, Darrell displayed a boyish curiosity about what went on behind the scenes of filming a series.

As I listened to them talk, I was surprised at how knowledgeable Taylor was about not only set decoration, but also about lighting and photography. Initially, Taylor had visited the set of *The Happiest Girl* because she was taking a class in anatomy, and Roy Brodnitz felt she could learn a great deal about body movement from watching the dancers whose actions would serve as models for the movie's computer-generated images.

When she continued to spend part of every day at the production studio, I assumed she was drawn to the set by her growing friendship with Vale, but seemingly, the art of filmmaking had also been an attraction. Taylor had always been fascinated by process — anything from preparing lasagna to building an inuksuk. As she told Darrell about what she'd learned of the processes behind the making of a movie, our daughter's dark eyes shone and her long-fingered hands, so much like Sally's, never stopped moving.

The party was animated, but when lunch was over and it was time to look at Sally's self-portrait as the sole student of the Academy of One, we were subdued. Darrell had packed the painting carefully, and as he removed the final layer of bubble wrap and set the painting on our dining room table, only Taylor and Georgie looked directly at the canvas. Darrell, Ben and I were all watching my daughter's face.

Her expression revealed nothing as she examined the painting of Sally at fourteen lying on the hood of a yellow convertible in a blatantly sexual pose. Behind her a motel stuccoed in hot pink offered vacancy. We were all silent, waiting for Taylor's response. When it came, her words were a surprise. "Jo, tell me what I was like when I was that age."

I took a breath. "Well, except for the fact that you were already a working artist, you were a normal fourteen-year-old. You, Isobel Wainberg and Gracie Falconer were inseparable. You and Isobel went to all Gracie's basketball games even though you both hated basketball. You had sleepovers every weekend. You giggled a lot. You had secrets. The three of you always had a project. You made personalized scents for all your friends. The Wainbergs, the Falconers and your dad and I took turns driving you downtown every week so you could feed the feral cats. And when you were fourteen you decided you wanted to have a 'rustic Halloween party,' and I drove you all over the countryside so you could choose the perfect pumpkins."

"Which weren't as perfect as the pumpkins Martha Stewart had at the rustic Halloween party in her magazine," Taylor said. "You told me that Martha's pumpkins were probably airbrushed."

I smiled at the memory. "They probably were, and Taylor, everybody at your party had a lot of fun."

Our daughter's eyes stayed on the painting. "Sally never had any of that," she said tightly. "Jo, I'm grateful you asked Darrell to bring this painting. It will take Vale where she needs to be to play Sally, but I don't ever want to see it again."

Darrell and I exchanged a quick look. "I'll take care of it," I said. "Taylor, just have Vale let me know when she wants to see it."

Taylor swallowed hard. "Thank you, and Jo, thank you for agreeing to let them make *Sisters and Strangers*. People need to know . . ."

"Know what?" I said.

"Everything," Taylor said. She squared her shoulders and turned to Darrell and Ben with a smile. "Now, would you two like to come to the production studios, see the paintings I've made and meet some of the people working on the series?"

"I'm in," Darrell said. "I'm very keen to see what you've done with Sally's work."

Ben demurred. "May I take a rain check? Those studios are spread out over a city block and, my ankle isn't ready for a marathon."

After Taylor and Darrell left, I re-swathed the painting in its bubble wrap cocoon, called a friend of Taylor's who owned a small gallery downtown and explained the situation. She agreed to pick up Sally's self-portrait later in the day and keep it safe until Taylor decided what she wanted to do with it.

While I made the arrangements to store the painting, Ben and Georgie went back outside, and after I broke the connection, I joined them. I had splurged on really comfortable patio chairs, and Ben and Georgie were basking in the sun, cozy as Taylor's cats, Bruce, Benny and Bob Marley.

"I could stay like this forever," Ben said. "But we need to talk about where the production stands. I know you've had a few bumps in the road."

"More than a few," Georgie said. "And the road ahead is uncertain."

When I'd told Georgie about Hal's role in securing the initial financing for Sally and Joanne, her first reaction was concern for Hal. She'd worked with him before, and like Fawn, Georgie felt Hal was a fine man who would be suffering for creating a situation fraught with peril. After she'd explained the sequence of events that might result in Buzz Wells coming to Regina, Ben's concern was palpable. "You have to do everything you can to keep Wells away from *Sisters and Strangers*," he said.

I leaned forward. "Easier said than done, because Ainsley is carrying a huge burden, and Buzz Wells has the skills to lighten her load," I said. "Gabe's will left everything, including Living Skies, to Ainsley, and when Roy died, Georgie told me Ainsley inherited the summer home in Lennox, Roy's loft in New York and his investments. Ainsley will be knee deep in the paperwork that comes from settling two estates. Not to mention the fact that she needs someone to manage Living Skies and someone to produce *Sisters and Strangers*."

Ben frowned. "I thought you said Fawn Tootoosis was the production manager. She has an excellent reputation."

"And deservedly so," Georgie said. "But Ainsley's never worked with Fawn, and she says she needs someone in whom she has complete confidence."

"And that's Buzz Wells?" Ben said. "Forgive me, but if she divorced Wells, she clearly had some concerns about him."

Georgie raised an eyebrow. "Believe it or not, it was Buzz who wanted the divorce."

"I didn't know that," I said.

"I only found out last night," Georgie said. "When Ainsley called and started making noises about having Buzz join us, I pointed out that there must have been some friction between them or she wouldn't have divorced him. Ainsley was upfront about the situation. She said Buzz divorced her because he was tired of having Roy at the centre of her life."

"Now the centre of her life is gone," Ben said.

"And there's a vacancy," I said.

"A vacancy that Buzz Wells is eager to fill." Georgie rubbed her abdomen and took a deep breath. "I know I've been leading the brigade against Buzz, but there's something you need to see before we take our next step."

After Georgie disappeared into the house, Ben looked at me questioningly. I shrugged. "Your guess is as good as mine."

Georgie returned with her laptop and placed it on the end table between Ben's chair and mine. "This video of Ainsley rehearsing the actors for the Broadway production of *The Happiest Girl* is posted on YouTube."

The video was only six minutes long but it revealed an Ainsley I'd glimpsed only once — the night she and Roy had danced to "Begin the Beguine" at the gala for their former dance teacher and mentor. As Ainsley and Roy tapped together, their relationship, strong and deeply intuitive, seemed organic — two individuals, each with an instinctive awareness of what the other needed. As a director, Ainsley appeared to have developed that same bond with her actors. A slight nod of her head, a half smile, a touch on the cheek and the moment came into focus. Clearly hours of work had gone into creating this kind of mutual trust and intimacy.

When the video ended, Georgie turned to us. "I wanted you to see what Ainsley can bring to a production." Her smile was rueful. "I'd almost forgotten how good she can be."

"Her rapport with the actors is extraordinary," Ben said.

"Ainsley works hard at establishing that rapport," Georgie said. "Before rehearsals start, she gives each of the actors a binder stuffed with her research — sketches, photos and lines from poems, plays and novels — anything that she feels will help them get to the heart of their character. She includes a note making it clear that the materials in the binder are simply tools that the actors can use or lose at will."

"So the binder is a good faith offering showing Ainsley's belief in the actor and in their future relationship," I said.

"Exactly," Georgie said. "You could see from that video how calm and attentive she is with them."

"She rows with a steady stroke," Ben said.

"She does," Georgie agreed, "and there's never any doubt about where the boat is headed. But now Ainsley is being buffeted in so many directions that she's incapable of setting her course. The first day of principal photography for *Sisters and Strangers* is Monday, June 11. Ainsley knows she's not doing what she needs to do to prepare, and it's driving her crazy."

"If she could accept the fact that Fawn Tootoosis is eminently qualified to bring the production through on time and on budget, Ainsley would be free to direct," Ben said. "And you two could focus on the script. The only vacancy then would be general manager of Living Skies, and that position would be easily filled."

"You make it sound so simple," Georgie said.

"It is," Ben said. "But human emotions complicate simple things. Ainsley is caught in a maelstrom, and apparently Buzz Wells is offering her a lifeline. The level-headed professional we saw in that video would have no problem realizing that if she trusts Fawn Tootoosis to produce *Sisters and Strangers*, the rest will fall into place."

"I doubt that Buzz Wells is pushing Ainsley in that direction," I said.

Ben's laugh was short and resigned. "I'm sure you're right. I guess if Wells does show up, all you can do is remain vigilant. On that cheery note, shall we move along? Would it be possible for me to look at what's been written so far?"

"Better than that — let's do a read-through," Georgie said. "Ben, you read the male actors' lines. Jo can read stage directions, and she and I will work out the women's lines as we go."

Hearing the dialogue aloud was absorbing, and the three of us were surprised when Darrell and Taylor returned and Darrell announced that it was time for them to hit the road. He was attending an opening at Saskatoon's Remai Gallery that night and needed time to get ready.

After we said our goodbyes, Taylor went out to her studio, and Georgie turned to me. "Do you believe that Buzz Wells coming aboard is a done deal?"

"I don't know, but speculating isn't going to change anything," I said. "That read-through with Ben gave us plenty of food for thought."

"It did," Georgie agreed. "But I'm tired of thinking. Let's

talk about the wedding. I saw an outfit online that I'd like your opinion on."

"Then get your laptop, and we'll sit down at the kitchen table and make decisions."

The suit Georgie showed me was stunning: pale dusky pink silk shantung, graceful, and chic.

"It's gorgeous," I said. "And with your colouring it will be perfect."

"But it's pink, and I've never been a girly-girl."

"It's a very muted pink, and the design is austere: no embellishments, just clean simple lines and precise tailoring. If you carry a bouquet of dusky roses and champagne orchids, you'll be a knockout."

Georgie's gaze was suspicious. "How do you know all that?"

"Taylor. She sees remedying my ignorance of fashion as her life's work. She was born knowing how to tie a scarf."

"Hal is a big fan of your daughter," Georgie said. "And of you." She paused. "Joanne, Hal told me about the role he played in getting the seed money for *Sisters and Strangers*. He's sick about it."

"I know," I said. "And I understand. Gabe had done a huge kindness for Hal by hiring him when everyone else had written him off, and Buzz had caused Hal's sister grief by using her concept to keep *Broders' Annex,* the show she'd created, running for four seasons after he'd forced her off the writing team." I touched Georgie's arm. "I understood that Hal couldn't have anticipated the outcome, and I told him that the day we met in the writers' room."

"And he was grateful," Georgie said. Suddenly she narrowed her eyes. "Joanne, I don't know why this didn't cross my mind before. Do you think Ainsley knows where the financing for *Sisters and Strangers* came from?"

"Gabe was an egotist. I can't imagine him telling Ainsley that he got the money for his shining new venture by having her ex-husband's creditors put the squeeze on him and by selling them stock in the company they owned."

"That does seem unlikely," Georgie said. "There's one way to find out." She took out her phone and placed the call. When Ainsley picked up, Georgie waded right in. "There's something you should know about how Gabe acquired the start-up financing for *Sisters and Strangers*," she said. That was as far as she got. As Ainsley gave her an earful, Georgie grimaced and mouthed the words "she knows"; after she'd listened a little longer, Georgie mouthed the words "she doesn't care."

She and Ainsley talked for a few more minutes and then Georgie ended the conversation, "Okay we'll see you tomorrow at two o'clock. Safe flight." She slid her phone back into her bag. "I'm assuming I don't have to tell you that did not go well."

"I picked up on that."

"Okay, well, in a nutshell, Buzz had a lousy hand but he played it well. He told Ainsley the truth and didn't spare the gory details. He said that at the moment, they were both in a difficult place, but they could help each other."

"And she agreed."

"She did. Ainsley says Buzz is just coming to Regina to

get the lay of the land, familiarize himself with the situation and explain his strategy for seeing *Sisters and Strangers* through to post-production. After that, if they can strike a mutually beneficial arrangement, Buzz will sign on for the duration. They'll arrive in Regina on the early flight, and Ainsley wants a table meeting, all hands on deck at two o'clock tomorrow afternoon. She's calling Fawn now to arrange it." Georgie pulled her laptop closer. "Nothing we can do till then, so let's see if we can find you something that Taylor will approve of."

I have never been a shopper but shopping online with Georgie was fun, and when we finally settled on an oyster silk shantung suit that was the perfect complement to Georgie's outfit, we moved onto possible dresses for Chloe, and from there to floral arrangements and wedding cakes. After we'd ticked off all the boxes, Georgie leaned back in her chair. "I call this a good day's work," she said. "I'm going home to nap. Since you have to be at the table meeting tomorrow afternoon, you should take the morning off."

"That works for me," I said. "Zack and I are spending the weekend at Peter and Maisie's farm looking after our grandsons. I can use some of that extra time to dig through the girls' toy boxes and pull out the old favourites."

Georgie rested her elbow on the table and cupped her cheek in her palm. "So what are the old favourites?"

"Let's see. Madeleine and Lena never seemed to tire of the parking garage with an elevator for cars. They spent hours arranging the livestock on their farm in various permutations and combinations. They were serious about their wooden building blocks, and they had matching Corn Popper push toys."

"I saw Charlie in action at the Easter egg hunt," Georgie said. "I'm no expert, but I'm guessing he could turn a corn popper push toy into a lethal weapon."

"You're probably right."

"Maybe you should keep the matching push toys in reserve in case Rumpel goes on a rampage."

"Maybe," I said, "but I'm guessing he'll start with a full-scale charm offensive."

Georgie shuddered. "I've seen Buzz turn on the charm, and he's positively oleaginous. I always felt like I needed to take a shower after he left the room."

"I hate slimy," I said, "but let's jump off that bridge when we come to it. In sixteen days you and a wonderful man are getting married, and by Christmas you'll have a child. This is a happy time. Don't let Buzz Wells cast a shadow over it."

* * *

As soon as Georgie left, I called Charlie D. "Guess who's coming to town?" I asked.

"Buzz Wells?"

"Now you've spoiled the surprise."

"Just the first one. From what I've heard Buzz Wells is full of surprises."

"That news does not gladden my heart," I said. "Anyway, the story is that Buzz is coming to assess *Sisters and Strangers,* and if he and Ainsley agree that he can make a contribution, he's on board."

Charlie D chortled. "And you'll have a front-row seat to watch Wells's performance as the reluctant genius selflessly shelving his own plans to save a troubled project. I'm not going to miss out on this, Jo. I'm calling the great man to arrange for an interview."

"Do you think he'll talk to you?"

"Are you kidding? The guy has a massive ego, and in addition to the fact that our show is heard Canada-wide, it's now aired in twenty-eight American stations with desirable media markets."

"How are you going to approach the interview?"

"The same way I approach every interview. I'll do my research. I'll go through everything we have, and then I'll visit the land of castaway dolls."

"You've lost me."

"It's just a term my producer uses for the people who played significant roles in the past of the person we're focusing on, before the person moved onward and upward. In Buzz's case, I'll probably start with the people who worked with him on *At the Algonquin*."

"I bet they'll have stories to tell."

"Agreed," Charlie D said. "That must have been a tumultuous ride. Anyway, after the research it's the usual drill: I come up with questions that I hope will evoke a thoughtful response, I listen carefully to Wells's answers, and if I think a follow-up question will shed more light on what's happening with *Sisters and Strangers*, I'll ask one."

"No gotcha questions."

"Not my style," he said. "Anyway, in this case unnecessary. Guys like Buzz Wells have a habit of painting themselves into a corner without any assistance from me."

"Are you going to tell him you're my son-in-law?"

"Sure. I believe in full disclosure. I also think Buzz will give me more if he thinks he can get to you through me."

"Buzz and Ainsley are arriving here tonight, and there's a table meeting of all the department heads tomorrow at two o'clock, so Buzz can get up to speed."

"Our New York office will find his number, and I'll call Buzz tomorrow before the meeting and ask for an interview at his earliest convenience. Give him that extra jolt of confidence he needs before he bulldozes his way into *Sisters and Strangers*."

"Hey, whose side are you on?"

Charlie D's tone was no longer lighthearted. "I'm on your side, Jo — always — but Buzz Wells has a lot at stake here; so do you, and we can't afford a misstep."

* * *

Taylor blazed through as I was setting the table for dinner. She said that when she'd seen Kyle at the studio that afternoon, he seemed better, and they'd arranged to have a quick burger and work on the apartment. I removed her place setting and Zack and I sat down to our chicken chili and cornbread alone.

Zack ate with gusto. "This is fantastic," he said. "We haven't had this before, have we?"

"No. It's from craft services. Georgie brought lunch and we're having leftovers."

Zack buttered his cornbread and grunted appreciatively. "Movie people eat well."

"They do, and because of the long hours and the various dietary restrictions and likes and dislikes, craft services has to work hard to keep everybody happy."

"This dinner is making me happy. How did your day go?"

"Mixed," I said. I gave Zack an overview of our day, ending with the news that Buzz Wells would be accompanying Ainsley when she returned to Regina.

"And that does not augur well?"

"I honestly don't know. This afternoon Georgie showed Ben and me a video of Ainsley rehearsing the actors for the stage version of *The Happiest Girl*. She was relaxed, radiant and brilliant with the actors. Zack, it was hard to believe she was the woman we've been dealing with since November. Even I could recognize that *Sisters and Strangers* needs what Ainsley can bring to it. Since Roy and Gabe died, Ainsley's been overwhelmed. Suddenly, she has the responsibility of running Living Skies, making decisions about the rough cut of *The Happiest Girl* and trying to visualize the screenplay of *Sisters and Strangers* when she has only a partial script to work with. And she is mourning the death of the person who was like a part of her for thirty years."

"And as the song says, 'Something's gotta give.'" Zack dipped his spoon into the nearly empty bowl.

"Ben says that if Ainsley let Fawn take over as executive producer, we could all get on with doing our jobs. Living Skies would need a general manager, but Ben didn't feel that would be an insurmountable problem."

"No. In fact, not a problem at all. Falconer Shreve handles Living Skies' legal affairs, and we're front and centre now protecting their interests as the fire investigation continues."

"No smoking gun there?"

"Nope. Fire and Protective Services are keeping their cards close to their chest, but everything we know seems to point to arson. Anyway, Maisie jumped in and took a potential client I didn't want off my hands today, so I have some time. Given everything, I may step into the management of Living Skies myself."

"And leave your law practice?" I said. "That's crazy."

"It would be," Zack agreed. "I'm just talking short term — a couple of hours a day to make sure the company's in fighting trim."

"And to keep Buzz Wells from getting his hands on it," I said. "It's a terrific idea. Are you sure being a part-time lawyer won't make you crazy?"

"It won't be for long. It will plug a hole that Buzz Wells might burrow in through, and it'll give us time to get somebody first-rate to take over."

"So where are you going to start?"

"With Georgie. She's still nominally executive producer, so we need her onside."

"She will be," I said. "I'll call her as soon as we're finished here. What's the plan of action?"

"We need to buy back the Living Skies stock Gabe gave to Buzz Wells's creditors as an incentive to get them to force Buzz to pay his debts. Life's complicated enough without having loan sharks as stockholders. And on another front, Jo, how would you feel about me sitting in on the table meeting tomorrow?"

"I'd feel immensely relieved. Buzz has had Ainsley to himself since Monday. If they've formed a bond, they'll have the upper hand at the meeting tomorrow. Georgie shouldn't have to face them alone. This is a high-risk pregnancy. Georgie's forty-four — her doctor is already concerned about her blood pressure. I'll fight the good fight with her, but we could really use backup."

Zack covered my hand with his. "You've got me."

"The three best words in the English language," I said. "Thanks. I love you."

"The other three best words," Zack said, and he held out his arms to me.

CHAPTER FIFTEEN

When Pantera, Esme and I came back from our walk Friday morning, the dishwasher was chugging, the aroma of coffee drifted through the air, and my husband and our daughter were sitting at the kitchen table in their robes with the satisfied expressions of cats who got the cream.

"Good morning," I said. "Obviously, you both started your days sunny side up."

"We did," Zack said. "Taylor and I have made an offer for that stock in Living Skies that Gabe used to induce Buzz Wells's unsavoury acquaintances to put the squeeze on him."

"You move fast," I said. "How did you find out who owned the stock?"

"Through the firm's files. Transfer of stock has to be recorded, and it was. The owner of thirty percent of Living Skies was a company called Murray2193 in New York City.

It's a shell company, but there was a contact number. I called and a very pleasant-sounding woman picked up. I told her I was interested in buying the stock because I lived in Regina and I was thinking I might like to dabble in movies in my retirement. She said she'd get back to me — and she did in less than ten minutes. The price she asked was exorbitant but manageable, and I wasn't about to dicker. So Taylor and I gathered our pop bottles together and took the plunge."

I turned to our daughter. "How come you're involved?"

"Dad thought a family purchase would seem less aggressive."

"Your dad's a smart guy."

"Thank you." Zack wheeled his chair back. "Time for me to get ready for the office and for my new gig as a movie mogul."

"Wear that grey suit you wore to Peter and Maisie's wedding, and the tie with the swirl of colours that always makes me think of Scheherazade," I said. "Show Buzz Wells he's out of his league."

When I called Georgie about the stock transfer, she was enthusiastic. "A nice preemptive strike and a necessary one. As I said last night, I'm glad Zack's stepping in. I'll save you places next to me at the meeting."

I'd just broken the connection with Georgie when Charlie D called. "Buzz Wells has agreed to a live interview Monday morning," he said.

"That was fast."

"Buzz jumped at the chance to 'introduce' himself."

"What's he like?"

"Cocky. Jo, Wells is not talking like a man who is being considered for a position. He's talking like a man who's in charge, and he has big plans for the series."

"So do we," I said. "Zack's coming on board. He'll be at the meeting today, and he has some announcements that might take the wind out of Buzz's sails, at least temporarily."

When I described Zack's strategy, Charlie whistled. "Take notes and call me when the meeting's over."

"Will do," I said. "So how are you preparing for the face to face?"

"I've already got phone interviews lined up with some of the players in the land of the castaway dolls. They seem very eager to talk about their experiences with Mr. Wells."

* * *

I was in the garage sorting through the girls' old toy boxes, when Peter arrived. I'd opened the garage door to let in the fresh spring air, and when Pete spotted me, he came in. He looked terrible: pale, exhausted and unkempt. My grandmother would have said he "looked like he'd been dragged through a knothole backwards." He gave me a one-armed hug. "So what are you up to?"

"Just going through the girls' old toys to find some things Charlie and Colin might have fun with this weekend."

Pete took a deep breath. "About this weekend . . . we're going to have to cancel, Mum. Maisie just took on a big case. It's complicated — the Crown says it was murder and the accused says it was self-defence. The accused fired his lawyer and the trial starts in two weeks, so Maisie will be pulling all-nighters until then."

"I'm sorry," I said. "Zack and I were looking forward to having time with the boys."

"Maisie and I are sorry too. We were looking forward to being at the lake," Pete said. "But this came up."

"Do you have time to come inside and talk?"

Pete tried a smile. "Actually, having a talk is the reason I'm here."

Remembering Maisie's misery after she and I had put Charlie and Colin down for their naps on the day we saw the crocuses, I felt a chill. I'd attempted to reassure her, but Maisie had never disguised her passion for the law, and I knew the cracks in her relationship with Pete were bound to deepen. As Pete followed me into the kitchen, I was certain he'd come to tell that he and Maisie had decided to separate, and I was heartsick.

"Can I get you anything?" I said.

"Thanks," he said, "but I'm fine. Actually, Mum I really am fine, and so is Maisie, although she doesn't look much better than I do this morning."

I took the chair across from him. "You had a bad night?"

"The worst," Pete said. "We never fight, but last night we did, and it was terrible. Maisie came home late from the office. The boys were already asleep. She said we couldn't go to the lake because she had a new client. You know that I'm a no-drama guy, but I was tired too, and I blew up. We both said things — cruel things that we'd obviously been feeling for a long time. And it didn't stop — the words just kept on coming. It was the worst night of my life, and then suddenly Maisie and I just looked at each other and realized what we were about to lose and we both said, 'This can't happen!' Exactly the same words at exactly the same moment. I don't know how to explain it — it was as if the wall we'd built between us fell down, and we were on the same side again."

Relief washed over me. "You've found a way forward?"

Pete nodded. "We laid out our priorities. We love each other. We love Charlie and Colin. We both love our work. Once we'd established that, we knew we had to find a way to protect what mattered most to us."

"And you did . . ."

"We did, and that meant facing the fact that our decision to live on the farm was a mistake." Pete paused, watching my face for a reaction.

"That's a big decision," I said. "You're not simply changing your address, you're changing your way of life."

"We know that," Pete said, and his voice was firm. "Mum, there was no other answer. It's only an hour's drive into town, but Maisie and I are both making that drive twice a day, and half the time we have the kids with us. Often by the time Maisie gets behind the wheel to come home, she's put in twelve hours at the office. Last night she told me that more than once she's caught herself just as she was falling asleep."

My breath caught in my throat. "That's terrifying."

"It is, and the odds that one night she might not wake up in time were against us. We examined all the possibilities, but the only one that made sense was to move back to Regina."

"But you love the farm, and Maisie grew up there. She

says when she's in that house she feels that Lee is very close to her."

"Maisie and I talked that through. Taking over Lee's breeding program was a joy for me. I love the work, and I love the life, but I love Maisie and our sons more. And Maisie knows that moving from the house where she and Lee shared their lives will be painful, but last night we realized that unless we sacrificed something, we could lose everything."

The bands of tension that had been tight around my chest since Pete walked into the garage and said he'd come to talk to me had begun to loosen. "So the decision is made," I said. "What's next?"

"We may be in luck on that score," my son said. "There's already at least one potential buyer. Vince Treadgold has already asked me to keep an eye out for a farm like ours."

"So Vince is serious about changing course."

Pete grinned. "He is, and it's fun just being around him. He's smart, he's passionate, and he says that for the first time in a long time, he can't wait to get up in the morning."

"Okay. So do you want me to start checking out real estate listings here in the city?"

"That would be aces," Pete said. "Now I'd better get a move on. I'm picking the boys up from child care early. When they go down for their naps, I'm going with them."

"You have no idea how relieved I am that you and Maisie have worked this out," I said. "We all love you and Maisie and the boys so much."

"And we love you," Pete said, and his voice was rough with emotion.

* * *

As I walked to the Living Skies offices for the table meeting, I was surprisingly relaxed. I had been apprehensive about meeting Buzz Wells, but Zack was a formidable ally and Peter's good news had buoyed me. I knew that Gracie Falconer, the daughter of Zack's late partner, Blake, was ready to sell the big Tudor home in which she'd grown up, and I was weighing the pluses and minuses the house presented for a busy young couple with very active twin boys, when Danny Kerrigan burst out of the production studios' entrance and jogged towards me.

Danny was painfully awkward, both physically and socially. That afternoon, he greeted me with a disarmingly open smile. "Nick told me you were coming to the meeting today, Mrs. Shreve, and I've been waiting for you."

"Well, I'm here now."

"I wanted to tell you that nothing bad will happen to Taylor and Vale."

"I'm glad to hear that," I said. "I know you and Lizzie were concerned about them."

Danny's face creased with pleasure and he took my hands in his. "We're not concerned anymore. Pastor Kirk always says, 'Why worry when you can pray?' and he's told everyone at the Church of the Bountiful Gifts to pray that Taylor and Vale will be delivered from evil and see the light."

Danny watched my face expectantly, waiting for my response. I was speechless, but finally, the words came. "I'm praying that same prayer for you, Lizzie and for all your friends at the Church, especially Pastor Kirk."

"I'll tell him. Mrs. Shreve, isn't it funny that we have exactly the same prayer?"

"It's a good prayer," I said. "And I'm going to keep saying it."

***

The meeting was scheduled for two o'clock, but the room was already almost filled. Georgie waved me to the place beside her. As acting executive producer she'd taken the chair at the head of the table. I noticed she'd put her bag on the chair next to her, reserving the place for Zack's wheelchair.

"I'm glad you're here," she said. "Buzz came knocking at my door this morning. You were right. He's going with the charm offensive. He brought me an extra-large latte from that chi-chi place around the corner and asked if he could come in and 'run a few things by me.'

"There was no way I was going to let him through that door, and Buzz must have known that, but he'd apparently banished the memory of what a total turd he was when he was the showrunner on that sitcom I wrote for. For Ainsley's sake, I was polite. I explained that I was getting married at the beginning of May, and I had a full morning planned. He gushed about my bridal glow and what a lucky guy my groom was, said he'd catch me later and slithered back upstairs."

I groaned. "And Ainsley is bringing him to this meeting. Katy, bar the door."

"Too late," Georgie said. "Cast a discreet look at the front of the room. Buzz has already entered the building."

Wearing what I'd come to believe was the uniform of the boy-men in the movie industry — closely fitted blue jeans, black t-shirt and top-of-the-line runners — Buzz was as tanned, chiselled and carefully coiffed as he was in his photo on the web page. But there was a surprise. From the photo, it appeared that, like many actors and politicians, Buzz Wells had a large head, and I'd assumed he would be a towering presence.

Georgie gave me a sidelong glance. "So what do you think?"

"I don't know. I guess I just assumed he'd loom larger."

"I told you he was like Rumpelstiltskin," Georgie said. "Diminutive — 'a manikin.' But don't let his size fool you — Buzz may be tiny, but he fights dirty."

"Rumpelstiltskin came to a bad end," I said. "After the young queen proved that she knew his name, he stomped so hard his entire leg went into the earth and when he tried to pull it out, he tore himself in two."

Georgie lowered her head to hide her smile. "We shouldn't be making light of this."

"Why not? Look at him, working the room." Politician-style, Wells was walking around the table, introducing himself, shaking hands. "The charm offensive," I whispered.

Buzz had barely managed to make it halfway down one side of the table when Zack appeared in the doorway. A powerful man in a wheelchair is a magnet, especially when he's wearing a tie with a swirl of colour vibrant as a sultan's treasure. Georgie murmured to me, "I believe the focus in the room just shifted."

Buzz had left Ainsley alone, and Zack wheeled over to her. They greeted each other warmly, leaving Buzz stranded, with three-quarters of the people in the room still to charm. As Zack approached us, Georgie took her bag off the seat of the vacant chair and pushed the chair out of the way. When Zack wheeled in next to her, Georgie didn't miss a beat.

She rose to her feet and in a carrying voice said, "We're ready to begin. For those of you who haven't already met him, this is Zack Shreve, the senior partner in Falconer Shreve Altieri Wainberg and Hynd, the firm that handles Living Skies' legal business. In the past four months, Living Skies has been in a state of flux. As our lawyer and as the new owner of a significant percentage of Living Skies shares, Zack is assessing the health of the production company and our options for the future. But before I hand the meeting over to Zack, I'd like to welcome Ainsley's friend, Buzz Wells, to our meeting." Georgie's smile was sweetly innocent. "He's visiting from New York." Buzz, still frozen mid-greeting with Edie Gunn, the locations manager, tried a jaunty wave, but Georgie had already returned her attention to Zack. "Your turn now," she said.

As she took her seat, I murmured, "Well executed."

Zack leaned forward in his chair, and it was clear from the beginning he was operating in full courtroom mode. "I'll get right to it," he said. "I know some of you already, and I hope to know the rest of you soon. I've just begun my appraisal of the company, but I have rectified one situation that concerned me. Thirty percent of Living Skies stock was owned by Murray2193, a New York company with a questionable reputation. My wife, my daughter and I purchased the stock this morning, so Living Skies is once again wholly Canadian owned.

"I've learned that the production of which you're all a part has a personnel problem, but it's not an insoluble one," Zack continued. "The deaths of Gabe Vickers and Roy Brodnitz created a situation where people were being asked to assume responsibilities on an ad hoc basis — that's never good for morale or for effective management. Clarifying job descriptions would simplify everything. Once the responsibilities of every position are delineated, it's simply a matter of putting the right person in the right place and letting him or her do the job.

"Fawn Tootoosis has an impressive résumé as line producer, producer and executive producer. More significantly, in the months since Gabe Vickers's death, Fawn has kept a steady hand on the tiller. However, despite her experience and her exemplary performance Ms. Tootoosis is still referred to as acting producer. This is an insult to her, and it blurs the lines of responsibility. I suggest a formal announcement to the media that Ms. Tootoosis is now the executive producer of *Sisters and Strangers*. This would free up Georgie Shepherd to devote her skills full-time to writing the script for the series. After that, the one position that would remain vacant is that of general manager of Living Skies, and as I speak,

Brock Poitras, the MBA who manages Falconer Shreve, has a headhunter searching for the right candidate."

Ainsley remained impassive during Zack's presentation. Buzz Wells did not. Georgie scribbled something on her agenda and slid it to me. I smiled when I saw what she'd written. "Rumpel is about to spontaneously combust."

Zack was finishing his report. "I know this has been a difficult time for all of you, but everything I've heard about your work and your commitment is overwhelmingly positive. We all have good reason to be optimistic about the future of both Living Skies and *Sisters and Strangers*. You have my contact information. If you have questions or concerns, feel free to get in touch."

Georgie reached over and patted Zack's hand. "Thanks, Zack, for what you've done and for what you continue to do. I know how busy you are, so if you'd like to get back to your day job, we'll understand."

"Actually, if no one objects, I'd like to stick around," Zack said. "Joanne tells me that table meetings are where all departments report on what they've been doing, and I'd like to learn about that."

"I'm sure we'll all be delighted if you stay, Zack." Hal Dupuis's rich and resonant voice made what might have seemed simply a polite response, sound heartfelt. "Everyone at this table works in a different field," he said, "but we're all show-offs and we welcome the chance to strut our stuff, especially in front of a newly minted minority shareholder."

Zack grinned and settled back in his chair. "I'm ready when you are."

Presentation folders lay in front of each place at the table. Hal picked up his and waved it. "Everyone please, open your folders. Looks like Costume Design's up first. The drawings you're about to see are of the gowns worn by the principal female actors in the scenes at the Valentine's dinner celebrating Sally Love and hosted by the Mendel Art Gallery.

"As you know, the evening ended tragically. In addition to a large staff, there were one hundred and eighty guests present when Sally and Izaak Levin died within minutes of each other. People were still at their tables eating, so there was great confusion. It was difficult to track down photos of the evening, but Joanne Shreve managed to find some photos of herself and of Sally, Nina and of Nina's lover, Sally's ex-husband, Stuart Lachlan." Hal turned towards me. "I'll be forever grateful for those photos, Joanne. They made my work much easier, and, more significantly, they made it true."

I nodded.

"In movies, everything an actor wears makes a statement," he said. "The first drawing is of a form-fitting, high-necked gown of red silk shot through with gold, which will be worn by Rosamond Burke. Zack, Rosamond plays the documentary filmmaker and friend for decades of both the Love and Ellard families. She's seen this sketch, and she's ecstatic about the dress and about the insight it will give the audience into her character, a stunning woman who knows who she is and celebrates her identity."

"The next drawing is of the gown Joanne wore that night, classic design in lipstick-red satin, backless with a square neckline."

Zack drew me towards him. "You must have looked beautiful in that dress."

"That was the only time I wore it," I said. "As soon as I got home that night, I took the dress out to the back alley and buried it in the trash."

Zack's dark eyes were concerned. "Jo, if this is too much for you, we don't have to stay."

"No, I knew this remembrance of things past would be painful, but I promised myself I would see this through, and I will," I said. Brave words, but when I turned to the next drawings, my resolve melted.

"These two designs are my prize," Hal said. When he glanced in my direction, I knew he was concerned about my reaction, but I nodded encouragement. "That night, Nina and Sally both chose dresses from the '60s. Nina's was a slim, sculptured Balenciaga gown of lustrous red velvet, a classic gown that paid homage to the timelessness of good design. Lovely, but I imagine that after her daughter arrived wearing Rudi Gernreich, no one gave Nina a second glance."

Rudi Gernreich was an advocate for advancing women's sexual freedom, and Sally's outfit was blatantly sexual, a one-piece jumpsuit of white lace, appliqued on a sort of stretchy net with matching leggings. There wasn't much lace in the jumpsuit, but there was a lot of net and a lot of Sally. And Hal was right, Nina had been eclipsed once again. That night I hadn't known that Nina and Stuart Lachlan had become lovers, but from the moment Sally walked in, Stuart seemed mesmerized, touching her arm, stroking her hair and leaning his face close to hers when she talked. Nina and I were standing together, and her small, carefully toned body radiated fury.

"That jumpsuit must have been a poke in the eye for Nina," Georgie said quietly.

"It was," I said. "And I'm sure Sally chose it for that very reason. She and Nina knew each other's vulnerabilities. They knew where to strike."

After Hal finished, Kyle Daly stood. Buzz Wells pushed his chair back and pivoted to watch Kyle. Buzz's gaze was sharp and appraising, and Kyle, obviously unnerved, shifted to avoid his scrutiny. Kyle's voice was strained as he began describing the table settings: the tiny stylized hearts hand-drawn on the individual place cards, the placement of the five-cylinder pillar candle vases, and the species of rosebuds chosen because their crimson petals were an exact match for the rich red of the strawberry sauce on the *coeurs à la crème* that would be served for dessert. Eyeballs were glazing over, and when Kyle noticed, he laughed nervously. "Like the great Nicolas Poussin, '*Je n'ai rien négligé* — I overlooked nothing.' Since I can't overlook the fact that you don't share my obsession with table settings, I'll move along.

"The real excitement in the Art Department is the work Taylor Shreve is doing replicating her birth mother's paintings. We've been keeping the pieces Taylor has already completed in set storage, but Taylor and I have decided they should be out where people can enjoy them. When we're through here please stop by our workspace and indicate your first and second choices. A member of our crew will come around Monday morning to hang the paintings, and we'll switch them off every couple of weeks, so everyone will get a chance to enjoy all of Taylor's work."

When there was a round of good-natured applause, Kyle seemed to relax. He bowed. "The paintings are your reward for not giving me the hook during my explanation of the placement of the five-cylinder pillar candle vases."

As the presentations wore on, the afternoon sun poured in, turning the air gold and making the room slumbrous. The last to present was Edie Gunn and her news was positive. She had locked in dates when the cast and crew could use the MacKenzie Gallery and she'd booked accommodations within driving distance of Lindner Island for three weeks in summer and two in autumn. "We're good to go," she said in a cheery, gravelly voice that reminded me of my basketball coach at Bishop Lambeth.

Georgie had been daydreaming, but she was suddenly alert. "Anybody have anything else?" she asked. When there was no response, she said, "Then I guess that's a wrap. Thanks all."

However, as it turned out there were two more scenes to play out, and they were ugly ones. Buzz Wells was on his feet. His colour was high, and his tone, aggressive. "I have a question about Joanne Shreve's option contract. It includes a clause that gives her the right to put a stop to the production if she doesn't like the direction in which the project is heading."

Zack's voice was even. "I wrote that clause, Mr. Wells. It's not lengthy, but brief as it is, you missed a part. The contract becomes null and void only after Joanne Shreve and the 'contractor,' originally Gabe Vickers, but now Ainsley Blair, have made every effort to resolve the problem and mutually agreed that there is no resolution.

"Gabe Vickers read every word in that contract with great care before he signed. Vickers had flaws, but when it came to producing movies, he was admirably professional. As an executive producer, Vickers routinely handled large sums of money, and there was never a hint of financial malfeasance. Investors trusted him, because they knew he was scrupulous, and he could, if called upon, account for every penny." Zack's voice hardened. "He was not a gambler. He knew that gambling with money entrusted to him violated not only the law but also the covenant between him and his investors. Do you have any further questions, Mr. Wells?"

Buzz's features had hardened into a grim anger.

Zack waited a full and tense minute before he said, "In that case, we're through here," and turned his wheelchair towards the door. "Jo, I'm going to check in at the office. I won't be long."

"I'll meet you at the door, martini in hand."

Georgie and I picked up our presentation folders. "Does that zinger Zack just delivered qualify as a shot across the bow?" she said.

I shrugged. "We'll have to wait and see how Wells responds. If we're lucky he'll wave the white flag and leave town."

Zack had stopped to talk to Nick Kovacs. They were to the left of the door and as Buzz exited, he deliberately clipped Zack's wheelchair with his hip. When Nick started after Wells, Zack stopped him.

"There's our answer," Georgie said. "The battle's on. And

that rat Rumpel just left Ainsley sitting there alone to deal with his mess. I'd better check on her. I'll call you later."

Zack and I came out of the room together. We were just in time to catch the next skirmish. Kyle Daly was walking swiftly down the hall, but when Buzz caught up with him and grabbed his arm, Zack and I picked up the pace and we were close enough to hear a brief and disturbing exchange. Still holding Kyle's arm, Buzz moved close to Kyle's ear and said something.

Kyle shook him off. "Let it go," he said. "If you stay it will just get worse."

When Kyle turned to go into the men's room, Buzz followed him, and Zack was right behind. I stood outside the door, waiting and wondering. It wasn't long before Kyle came out, clearly distraught. He stopped in front of me. "I've made a terrible mistake," he said.

Suddenly, Wells was there. He glared at Kyle. "Shut up," he said. "You and I are in this together, and you can't walk away."

It was a few minutes until Zack returned. "Sorry to keep you waiting," he said. "I thought since I was there, I might as well use the facilities. Did I miss anything?"

"You did," I said. "But it will keep until you get home."

I'd just had time to let Esme and Pantera out and check the mail when my phone rang. It was Charlie D. "I have news," he said.

"So do I," I said. "There was a dust-up at the table meeting this afternoon."

Charlie D laughed. "You win. Your news is hotter than mine. You go first." After I'd described how Zack thwarted

Buzz's clumsy attempt to humiliate him, Charlie D was thoughtful. "That may explain the call I just got from Buzz Wells. He backed out of the interview he'd been so keen to do on Monday."

"Did he reschedule?"

"Nope. He just said his plans had changed. Maybe Zack's not-so-veiled comments about unethical producers playing fast and loose with investors' money spooked him, and he's packing his bags and hitting the road."

"No such luck," I said. "Buzz Wells is far from finished. He left the meeting in a foul mood. On his way out, he deliberately bumped against Zack's chair and then he accosted Kyle Daly and said they needed to talk. Kyle tried to brush him off, but Buzz was having none of it. Buzz told Kyle that they were in this together, and he couldn't walk away."

Charlie D whistled. "That sounds ominous," he said. "But at least one question has been answered. We knew someone working on *Sisters and Strangers* was a conduit for information to a person or persons who didn't wish the production well. At least now we know the identity of the mole."

"And I wish we didn't," I said. "I'm fond of Kyle."

"He's been helping Taylor decorate her new apartment, hasn't he?"

"He has, and Taylor's been working on the paintings that Set Decorating will use for the series. She and Kyle have spent a lot of time together, and lately Taylor's been worried about him. One night last week he and Taylor and Zack and I watched the rough cut of *The Happiest Girl*. It's amazing, Charlie D — beautiful and very powerful."

"Expectations are high for that movie," Charlie D said. "Roy and Ainsley did our province a great service by insisting that it be filmed here."

"They did," I agreed, "but that decision brought them both nothing but grief. And now Kyle is suffering. When we turned on the lights after watching the rough cut, Kyle had an 'episode.' He seemed dazed, and he said he was sorry and ran out of the house. Taylor went after him. Zack and I had no idea what was going on. We thought it might have been a panic attack. When she came home, Taylor told us that Kyle said it was PTSD. He told Taylor he's been reliving that moment when he and Ainsley found Roy on the island and Roy was in such a terrible state."

Charlie D was sanguine. "To see a man like Roy suddenly reduced to a creature who was barely human would be traumatic for anyone."

"It would," I said. "And Taylor tells us Kyle is getting professional help, but I have a feeling that Kyle might have been more than a witness. After he and Buzz confronted each other today, Kyle told me he'd 'made a terrible mistake.' Buzz cut him off before he could say more."

"Are you going to pursue this with Kyle?"

"No," I said. "He's on the edge, and I don't want to push him. I'll have to wait until he comes to me."

"You think he will?"

I shook my head. "No, but we live in hope."

CHAPTER SIXTEEN

The last week of April brought weather that was temperate and benign. The daffodils and the Red Dynasty tulips burst forth in a show of beauty almost as impressive as the photos in the bulb catalogue. Taylor and I moved the table and patio chairs close to the flower bed so our family could feel the presence of spring while we ate.

The rhythm of our lives slowed to a steady predictable beat, in large part because Buzz Wells had not appeared in public since his dismal Regina debut at the table meeting. He was still living in the top floor of the duplex with Ainsley. Georgie reported that delivery people regularly appeared with takeout food, and she could hear Buzz pacing and prowling at all hours of the day and night; however, she had seen neither hide nor hair of Buzz since he huffed and puffed out of the meeting. Georgie said that for her every day without Buzz was a day filled with sunshine.

When Hal Dupuis called me with a question about a particular outfit of Nina's, he reported that, thanks to Fawn, the pre-production process was progressing smoothly, and Ainsley was putting in full days at the production studios, talking to department heads and working on her preparation binders for the actors. Georgie and I continued to work steadily and productively on the script, using our breaks to chat about the wedding and search online real estate listings for a house for Peter and Maisie.

And the news on that front couldn't have been better. Zack and I had just finished dinner on Thursday when Peter called. He was exuberant. "Vince Treadgold wants to buy the whole operation. His daughter Celeste hates her job in Ottawa and the idea of working on a farm with her dad and their salukis appeals to her. Vince is over the moon about that. I guess he and Celeste have never been close."

"Vince's second wife didn't like children," I told him. "Celeste was in boarding school in Toronto from the time she was six, and after that she went to University of Toronto. This will give Celeste and her father a chance to make up for lost time."

Pete shook his head. "So much depends upon chance. If you and Vince hadn't been sitting next to each other at Nick Kovacs's birthday party . . ."

"You and Maisie would still have found a way to make it work," I said. "Vince's involvement just simplifies matters.

But the farm does give Vince and his daughter a second chance, and that is serendipitous."

The Falconer house in the Crescents was not yet listed, but Zack had a copy of the keys and Georgie and I played hooky one afternoon to check it out. It was a beautiful old place, and not surprisingly, Georgie fell in love with it. It had everything she, Nick and Chloe could want in a house: large, light-filled rooms, a room adjacent to the main bedroom that would be perfect for a nursery, a good-sized bedroom and bath for Chloe and a separate suite on the main floor for Mrs. Szabo. But when I urged Georgie to take pictures she demurred, saying marriage and a new baby would be change enough for Nick without expecting him to move from the home that he'd lived in all his life, so we agreed to let the matter drop.

* * *

Madeleine, Lena and Taylor flew to Vancouver on the morning of Thursday, April 26. When they returned late Sunday afternoon, Vale would be with them, and she and Taylor would move into their new home on Monday.

Two full days and two half days aren't much time to take in a city like Vancouver, but Madeleine and Lena had a list of must-sees and it tilted heavily towards visits to the set of *Riverdale*, home of a very different Archie, Veronica, Betty and Jughead than I remembered from my comic book days. Mieka had drawn up her own list of suggested must-sees — Stanley Park, the Vancouver Aquarium, the Seawall, False

Creek and Granville Island. It must have been a stretch, but pictures don't lie, and the pictures that kept popping up on our phones showed that the four young women had ticked off all the boxes.

At Mieka's request we drove straight from the airport to their house. Three days of non-stop fun was catching up with her daughters, and Monday was a school day. Taylor and Vale were staying with us. I assumed they'd want to make an early night of it because they were moving into their new apartment the next morning, but when we arrived home Taylor went into the kitchen, put the kettle on and said, "We haven't had a chance to visit. Are you guys up for some chamomile?"

Zack and I exchanged a quick glance. "Absolutely," I said. "We need a little time to get accustomed to Vale's new hair colour."

Vale's natural hair colour was auburn, and since we'd known her, her hair had been not quite shoulder length, shining and straight. Now it was longer and lighter, a satiny honey blond with platinum highlights framing her face. When she turned to me, Vale's eyes were anxious. "The hair stylist on our movie and I went by the videos of Sally at the lake." Vale held out a strand of platinum hair. "These micro highlights took forever, but the stylist said my hair had to be 'summer blond,' like Sally's. Did we get it right?"

"You did," I said. "It's perfect."

"I'll text him," she said. "He takes his work very seriously, and he was worried."

"This may put me in the category of the unevolved male," Zack said. "But does the hair matter that much?"

Vale squeezed Zack's shoulder. "You're not unevolved, Zack. It's an actor thing — maybe it's not a thing for all actors, but it's a thing for me. Acting is all about what's happening inside you. I need to know what's happening inside Sally every single moment she's onscreen, but getting there is a process. I need the externals in place. For me it starts with how my character looks, how she dresses, especially how she walks. I know that Sally was a beautiful young woman who was aware of the power of her beauty but at ease with it. The audience needs to feel that from the moment she comes onscreen. And they need to feel Sally's passion for her work and for the people who fuel her art. They also have to understand why as soon as Sally feels someone has nothing left to give her art, she walks away. Terrible things are done to Sally, and Sally herself does terrible things, but she's not a victim and she's not a villain. I have to signal to the audience that no matter what the cost, Sally has to protect her art, because after Des dies, it's all she has left of him."

As she described her process, Vale seemed to strip herself bare. When she saw our faces, she realized her intensity had been overwhelming, and Vale smiled apologetically. "Zack, I'll bet you're sorry you asked."

"Not at all," Zack said. "You've become a very large part of Taylor's life and that means you're a very large part of our lives. Joanne and I want to come to know you better."

"And I want to come to know you better," she said. "Now it's your turn. What have you guys been up to while I was in Vancouver?"

Taylor's move to Dewdney Avenue would be a simple

one. Zack and I hadn't seen Kyle since I witnessed the argument after the table meeting, but he and Taylor had taken her clothing, books and cache of personal care items and treasures to the new place together, and Taylor said that Kyle was quiet but appeared to be calm. Cronus's colour choices for his apartment were idiosyncratic, but the furnishings he'd chosen were tasteful and well-crafted. Kyle shipped the oversized photographs of Ava Gardner to a friend who had been enamored of Ms. Gardner since he heard her say, "Deep down, I'm superficial," in an interview. The dozen tanned exotic animal skins mounted on the walls turned out to be the real thing, and Kyle found a buyer online who was both eager and generous. Saying "we can always use weird stuff," Kyle took the mirror that had hung over the bed to Set Decoration. The rest of Cronus's purchases fit smoothly into the new spaces and the new colour scheme.

Only Taylor, Kyle and a handful of members of the Set Decoration crew had witnessed the transformation of Cronus's masculine lair into a home for two young women with busy lives. But I was familiar with the colour scheme.

Taylor had wandered into the home office one day when I was working and spied the swathe of silk Hal Dupuis had given me as a souvenir of my first table meeting. As she picked up the fabric, her face lit with delight. "I have pored over dozens of colour charts and nothing was right, but this is it. This is the perfect colour for the walls in the living room of the new place. This shade will set off everything — that warm brownish red of the exposed brick, the white oak floors, the tan leather couch and chairs, the black lacquered room dividers and all that art we're bringing in. Jo, this is just so right!" She examined the fabric more closely. "Where did this come from?"

When I explained, Taylor's face grew serious. "If painting the walls Prussian blue is going to bring back memories you would rather keep buried, I can find another colour."

"No. It's a gorgeous colour, and you're right, it will pull everything in the living room together. And seeing you and Vale in that room will make new memories for me — happy ones."

"You're sure?"

"I'm sure."

Taylor grinned. "In that case, I'm going to call Kyle and see how much paint we need. We're going to have to work fast."

Like everyone her age, Taylor was an inveterate smart-phone photographer, but she was determined that no one would see the place before Vale did, so there were no photos.

Zack's birthday was on May 1. It was a good fit for a man with a lust for life's pleasures, and we always cele-brated with a shindig, but Georgie and Nick's wedding was on the 5th, so Taylor had suggested that we have a com-bination birthday party/housewarming at their apartment on Tuesday. The gathering would be small: just our family, kids and grandkids included, and Kyle because he'd been part of it all.

* * *

Monday morning when I came back from walking the dogs, Vale and Taylor were dressed and waiting for me.

"Are you taking off already?" I asked. "At least have breakfast."

"We had juice," Taylor said.

Vale's blue-green eyes were shining. "And I couldn't wait to see our new home. We said goodbye to Zack and now . . ." She held out her arms to me. "Thank you for everything, Jo."

"We'll call as soon as we're settled in," Taylor said. "And we'll all be together tomorrow night. Now I'd better get my cats."

"You're taking the cats?" I said.

Taylor laughed. "Did you really think I was going to leave them?"

"Of course not. I just wasn't thinking."

"You were in denial." Taylor's voice was small and sad.

"Maybe I was, but I'm not anymore," I said. "Round up Benny, Bruce and Bob Marley, so I can say goodbye."

I stood on the front porch, waving until Taylor's car turned onto Albert Street. Then I closed the door, walked into the kitchen, sat down at the table and had a good cry.

I've always seen the wisdom of Catharine Parr Traill's observation that when disaster strikes, it's useless to wring one's hands in misery — it's better to be up and doing. Our daughter leaving home and moving ten minutes away from us hardly qualified as disaster, and I'd never been a fan of hand-wringing, so my path was clear.

I poured myself a cup of coffee, went to my office and turned on my laptop. There was a brief note addressed to

Georgie and me from Ainsley. "I showed Roy's script and your additions to Buzz. He volunteered to 'bring it home,' and he has. We're sharing his complete script for *Sisters and Strangers* with you both in a Google Doc."

"She let him rewrite Roy?"

As I opened the document and began to read, I felt as if my chest was being flooded with cold air. Buzz had replaced the gentle opening of the raft scene with the sounds of a woman gasping desperately for air as she dies slowly and in mortal terror from anaphylactic reaction to powdered almonds in the dessert she'd been served at a banquet in her honour. The caterer had been aware of the severity of Sally Love's allergies and had chosen his menu with care. There were no powdered almonds in the dessert he had prepared for Sally. Nina had added the almonds and she had removed the epinephrine kit from Sally's purse. Nina, a stickler for perfection, had ensured that her daughter and lifelong rival would never again eclipse her.

It was a riveting opening, but it wasn't Roy's tender pointillist introduction to Sally and Joanne as girls on the cusp of adulthood, and the structure and tone of the story had been radically altered. Rosamond Burke, who cared deeply for Sally, had asked to play a role in the series, and Roy had created a character loosely based on Ben Bendure for her. The new character, Margaret Nightingale, shared Ben's affection for the Love and Ellard families but was clear-eyed about their weaknesses and strengths individually, and about the complex dynamics of their relationships.

In addition to her onscreen presence in the lives of Sally and Joanne in middle age, Rosamond would provide the voice-overs, her splendid contralto deepening the audience's understanding of the story and offering them a narrator they could trust to convey knowledge and judgment.

In Wells's script, the audience learned the details behind Sally's death through police interrogations and flashbacks narrated by a character who Buzz describes as "seeing the main characters in bitingly satirical terms." The lines he wrote for Margaret Nightingale showed a condescension towards the characters that I found chilling, and when my phone rang and I heard Rosamond Burke's beautifully modulated voice, I wasn't surprised.

"This can't be allowed to happen," she said. "That script is an abomination, and it's a betrayal of Roy Brodnitz as an artist and a human being."

"I agree," I said. "It's nine a.m. here. I've only had a chance to read episode one, but I've read enough to know that you're right. What time is it in London?"

"A tick after four in the afternoon," she said.

"Let me talk to Georgie Shepherd," I said. "I know she'll feel as we do about what Buzz has done with the script. To be honest, I can't understand why Ainsley would send it out."

"Ainsley is too knotted in her grief to think clearly," Rosamond said. "I spoke to her after I heard the news about Roy. She was an automaton. When we worked together on *The Happiest Girl*, Ainsley and I had a fine relationship. She's a superb director, and I know that what this man Wells has written does not reflect her vision of *Sisters and Strangers*."

"No, it doesn't, Rosamond. Georgie and I work here, at my house. I'm expecting her soon. After we've talked we'll call you and the three of us can come up with a way to respond."

"Excellent. I'll fix myself a gin and Dubonnet while I wait."

"Queen Elizabeth's favourite."

"It's a pleasant drink for an afternoon," Rosamond said, "but the Queen and I both prefer something more robust after the sun goes down."

* * *

By the time Georgie arrived, I'd read episode two, and I was gnashing my teeth.

Georgie took my measure and gave me a fraction of a smile. "I see you've waded into the steaming pile of doo-doo Buzz produced."

"I have, and Rosamond has already called and said, 'This can't be allowed to happen.'"

"Rosamond has given us our mission statement," Georgie said. "So where do we go from here?"

"I guess we read the rest of Buzz's script."

We read the script aloud and without comment. When we'd finished, Georgie yawned and stretched. "So what do you think?"

"You mean once I put aside the fact that Buzz ripped up our script to make his own creepy collage?"

Georgie laughed. "Yeah, once you've cleared that hurdle."

"I hate it," I said. "It's slick, it's derivative, it's generic, it's forgettable, and it will probably get great ratings."

"That's pretty much my take," Georgie said. "I think we should forget we ever saw it."

"The Bobby Kennedy strategy during the Cuban Missile Crisis."

Georgie frowned. "When the Soviets were going to launch missiles at the U.S. from Cuba, and the U.S. set up a naval blockade to prevent more missiles from reaching Cuba."

"A classic case of brinkmanship," I said. "Khruschev blinked first. He sent a letter to Kennedy saying that if the U.S. pledged never to invade Cuba, Russia would remove the missiles. The next day Khruschev sent a second letter adding another condition: the U.S. would also have to withdraw their missiles from Turkey. Bobby Kennedy ignored the second letter, embraced the proposals in the first letter and Khruschev went along with it."

"That's a great story," Georgie said.

"It is. History has sandpapered the facts a bit, but that said, I think we should treat Buzz's script as the second letter and carry on as if it didn't exist."

"More brinkmanship."

"Yes. And you can discreetly let the department heads know they should continue working on the draft of Roy's script that you and I've been writing."

"You do realize that can't go on forever."

"I do, but at the very least it will buy us enough time to get our script finished and give Ainsley a chance to realize that Roy would hate what Buzz Wells has done to his last project."

"Okay, let's call Rosamond and tell her we're going with letter number one, and then I'll go to the production studios and skulk around."

"I hate that you're having to go through this," I said.

"I hate it too, but Roy deserves an advocate, and it seems you and I are it."

"One way or another it will be over by June 11."

Georgie's gaze was probing. "Joanne, if Ainsley insists on going with Buzz's script, are you prepared to pull the plug on *Sisters and Strangers*?"

"Between you and me . . . probably not," I said. "Last night Vale talked about what she wanted the audience to learn about Sally through her performance, and the thought and effort she's putting into preparing for the role touched me. Everyone at that table meeting on Friday has committed him or herself to making something beautiful and true. We have to believe that even if Ainsley goes with Buzz's script, we can salvage something."

"So I should let people know that no matter what happens, you'll let the project go ahead."

I paused. "No, our message is that we're working on Roy's script, and we won't compromise. We're saying *Sisters and Strangers* will honour Roy's vision or it won't get done at all. We may have to bend later, but no one needs to know that now."

After Georgie left, I was weighing the pros and cons of calling Charlie D and filling him in on the latest in the Buzz saga when Charlie D himself arrived at my door.

"The power of positive thought," I said. "I was thinking about calling you."

"Think no more," Charlie said. "I'm here. But not for long. People get anxious if I'm AWOL this close to airtime."

"Do you have time for coffee?"

"No, but a glass of ice water would be nice. Can I get one for you?"

"Please do, and let's go out to the back patio. A family of ducks appeared on the creek this morning. I'm hoping they'll stick around."

We walked to the bottom of out property that gave us the best view of the creek. Charlie D scanned the water. "No ducks in sight," he said. "What's up?"

"Buzz Wells," I said. "Since his flame-out at the table meeting, Buzz has been a busy boy."

When I'd finished the story of the script, Charlie D groaned. "I don't get this at all," he said. "From what you say, Buzz not only ran roughshod over what you and Georgie wrote, he changed everything, including the episodes Roy created. Why is Ainsley Blair going along with this?"

"Rosamond Burke says Ainsley is 'too knotted in her grief to think clearly.' That's as good an explanation as any."

"Are you and Georgie just going to roll over and play dead?"

"No, we have a plan that will buy us some time. Georgie and I are counting on Ainsley to eventually see that Buzz is using her. We're just hoping that happens sooner than later."

"I may be able to kick-start the process," Charlie D said.

"Georgie sent us the CV of everyone working on *Sisters and Strangers* to check for a connection with Buzz Wells. Jo, you're not going to like this, but Kyle Daly worked on a series called *Broders' Annex* that Buzz Wells executive produced. We know that Buzz was getting information from someone working on *Sisters and Strangers*. Kyle Daly is the most likely possibility. This may mean nothing, but I don't think we can disregard it."

"No, we can't," I said. "I've had concerns about Kyle myself. After Roy's death, Georgie asked him to clear Roy's things out of the main floor of the duplex he and Ainsley shared. Kyle brought me something that has nagged at me ever since." I went to the mudroom, retrieved Taylor's book about the life and art of Ernest Lindner and brought it back to Charlie D. "Kyle said he found this on Roy's desk," I said. "When Roy was struck with the idea of seeing *Sisters and Strangers* through the lens of magic realism, he called Taylor and asked if he could borrow her book about Lindner. At that point, Roy had withdrawn from all of us and Taylor hoped Roy's request meant he was ready to invite her back into his life. It didn't work out that way. She took the book to his place, he thanked her and closed the door."

"And nothing changed."

"No, and as you can see, Taylor's book had been destroyed."

As Charlie D leafed through the book's pages, his face was etched with concern. "Roy must have been in agony," he said finally. "All these markings obviously had a meaning for him, but they're not recognizable as letters of the alphabet or symbols. You worked with Roy. Did he ever use some sort of private shorthand?"

"No. His handwriting was unremarkable, but always legible. Never anything like this."

Charlie D shifted his gaze to me. "I get why this book disturbs you, but you said it nags at you. Why?"

"The timing," I said. "Ainsley told me the last time she spoke to Roy on the island he said he'd left the Lindner book he intended to bring for her at home, but as soon as they got back he'd give it to her."

"He didn't remember defacing the book?"

"Apparently not. Charlie D, something is very wrong here. Roy called me just after he and the rest of the crew arrived on the island that morning. He was ebullient, like his old self: excited about being on the island, filled with plans for the series. He even alluded to a shared joke of ours. If he had defaced the book Taylor loaned him, the man I talked to that morning would not have left the book in plain view on his desk."

"But Kyle Daly told you that's exactly where he found the book — on the desk, in plain view. And he was the one who brought the book to you. Do you think Kyle was the person who defaced Taylor's book?"

I felt a sickness in the pit of my stomach. "I don't want to, but suddenly everything's coming together for me," I said. "Kyle was the one who went into the woods with Roy, and he was with Ainsley when she found him. And something else — Kyle has been suffering from what he describes as PTSD episodes where he relives the moments after he and Ainsley found Roy in the forest."

"You think it's guilt."

"I'm beginning to wonder. I like Kyle," I said. "And Taylor is very close to him. He's a decent man. I can't imagine him being part of any of this unless . . ."

"Unless Buzz knows something that gives him leverage over Kyle," Charlie D said. "But finding what that leverage was will be looking for the proverbial needle in the haystack."

"Not necessarily," I said. "Hal Dupuis's sister, Stella Delacroix, worked on *Broders' Annex*. She wrote the pilot and then Buzz took over and steamrolled her, but Hal said Stella was around for the first season."

Charlie D gave me a lazy smile. "Still a needle in the haystack," he said. "But the haystack just got smaller."

"Georgie will have Hal's number," I said. "I'll call and ask him for his sister's contact information."

Charlie glanced at his phone. "Time for me to skedaddle. Keep me in the loop and Jo, if the duck family shows up, tell them to stick around, and I'll bring the girls over to see them."

"Madeleine and Lena may be a little old for that."

"No one is ever too old for ducks," Charlie D said, and he started walking towards the house.

* * *

Hal Dupuis, remorseful about the role he'd played in bringing Buzz Wells into the production of *Sisters and Strangers*, called his sister, urging her to help Charlie D in any way she could. I was apprehensive about what Stella Delacroix might know about Kyle's relationship with Buzz Wells, but I believe in the adage "the truth will set you free."

Kyle Daly was suffering. The information Buzz Wells was hanging over Kyle's head had brought Kyle to the breaking point. However painful the truth was, if it came to light, Kyle would at least be free of Buzz's threats. And knowing the truth about what had happened in the last hours of Roy Brodnitz's life might answer the dark and troubling questions with which his death had left us all.

CHAPTER SEVENTEEN

Zack's fifty-fifth birthday began the way the best birthdays often do, with unhurried world-class lovemaking. We followed that with breakfast: fresh blueberries, smoked salmon and Zack and Nero Wolfe's favourite, eggs with *beurre noir* — indulgences that cut the time Taylor's father spent mournfully eyeing her empty place at the table in half. Just as I was putting Esme and Pantera on their leashes, our younger son, Angus, called from Calgary to wish Zack a happy day. Like Zack, Angus believed the law was a "kick-ass" profession, and when the dogs and I left for our walk, Zack was beaming as he listened to Angus ramble on about a case.

Zack was still on his phone when we got back. After he hung up, I said, "Were you talking to Angus all that time?"

"No, that was Taylor. She called to let us know that they're loving their place on Dewdney and that everything's set for the party tonight. She and Vale are going over to the production studios this morning. Vale wants to say hello to everybody, and Taylor's tagging along so she can surreptitiously check on Kyle's condition." Zack cocked his head. "She and Kyle are just friends, aren't they?"

"Yes, just friends."

"That's a relief," Zack said. "Vale's a keeper, and I wouldn't want our daughter to change horses in midstream."

"Whoa! Did you hear what you just said? That metaphor is weird on so many levels."

"It's my birthday and it's my metaphor, so let it go. Now, if you change your mind about coming to the 'surprise birthday' lunch my partners are hosting at the Scarth Club, come ahead."

I bent to kiss his head. "Thanks, but Georgie and I still have a lot of ground to cover."

As I stood on the porch to wave goodbye to Zack, I felt a twinge of guilt. My husband and I didn't keep secrets from each other, but reasoning that there had been turmoil enough, I hadn't told Zack that Charlie D was looking into Kyle's past. This was his day, and he deserved to enjoy every minute.

* * *

Georgie was having a final fitting on her wedding outfit that morning, so we got a late start.

We were just hitting our stride when Taylor and Vale arrived. "I didn't think I'd see you two till tonight," I said. "This is a pleasant surprise."

Taylor and Vale exchanged a quick glance but remained silent.

"Something's wrong," I said.

Taylor knew that Zack's health was always my first concern. "It's not Dad," she said. "It's about *Sisters and Strangers*."

Vale reached into her messenger bag and pulled out a script. "Taylor and I were at the studio chatting with Nick Kovacs, when a man came up, introduced himself as Buzz Wells and gave me this." Vale handed me the script. "He told me that from now on this was the version we'd be working with."

Georgie scanned the title page and scowled. "*Sisters and Strangers*," she said. "And lookee — the writers' names are in caps! BUZZ WELLS and ROY BRODNITZ."

I tried to keep my voice even. "Vale, were you the only one Buzz gave the script to?"

Her head shake was vehement. "No. He was passing them out to everyone and telling them that Ainsley had okayed the revised script and they were to adjust their notes to accommodate it."

I had never heard Georgie swear. Obviously she'd been saving up for the right moment, and this was it. After she'd uttered a daisy chain of expletives, she breathed deeply. "Ah that's better. The nuns always told us not to use gutter language but the good sisters of Saint Thérèse of Lisieux never met Buzz Wells. I'll call Fawn and ask her to tell everyone the matter of the script is being decided and until further notice they should work with the old script."

"I think she already tried that," Taylor said. "When Buzz

was handing around the scripts, Fawn came in and said that Ainsley wanted people to be open to all options."

"How did that go over?" I said.

Vale was clearly troubled. "Except for Danny Kerrigan, everyone was pretty quiet. He was really upset. He said he'd read the original script so often he dreamed about it. He knew exactly how the scenes were going to look and sound. The script was perfect as it was, he said, and no one should be allowed to ruin it."

"*Sisters and Strangers* means a lot to Danny," Taylor said. "I told him not to worry, that you held the option, and you wouldn't let the project go ahead if it wasn't perfect. I was trying to reassure him, but my words seemed to upset him even more. He said that if Buzz didn't back down then everything would fall apart, and he wouldn't be able to do what he had to do."

Life had taught me never to ask a question if the answer might bring me grief, but remembering Lizzie's fervour about the mission she and Danny had to save Vale and Taylor from eternal damnation, I pressed on. "Did Danny explain exactly what he had to do?"

"No," Vale said. "He was beside himself, but he didn't want to break down in public, so he left."

"Kyle's having problems too," Taylor said. "He's not coming to the party tonight. He says he doesn't want to spoil the celebration. I told him I wanted him there because he's done a great job and he deserves to hear the praise. Jo, Kyle's angry at himself because he knows his behaviour is fuelling the rumour that's going around."

"What's the rumour?" Georgie said.

"The rumour is that this production is cursed," Vale said. "First Gabe, then Roy and the fire, and now Ainsley and Kyle are faltering, and Danny's spinning out of control. People are saying that *Sisters and Strangers* is in trouble."

"Then we have stop the rumours with the truth," I said. "This production is not cursed. Someone doesn't want it to succeed, and they are doing everything they can to ensure that it fails. It's that simple. Our job is to find out who's undercutting us and make them stop."

Vale and Taylor had instinctively moved closer to each other. "Taylor and I will go back to the production studios and tell people what you just told us," Vale said, and the tilt of her chin was defiant. "We have a chance to make something beautiful and true. *Sisters and Strangers* is worth fighting for."

As soon as the young women left, Georgie turned to me. "Way to rally the troops!" she said. "I could feel your knees shaking, but that was only because we were sitting across the table from each other. I'm sure Vale and Taylor didn't notice."

"Good," I said. "I didn't realize how widespread the rumours had become."

"I'm certain Buzz is out there fanning the flames," Georgie said. "But let him fan. We have work to do."

Taylor and Vale's party for Zack was scheduled to start at five p.m. — early even by prairie standards — but not early when two of the significant guests are nineteen months old. The plan was to devote the first hour of the celebration to the housewarming with tours, antipasto and visiting; the second hour to lasagna, salads and more visiting, and the final hour to cake cutting and present opening. After the guests of honour had been feted and everyone was sated, we'd be out the door by eight o'clock.

The day had already seemed long to me, and I was about to suggest that Georgie and I knock off early, so I could have a nap and a shower before the party when my phone rang. The area code was unfamiliar, and I held up my phone to Georgie. "Do you know where 718 is?"

"Brooklyn, Queens and Staten Island," she said.

I picked up. Stella Delacroix's speaking voice was lovely: low and filled with music. After she'd introduced herself, she went straight to the business at hand. "You can speak freely, Joanne. My brother has been open with me about the role he played in involving Gabe Vickers in *Sisters and Strangers.* Hal is sick about the collateral damage his rashness has caused. Hal is not given to vengeance, but I'm his sister. He knew I was wounded by what Buzz Wells did to *Broders' Annex,* and Hal has always been protective."

"You two are lucky to have each other," I said, watching as Georgie packed up her bag but didn't leave yet.

"We are," Stella said. "And now it's Hal who's hurting. How can I help?"

"Could we start with the first year of *Broders' Annex* when you and Kyle Daly were both working on the series? I know the animus Hal feels towards Buzz Wells is rooted in the past, but I have a feeling that the problems plaguing our production now grow out of that time too."

"That wouldn't surprise me," Stella said. "That set was a snake pit. The Buzz-saw, as everyone called our executive producer, encouraged rivalries. He felt mistrust and fear made people strive to outperform their colleagues and achieve excellence. All his philosophy did was divide us. People kept their heads down and did their jobs. Kyle was the exception. He had a smile and encouraging words for everyone."

"Even Buzz?"

"Even Buzz," Stella said. "And the Buzz-saw lapped it up. He adored Kyle. Of course the assumption was that the relationship was sexual, but it wasn't. Kyle and Buzz are both straight; they just shared a passion for their work. Kyle was young and fairly new to the business. There were things he needed to learn, and Buzz had years of experience to draw on. The term 'mentor' is overused, but I would characterize their relationship at the beginning as that between a mentor and a gifted associate."

"But that changed?"

"It did. A situation arose around Kyle that was potentially very dangerous, and Buzz, usually the most selfish of men, did everything in his power to protect his friend."

"What happened?"

"Kyle was the victim of a stalker, and to complicate matters, the stalker was an executive on the network that had picked up *Broders' Annex*. Her name was Heather Hurworth, and she was at least two decades older than Kyle. She was attractive and fashionable — she always wore those funky, retro glasses with the oversize round black rims — and very mod. At any rate, Heather was known to flit from passion to passion — a man would be her be-all and end-all one day, and by the next day she would have moved on."

"But she didn't move on from Kyle."

"No. I had my own woes at the time, but Heather's bizarre behaviour generated the real drama. Kyle and Heather had a fling, but when Kyle tried to end the relationship respectfully, Heather refused to accept his word that the affair was over. We shot the series in North Caldwell, New Jersey, the same town where Tony Soprano lives. It's an hour or so from New York, but in our business the working day is long, so the production company rented a couple of motels to accommodate us. Heather's office was in Manhattan, but periodically she'd be waiting outside Kyle's motel door in the morning. She'd always pick a day when the weather was wretched, so Kyle would have to let her ride with him to the set. People tried to talk to her, but she ignored them. A restraining order was out of the question: Heather was a network executive, and we were a young and vulnerable series. It was a hot mess.

"Kyle tried to wait it out, but it didn't end, and one day he snapped. He and Heather had a loud and public quarrel. Kyle said she was acting like a crazy person and then he went outdoors to cool off. When he came back in and started towards the set, a light stand fell, missing him by a fraction. Heather had been standing by the light stand, and everyone within earshot had heard her say, 'Don't make me do something we'll both regret.'"

"How did the situation resolve itself?"

"Heather Hurworth died. *Broders' Annex* was still shooting, but my part of the writing was finished and I'd hightailed it back to Brooklyn, so this information is second-hand, but

I trust my source. The accident happened not long after I left. Heather was waiting outside Kyle's motel room. To avoid her, Kyle sprinted to his car, jumped in and started the car. Heather was waving her arms to stop him, but the parking area was icy and she slipped and fell in front of Kyle's car, and he ran over her. The coroner said she died instantly.

"The police investigated, of course. But luckily, there was a bystander who was able to fill them in on Heather's unstable behaviour and the threats she'd uttered against Kyle Daly. Even more luckily, he had witnessed exactly what happened and he swore that Kyle was blameless."

"I take it the eyewitness was Buzz Wells," I said. When Stella murmured assent, I continued. "Kyle was lucky that Buzz Wells lived in the same motel he did."

Stella laughed. "Buzz Wells definitely did not live at the Stardust Motel with the crew. The phrase 'we're all family' is bandied about a lot on movie sets, but there's a hierarchy, and Buzz was at the top of the heap. He spent the shoot ensconced in the finest lodgings North Caldwell, New Jersey, had to offer."

"So what was he doing in the parking lot of the Stardust Motel that morning?"

"Your guess is as good as mine," Stella said. "But Kyle will know." She paused. "Joanne, you and Hal and I are all very fond of Kyle. But my brother tells me your daughter, Taylor, has grown close to Kyle, and given everything, it might be wise to suggest that she put some distance between Kyle and her. Hal and I both feel that Buzz is using Kyle as a pawn to get what he wants out of *Sisters and Strangers*. Hal says that Kyle is already paying a terrible price for something he's done, and Buzz Wells is not finished. If he needs to, he'll use Kyle again. Hal believes Taylor should get out of the line of fire, and I believe that too."

I was badly shaken, but my voice was steady as I thanked Stella Delacroix for her concern and told her I would talk to Taylor and keep Hal apprised of developments. I ended the call and turned to face Georgie.

She looked stricken. "More bad news?"

"Yes," I said. "Georgie, why don't you let me handle this? You're getting married in four days, and you're having a baby in seven months. You don't need this stress. Take the rest of the afternoon off. Go home, have a bubble bath and take a nap."

Georgie's smile was weary. "You almost had me at 'bubble bath,' but that day when you were dyeing Easter eggs and I came to tell you about Roy's breakdown, simply talking to you made me realize the truth of that old saw that a burden shared is a burden halved." Georgie covered my hand with hers. "We're in this together, Jo. So fill me in and halve your burden."

As she listened to my account of Kyle's relationship with Buzz Wells, Georgie's grey eyes were troubled. When I finished, she said, "I'm with Stella on this. You have to tell Taylor everything we just learned and urge her to stay away from Kyle."

"I'll do what I can," I said. "But Taylor is fiercely loyal to her friends, and Kyle is her friend. She's already worried about him. I'm almost certain I won't be able to convince her to walk away from him when he's in trouble. If Stella's right, Kyle is in deep waters already, but Buzz is desperate, and his desperation means more grief ahead for Kyle. Georgie, I'm almost certain that Kyle was responsible for giving Roy the hallucinogen or whatever he ingested that destroyed him. I don't believe that Kyle was ever aware of what the drug might do. Roy's emotional problems were well known. Buzz could have told Kyle he was concerned about Roy's writers' block and suggested LSD to get the creative juices flowing. It's possible Buzz provided the drug himself. Kyle goes back and forth to New York periodically. I know from a case Zack had that LSD is the ultimate smuggleable drug — it has no smell, no taste, no colour and it is dosed in micrograms. Whether Kyle gave Roy a drug he'd requested and Buzz provided or slipped the acid into Roy's water because Buzz said he wanted to help an old colleague is a moot point.

"What matters now is what Kyle does next. Our only hope is that he tells Ainsley that Buzz was behind the plan to give Roy the hallucinogen that led to Roy's fatal heart attack. If Ainsley knows the truth, she'll have Buzz on the next plane out, and our problems with him will be over."

"But Kyle will be in a world of trouble. Joanne, we don't know exactly what happened in that motel parking lot. If Kyle ran over that woman deliberately, he'll be charged, and his life as he knows it will be over. Why would he open himself up to that?"

"Because it's the right thing to do?"

"Dream on," Georgie said. "Kyle is not a saint. He's a human being and like most of us, he does what it takes to protect himself."

"People aren't always driven by self-interest," I said. I thought of Cronus's decision on the last day of his life. "Sometimes we're able to see past ourselves and know what we have to do. I'll talk to Zack and see if he can come up with a way around this." I started straightening the papers in front of me on the table. "But I'm not telling anyone anything tonight. Taylor, Vale and Zack deserve a happy evening. I'll make certain Taylor comes by the house tomorrow morning, so we can give her the full picture."

Georgie reached over and squeezed my hand. "We'll get through this, Jo." The smile she gave me was endearingly crooked. "After all, we have an elegant yet intimate wedding to plan."

* * *

Zack and I arrived at the apartment on Dewdney Avenue at five on the button, but the party was already in full swing. Vale met us at the door with a hug. "Say hi to everybody, and then it's my turn to lead the tour," she said.

"Madeleine and I can help," Lena said. "We've already been on the tour three times."

I turned to Mieka. "When did you get here?"

Mieka's expression was sheepish. "Twenty minutes ago. The girls couldn't wait to see the new place. Neither could I."

She bent to embrace Zack. "Happy Birthday," she said. "You and Mum are in for a treat. This place is really something."

"When Lena and I get our first apartment," Madeleine said. "It will be like this — elegant but cutting edge."

"Cutting edge, eh?" Zack gripped the handrims of his chair. "We'd better get started, Jo."

Pete came over. "I'm the bartender," he said. "Your beverage of choice will be waiting when you return from the tour. What's your pleasure?"

"It's Zack's birthday, and we no longer have a resident designated driver," I said. "So I'll have sparkling water."

"And I will have a martini," Zack said. "But make it a double so I can give my new designated driver a sip."

Kyle and our daughter had worked magic on the formerly in-your-face red pleasure palace. The combination of Prussian blue walls, white oak floors and exposed warm red-brown brick in the living room was inspired, and Taylor and Kyle had stayed with shades of grey, blue and what Taylor called "greige" for the walls throughout the apartment. The guest bed and bathroom were a pale watery blue; Taylor and Vale's bedroom and bathroom were in a shade called River Gorge Grey that I would not have chosen in a hundred years but was stunning. The windowless room where Cronus and his consenting partners enjoyed S&M was now a shared office with icy blue-grey walls and a new good-sized window.

"Putting that window in the brick wall must have been a major structural undertaking," I said.

"I'm sure it was," Vale said, "but everything was completed and ready when I arrived. All I had to do was love it, and I do." She shook her head. "I really wish Kyle had come tonight. Taylor's sending him pictures, but it's not the same as being here."

"No," I agreed. "It's not. Now I take it this room is your office."

"Taylor got the idea from the office you and Granddad have," Madeleine said. "That long table in the middle is so Vale and Taylor can be together when they work, the way you and Granddad are."

"Mimi and I like the arrangement," Zack said. "More time together."

"That's what Taylor and I are aiming for too," Vale said. "I still can't believe this place is really ours. My mother and I were in the same apartment for years, but I don't remember us ever having it painted or even whether we had any pictures on the walls. It was okay but it was pretty much just a place to sleep and eat."

"And this is a place to live," I said.

"Yes," Vale said. "This is a place to live."

By the time we returned to the living room, the antipasto trays from Italian Star Deli had arrived and everybody was digging in. When Peter came over with our drinks, Taylor was with him. Her brown eyes, clear and unblinking, met mine and then Zack's. "So, what's the verdict?"

Zack grinned. "Madeleine pronounced the apartment 'elegant and cutting edge,' and in my opinion, she nailed it. You did a terrific job, Taylor."

"Thanks, but I couldn't have done it without Kyle and his crew. They worked in shifts, so there were people here

24/7, and of course, Kyle's people are experts, so no wasted time and no disasters. Now that Vale and I have figured out how to entertain, we plan to have Kyle, the crew and their significant others over for dinner."

"I'll bet the significant others will leave here with renovations in mind," Zack said.

"I've picked up a few ideas," I said. "Taylor, you were so wise to choose neutral colours so the art would be the focus."

"I knew you'd notice that," Taylor said. "We have a lot of seriously great art — from Sally and from Des and some pieces that I've bought myself. I cherish everything on these walls, and I wanted every piece to have its moment."

"And every piece does have its moment," I said. "There's such a good feeling about this apartment now — it's serene and solid and beautiful. This is the perfect first home for you and Vale."

Taylor swallowed hard and put her arm around me. "Let's get some of that antipasto before the Crawford-Kilbourns and the Kilbourn-Dowhanuiks start licking the trays."

That night was the twins' first meeting with lasagna, and it was love at first sight. Pete threw a plastic sheet over the white oak floor, set up Charlie and Colin in their portable booster chairs with trays, handed the boys their pasta and the photo taking began. After the boys had cleaned their plates for a second time, Pete and Charlie D took them to the guest bathroom to hose them down. The rest of us filled the dishwasher and brought out the cakes and presents.

When I noticed Maisie taking darting glances at the door, I said, "Are you expecting someone else?"

"One of our associates mentioned he might drop by," Maisie said.

"Fine with me," Zack said, "but I thought we were keeping this family only."

"He kind of invited himself," Maisie said. "Anyway, it's time for presents."

Vale and Taylor were both pink with excitement as they unwrapped their housewarming gifts: vibrant blue kitchenware from the Crawford-Kilbourns and the Kilbourn-Dowhanuiks and a gift certificate for Pawsitively Purrfect from Taylor's cats. Vale cooed appropriately over our gift — matching super-plush bath sheets from Portugal, snowy white, embossed with the number 42 in slate grey — but it was clear the number puzzled her. Taylor picked up on her girlfriend's confusion. "In *The Hitchhiker's Guide to the Galaxy*, 42 is the answer to the Ultimate Question of Life," she said. "Also somebody who can stay in control of virtually any situation is somebody who is said to know where her towel is." Taylor put her arm around Vale's shoulders. "So as long as you and I know where these glorious towels are, we're golden."

When there was a beep from downstairs, Taylor leapt to her feet and pressed the button that allowed the caller to enter.

"I guess the mystery associate decided to come after all," Zack said. He wheeled toward the door and opened it. Our son Angus was standing on the threshold. He'd come from

Calgary for the big day. "I heard some legal superstar was having a birthday," he said. "I'm here to touch the hem of his barrister's robe."

The next few minutes were a crazy chorus of laughter and half sentences. When the dust settled and we were finally ready for cake, some facts had been established. Angus was staying for at least six weeks and perhaps longer. Maisie had made all the arrangements with the Calgary office of Falconer Shreve. There had been friction between Maisie and the associate with whom she'd been working on the new and very high-profile case, but Maisie and Angus had worked successfully together before. They had talked, and he had agreed to come.

Zack could not stop smiling. He loved Peter and Mieka, but he and Angus had always had a special affinity, and as Zack blew out the candles on his cake I thought I'd never seen a happier man. When Lena asked him what he had wished for, Zack said, "Nothing. Everything I want is right in this room."

Taylor stepped forward. "Dad, you may not have wishes for this, but there's one more gift. It's from all your kids and grandkids and we're not taking it back. Close your eyes and we'll tell you when to open them."

She and Mieka and their brothers left and when they came back Taylor brought in an easel, which she positioned in front of Zack, and Mieka, Peter and Angus balanced the very large and striking woodcarving that they were carrying on the easel.

Madeleine and Lena were watching their mother and when she nodded, they said, "Okay, Granddad you can open your eyes." Lena was holding an index card from which she began to read. "The renowned Haida artist Don Yeoman created this work. It's called *Supernatural Eagle*, and it's hand-carved on red cedar and painted in part with acrylics. Price $10,000." Lena's hand flew to her mouth. "I wasn't supposed to read the part, was I?"

"No, but it's okay," Madeleine said, and then she began to read from her own index card. "For the Haida people, Eagle is a symbol of both power and prestige as well as a harbinger of peace and friendship. Eagle is one of the two main crests of the Haida. It symbolizes courage and bringing to light. Eagle also has a strong connection to harmony." Madeleine smiled at Zack. "We chose this carving because Elder Pelletier suggested it. I know you and he had worked together on Racette-Hunter and the campaign and it made us think of you, Granddad."

CHAPTER EIGHTEEN

The next morning, the dogs and I had just stopped to watch the duck family out for a leisurely swim when my phone rang. It was Georgie, and she was seething. "Have you checked your messages this morning?"

"No," I said.

"Check them."

"I can't. I'm talking to you."

Georgie groaned. "I thought pregnancy brain wasn't supposed to kick in till the third trimester. Anyway, there's a message from Rumpel — Jo, his attack on *Sisters and Strangers* just moved into high gear. There are two pieces of information that will curdle your blood: Number one, Ainsley has agreed to let him act as her surrogate in dealing with any problems that arise with you about the direction of the production. Number two, Ainsley has asked Buzz to serve as executive producer. Fawn Tootoosis has been demoted to her previous position as production manager."

"Buzz is desperate," I said. "Charlie D told me last night that Buzz's investors in *At the Algonquin* are growing restive, and Buzz has promised to have everything in place by the end of the month."

"So he needs money, and this is his last kick at the can."

"Yes, and it's ours too," I said. "Our only way out is if Kyle tells Ainsley that Buzz was behind what happened to Roy. If we approach her, Ainsley will dismiss our accusation as groundless — and it *will* be groundless. We have no proof. All we have is Stella Delacroix's account, and Buzz will brush that off by saying Stella is simply a disgruntled ex-employee with a grudge. No, Ainsley will believe Kyle for the very reason you and I talked about yesterday. Kyle is putting himself in jeopardy if he tells her about the role Buzz played in Roy's tragic death. If Kyle steps up and tells the truth, Buzz will be gone, and we'll be free to make *Sisters and Strangers* the series we want it to be."

"And if we can't convince Kyle to open up, it's game over."

"Pretty much," I said. "But I think Kyle can be convinced. He's miserable, Georgie. He's a good person, and after the last table meeting, he told me he'd made a terrible mistake. I'll see what Zack says about the possibility of getting Kyle out of this mess relatively unscathed and then I'm going to do what I can to convince Taylor that Kyle's only option is to tell the truth."

When the dogs and I got home, Zack, dressed for the day, was in our bedroom, sitting in front of the easel, wholly absorbed in his new carving. He gave me a brief smile and gestured for me to join him. "Look at this: a few swirls of red acrylic, a few swirls of black acrylic, some grooves carved into red cedar and it's all there — the power and the spirit of the eagle." He took my hand. "I can't stop marvelling at this, and I can't stop thinking about those speeches our granddaughters made."

"It was an unforgettable evening," I agreed. "But this is today, and I need your help. The situation with Buzz Wells is coming to a head, and unless some painful facts are brought into the open, *Sisters and Strangers* is in serious trouble."

Zack turned his chair to face me. "I'll do what I can."

"Good. Now here's what we know. Kyle Daly and Buzz share a history. Hal Dupuis's sister, Stella Delacroix, worked with Buzz and Kyle on a series she'd created. I talked to Stella yesterday and her story about an accident that occurred during the shooting of the series is troubling."

Zack's expression remained impassive as I described the circumstances leading up to Heather Hurworth's death, and when I finished, his appraisal of the situation was crisp. "So Buzz is threatening to recant his story of what happened in the motel parking lot if Kyle doesn't do as he's told."

"Right," I said. "And this is where you come in. We don't know what happened in that parking lot, but we do know that Kyle Daly has nothing to gain from sabotaging *Sisters and Strangers*, and Buzz Wells does. His creditors are closing in on him, and he's cornered. Blackmailing Kyle into doing his dirty work has offered Buzz a way out."

Zack's dark eyes were grave. "Jo, no matter what happened in that parking lot, Kyle is in trouble. He'll be confessing to giving Roy Brodnitz a substance that, albeit indirectly, led to his death. The role Buzz Wells played in facilitating that action will be key. If Kyle acted unknowingly, a good lawyer might be able to cut a deal with the Crown. But there's no grey area with arson. If Kyle set that fire, he'll have to plead guilty."

"If he was your client, what would you advise him to do?"

"I'd advise him to come clean," Zack said. "When Kyle ran out of our house the night we watched the rough cut, he was falling apart. If he were my client, I'd advise him to tell the truth because keeping what he's done secret is killing him. What he started to say to you after the meeting shows that he wants to confess. I think if he knows we're on his side, he'll open up."

"Good. Will you call Taylor and say what you just said to me? She and Kyle are close, and she'll do what she can to help him."

"I'll do that, but first, I'm going to call Ainsley Blair and in my capacity as Living Skies' lawyer, I'll point out that a contractor cannot simply hand off her rights to a surrogate."

"So no surrogacy for Buzz."

"No, and it's time to up the ante. I'm going to advise Ainsley that I've learned of a threat to *Sisters and Strangers* that needs to be investigated, and she should shut down the production until further notice. A lockout will slow Buzz's momentum and give Ainsley a chance to clarify her thinking."

"You really have nerves of steel."

Zack shrugged. "I'm just trying to prove I'm worthy of my eagle."

* * *

When I came back from showering and changing, I joined Zack in the office. He was on the phone, and when I came in, he mouthed Ainsley's name. I started to leave, but he gestured towards my chair. "Ainsley, Joanne just came in, and if you're okay with it, I'll put you on speakerphone."

"That's fine," Ainsley said.

"Good," Zack said. "Jo, Ainsley was concerned about the shutdown, but I told her that we know the threat is real, so we have to be proactive. She accepts that, and she just sent out an email telling support staff and crew that the production studios will be closed until further notice."

"That's a relief," I said. "Until we're certain the problem is resolved, we can't afford to take a chance."

"Of course not," Ainsley said. Her voice was cool but engaged. "Zack, I was planning to call you to apologize to you both for not checking about the legality of the proxy. Buzz volunteered to assume a number of responsibilities so I could focus on directing, and I was so anxious to get back to my own work that I jumped the gun." She paused. "Now, if there's nothing else . . ."

Zack turned to me. "Joanne, any questions or concerns?"

"No. We've done all we can do."

Ainsley's intake of breath was audible. When she spoke

her voice broke. "Let's hope it's enough," she said. "So much is at stake."

When the call ended, Zack said, "Jo, have you thought about what discovering Buzz Wells is the mastermind behind this attempt to take down *Sisters and Strangers* will do to Ainsley?"

"I have." My laptop was on our work table. I found the video of Ainsley rehearsing the actors for the Broadway production of *The Happiest Girl* and turned the screen towards Zack. "Take a look," I said. When the video was over, I said, "I'm hoping Ainsley will find that woman again — the strong woman who doesn't have to lean on a creep like Buzz to get through a crisis and whose joy in her work brings out the best in everyone around her."

"If Ainsley accepts that personnel plan we talked about at the meeting, everything will fall into place," Zack said. "Brock Poitras has already put together a short list of candidates for the position of general manager of Living Skies. He's planning to call Ainsley this week to arrange a time when she can sit in on interviews. Once that position is filled and Fawn Tootoosis is back as executive producer, Ainsley will be free to do what she loves."

"So the ball is in Ainsley's court," I said. "I'll phone Georgie and Charlie D and get them up to speed."

"I called Taylor earlier," Zack said. "She's going to suggest to Kyle that she pick him up and they come back here to her studio to talk things through. That way we're close by if they need us."

"Events are on the move," I said. "I guess now we just wait."

Zack had an appellate brief to prepare, and I had the script, so I made tea and we worked until we heard Taylor's car pull up out front. She and Kyle didn't come into the house. I beckoned Zack to the window and we watched the two of them walk across the back lawn to the studio. Taylor had her arm through Kyle's, and he was walking with his head down, clearly disconsolate.

"Kyle has a rough morning ahead of him," Zack said.

"He does," I agreed. "But Buzz's morning will be a hundred times worse, and his misery is just beginning."

* * *

It was almost an hour before we saw Kyle and Taylor walking back from her studio. When Zack gave me an inquiring glance, I said, "Let's sit tight and take our cue from them."

They came immediately to the office. Taylor embraced us both. "Kyle is ready to talk to you, Dad," she said. She gave Kyle an encouraging smile and held out her hand to me. "They need to be alone," she said to me. "Lawyer-client stuff, but I could really use some company."

When we went outside, Taylor collapsed on one of the chaise longues and closed her eyes. The sky was leaden, heavy with the rain the forecast predicted, but the air was cool and sweet with the scent of apple blossoms from the tree in our neighbour's yard. I lay down on the lounge beside her. My nerves were frayed, but if Taylor needed to discuss what was happening, I was there.

For several minutes, Taylor was silent, eyes shut tight, body tense. Finally she said, "That was brutal. Kyle's agreed to face this head-on. He knows that telling the truth will change how people see him, professionally and personally, but . . ."

"He also knows he has no choice."

"Kyle was wavering," Taylor said. "I was afraid he wouldn't go through with it and then — I don't know why — I told him Cronus's story, how after a lifetime as a slumlord exploiting people Cronus knowingly risked and lost his life to save Racette-Hunter, a project that offered the children of the community he'd exploited a way out. I also told Kyle that deciding to do the right thing brought Cronus peace."

"And that tipped the scales?"

"It did," Taylor said. "Just the way it did for Vale and me that night at the Sahara Club. The moment we heard that story, Vale and I both knew that Cronus's apartment, a place where a person who had made mistakes, but decided to live a life that grew out of those mistakes, was exactly the right place for us."

"You have no idea how much what you just said means to me and will mean to your dad. We both wish we'd had more time with Cronus. Knowing that his story saved another person is a legacy Cronus would be proud of. Are Kyle and Zack going to the police?"

"No, Kyle wants to see Ainsley first. He says she deserves to know the truth."

"So what is the truth?"

"It's close to what you and Dad came up with, but there are some differences that I've tried to convince Kyle are important. What Hal Dupuis's sister told you about Heather Hurworth stalking Kyle is true, and Kyle *was* behind the wheel of the car that ran over her. But Kyle says what happened was an accident. It was dark and according to Kyle, Heather Hurworth seemed to come out of nowhere, and then she just threw herself at the car. For a second, he saw her face and her arms flailing in his headlights, and then she was gone. He felt the impact of the car hitting something. He slammed on the brakes and jumped out of the car to see what had happened. As soon as he saw her, Kyle knew there was no way Heather Hurworth could have survived.

"Kyle was in shock, and he did something stupid. Instead of calling the police, he called Buzz Wells. When Buzz was almost at the motel, he called the police, told them he'd witnessed an accident."

"But he hadn't witnessed the accident," I said. "Why did Buzz tell the authorities he had?"

"Buzz said he wasn't certain that Heather Hurworth's death was an accident, and by saying he was an eyewitness, he was giving Kyle cover. Apparently, by the time the police arrived, Kyle was pretty well out of it, and Buzz took over. He told the police that Heather Hurworth had been stalking Kyle, and that morning he'd heard her shout 'You'll never be rid of me,' before she jumped in front of Kyle's car. The car was already moving. Kyle hit the brakes, but it was too late."

"And Kyle never went to the police to correct the story."

"He didn't see the need to. Kyle believed Buzz lied to protect him. Even after Kyle left *Broders' Annex* after the first season, he and Buzz remained friends."

"And Buzz used their friendship to convince Kyle to give Roy Brodnitz LSD."

"Yes." Taylor's voice was small. "He told Kyle they were doing it to help Ainsley. Buzz said that Roy's analyst had successfully used hallucinogens to treat patients suffering from creative blocks, and he believed a hallucinogen was the answer for Roy. Because Roy's experience with cocaine had made him wary, Buzz told Kyle the LSD would have to be given to Roy surreptitiously."

"And Kyle believed Buzz's story?"

"He had no reason not to," Taylor said. "He trusted Buzz, and Kyle knew enough about Ainsley's devotion to Roy to believe that she would go to any lengths to help him. The next time Kyle was in New York, Buzz gave him the tab of acid and told him that what he was about to do must be kept confidential and that Ainsley was very grateful. Kyle felt he was returning the favour Buzz had done for him when Heather Hurworth died."

"So he followed through."

"He did, but as soon as Roy was hospitalized in Saskatoon, Kyle called Buzz. He told Buzz he had to break his promise about keeping what he had done confidential, because the doctors needed to know that Roy had ingested a hallucinogen. When Buzz blew up, Kyle realized that the entire story about the analyst and Ainsley needing Buzz's help was a lie. And his nightmare began."

"Did Kyle set the fire at the production studios?"

"No. Buzz wanted him to, but Kyle refused. Buzz made other arrangements, and of course, Kyle couldn't say anything without starting an investigation that would eventually lead to him."

CHAPTER NINETEEN

When the rain started, Taylor and I picked up the cushions from the patio furniture and took them inside. We'd just finished piling everything in the family room when Zack came in. "Kyle wants to talk to Ainsley before we do anything else," he said. "I called Ainsley and explained enough to convince her she should talk to Kyle and me. She suggested that she meet us here. I had a feeling Buzz was in the apartment with her."

"I gather you'd like Taylor and me to make ourselves scarce," I said.

"If you don't mind."

"I don't mind," Taylor said. "Vale and I are going grocery shopping and she's really pumped about it."

"Vale's pumped about going grocery shopping?" I said.

"Wait till she sees the cat boutique at Pawsitively Purrfect."

For the first time that morning, our daughter smiled. I put my arm around her. "Taylor, this will work out. Let's just get through the day. Zack, I know Georgie's working at home. I'm going to go over there. If Buzz suspects things are falling apart, he may go to her place and start pressing her."

* * *

Georgie welcomed me enthusiastically. "I'm glad you're here, Jo. I've been getting a weird vibe from upstairs. Actually, it's more than a vibe. Ainsley and Buzz were fighting — raised voices, slammed doors, a lot of banging around. I've been trying to decide whether I should call her or go up."

"Ainsley's on her way to our place to talk to Zack and Kyle Daly," I said. "There've been developments."

When I finished Georgie raised an eyebrow. "Do you think it's possible that Rumpel may be on his way out?"

"A fairy-tale ending," I said. "We can only hope. In the meantime . . ."

Georgie and I had been working on the script for about twenty minutes when there was a loud thump on the floor upstairs. We'd both jumped, but when there was no further disturbance, we got back to work.

A few minutes later, Zack appeared at Georgie's door, clearly chagrined. "I felt Ainsley should not approach Buzz Wells without legal counsel," he said. "But Buzz Wells is on the second floor, and I don't do stairs."

Georgie was on her feet. "I'm no lawyer, but knowing

you're down here to take over will simplify things. I'll go with Ainsley."

"No, you won't," I said. "This is bound to be unpleasant, and your ob-gyn says no stress. I'll go."

"Ainsley's waiting in the duplex parking area," Zack said. "Jo, I feel terrible about this."

"Don't," I said. "As soon as Buzz comes down, Georgie and I will go to lunch somewhere that's guaranteed stress-free. We'll be fine."

Ainsley was standing by the outdoor staircase that led to the second floor. We greeted each other, and I followed her up the stairs through the back door into a bedroom. She called Buzz's name, and when there was no response, we started down the hall.

I followed Ainsley into the living room, until, without warning, she pivoted and bolted, almost knocking me over. She'd covered her mouth with her hands and was retching. The room was warm and when I took a breath, I choked on air heavy with the coppery, metallic odour of blood.

Buzz Wells was lying on his back, eyes open but unseeing. Danny Kerrigan kneeled beside Buzz with his hand over the slash in the side of Buzz's neck. Like Buzz, he was covered in blood. Ainsley stood in the hall with her back to the room, and I turned towards her. "Go downstairs and let them know what's happened. Tell them to call 911. I'll stay with Danny till help arrives." When Ainsley didn't move, I raised my voice. "Just do this one last thing," I said. "It's almost over."

My words had been confident, but I was light-headed and my knees were weak. It took an act of will to go to Danny. When I knelt beside him, I realized that he was attempting to stop the bleeding by putting pressure on Buzz's wound. I touched Danny's arm. "You can stop now," I said. "He's gone."

When Danny turned to look at me, his eyes were as dead and unseeing as those of the man on the floor in front of him.

"Danny, the police will be here soon," I said.

"I need to pray," he said. "Can you get Pastor Kirk?"

I was shaking so badly, I could barely pull my phone from the pocket of my slacks. Danny gave me the number. I entered it and crossed the room so he couldn't hear my words.

When Pastor Kirk picked up, I said, "This is Joanne Shreve. I'm a friend of Lizzie Ewing and Danny Kerrigan's."

"All of us at Bountiful Gifts are praying for your daughter and Vale Frazier," he said.

His baritone was smug, ingratiating and unctuous, and my throat tightened. "Thank you," I said. "But I'm calling about Danny. He needs your help. There's been a tragedy. A man is dead."

"And Danny is connected how?"

"I think Danny killed him. I don't know the details, but Danny is beside himself. He wants you to pray with him."

In the blink of an eye, Pastor Kirk's oily piety gave way to a tone of brisk dismissal. "Ms. Shreve, I'm late for a meeting with our leadership committee," he said. "We're revising the church's mission statement and my presence is critical."

"Danny's need is critical," I said, but it was too late. Pastor Kirk had already broken the connection. Like Pontius Pilate before him, the pastor had washed his hands of the matter.

When I joined him, Danny's eyes were anxious. "Pastor Kirk can't come," I said. "But Danny, I can pray with you."

A police officer once told me that police become inured to walking into bizarre situations. That said, I think even seasoned veterans of the force would have found the scene that morning in Ainsley Blair's apartment, surreal: a dead man, a murder weapon in plain view, and a young man and a much older woman praying together in a pool of blood.

* * *

The police had deferred questioning Ainsley and me until late afternoon, by which time we both had been examined by a physician, received short-term prescriptions for Ativan, showered under the watchful eyes of a female constable and dressed in Georgie's clothing. Zack never left my side.

The police interviewed us separately: Ainsley in the kitchen and me in the living room. It had been years since I'd seen Detective Robert Hallam, the officer who questioned me, but he was remarkably unchanged: a small, dapper man with a steel-grey crewcut, a luxuriant bush of a moustache, a prim mouth and an unshakeable belief that the world was divided into two camps — the good guys and the bad guys. In late life he married Rosalie Norman, the administrative assistant in the political science department where I was an associate professor. Rosalie was as prickly as her new husband, but she liked me well enough, so Robert Hallam had assigned me to the good guys camp.

I was sitting in a comfortable armchair with a cup of sugary, milky tea. Zack was beside me, and Robert Hallam pulled up a chair and positioned it so he could face me. He greeted me with warmth and concern. "How are you doing?"

I tried a smile. "As well as could be expected."

"What can you tell us?" Zack said.

"We've been able to piece together some information," Robert Hallam said. "Danny Kerrigan was quite vocal until the lawyer you arranged to represent him arrived."

Zack shrugged. "It's the law."

"I'm aware of that," Detective Hallam said. "You'll be relieved to hear that Mr. Kerrigan did not incriminate himself before his lawyer arrived. The first officers on the scene reported that Mr. Kerrigan was voluble but incoherent. We had better luck with a commissionaire at the production studios with whom Mr. Kerrigan spoke this morning. The commissionaire said Mr. Kerrigan was agitated but he gave what appears to be an accurate accounting of his activities.

"As he did every morning, Danny Kerrigan rode his bicycle to work. When he arrived at the production studios, he realized his phone was missing and retraced his route. As a consequence, he was over an hour late arriving for work. When he entered the building and discovered it was empty and the doors to all the departments were locked, he panicked.

"Mr. Kerrigan told the commissionaire that his sole purpose in life was to save Vale Frazier from eternal damnation.

He said that locating Vale Frazier was a matter of life and death and he had to find someone who could tell him where Vale was. The commissionaire told our officer that he'd pointed across the street to the duplex, told Mr. Kerrigan that Ainsley Blair lived on the second floor of the building, and since she was the boss, she would know where Vale was.

"That's all we know for certain. Mr. Kerrigan remembers going to the duplex and knocking on the door, but he has no memory of what happened after that."

"It would help me if I knew what happened before I walked in and saw Danny on the floor with his hand over the artery in Buzz Wells's neck that was spurting blood. I told Danny that it was too late to save Buzz Wells. Then he asked me to call his pastor to come and pray with him. I called Pastor Kirk, but he said he was too busy to come, so I told Danny I'd pray with him."

"All we can do is speculate, Joanne," Robert Hallam's tone was resigned. Buzz Wells's suitcase and messenger bag were by the door. The officers surmised that Danny had caught Buzz on his way out. Wells had a plane ticket. What happened between the two men is anyone's guess. But determining the cause of death requires no guesswork. Buzz Wells's carotid artery was slashed by Danny Kerrigan's cable-splicer's knife. When the officers arrived the knife was on the floor by the body. Mr. Kerrigan was still wearing his toolbelt and the space where the knife belonged was empty.

CHAPTER TWENTY

From that point on, as it always did, life continued. Katina Posaluko-Chapman, the lawyer Zack had called to be with Danny when he was questioned by the police, convinced the authorities that Danny should be hospitalized for a twenty-four-hour psychological assessment, and the police escorted Danny to Regina General Hospital, where he was admitted to the psychiatric ward.

Reasoning that living in the apartment directly below the active police investigation into Buzz Wells's murder would exacerbate an already nightmarish situation, Georgie packed overnight bags for Ainsley and herself and checked them both into adjoining suites at a downtown hotel.

I'd put off telling Taylor and Vale about the tragedy until I had at least some answers to the questions I knew they would have. When I finally told her the news, Katina

Posaluko-Chapman had already accompanied Danny Kerrigan as he was admitted to the psychiatric ward of Regina General Hospital, and Ainsley and Georgie had moved into the hotel.

Taylor listened in silence as I recounted the indescribable horror of finding Danny kneeling beside Buzz Wells's body with his hand over the slash he, himself, had made in Wells's neck.

When I finished, she said simply, "We're coming over," and her voice quavered.

The rain hadn't let up, and when the four of us went into the kitchen to talk, I switched on the overhead light hoping to dispel the gloom, but it seemed the pall of misery and remorse hanging over us was impenetrable.

"Danny did it to save my soul," Vale said. "And now . . ." Vale turned her eyes to Zack. "What happens to him now?"

When the situation called for it, Zack could radiate a masterful lawyerly calm. Taylor and Vale were reeling, and as he explained Danny's situation Zack was factual but positive. "I asked Katina Posaluko-Chapman to represent Danny. She's an excellent trial lawyer and she's experienced with cases involving the mentally ill. Katina was with Danny when he was questioned by the police, and she convinced them that Danny should be hospitalized for a twenty-four-hour psychological assessment."

"What happens if they decide Danny *planned* to kill Buzz Wells?" Taylor said.

"Then he'll be charged, and Katina will prepare him for trial. I don't believe the case will go that way. I expect the psychiatrists at Regina General will recommend transferring Danny to the provincial psychiatric facility at North Battleford for a thirty-day assessment to see if he's fit to stand trial."

Taylor pressed on. "And if the psychiatrists decide Danny is not fit to stand trial?"

"He'll remain at the North Battleford facility. The staff there is excellent."

Taylor fingered a small stain on the sleeve of her sweater. "How long do you think Danny will be there?"

"He'll remain in North Battleford until his psychiatric team is certain that he poses no threat to himself or others."

"And that could be years," Vale said, and her misery was palpable. "Danny's entire life has changed course because of me."

The horror and confusion in Vale's face was now eclipsed by guilt. Zack touched her arm softly. "No," he said. "The entire course of Danny's life did not change because of you. His fate was determined by something that happened long before he met you. Fred C. Harney, the old lawyer with whom I articled, used to talk about what he called 'the train of events.' Fred believed our fate is as accidental as it is inescapable. Something happens and suddenly we find ourselves on the train of events that leads us inexorably to our destination."

Vale nodded but it was clear from her expression she hadn't accepted it yet.

"No one understands exactly what happened today," Zack said. "We know that Buzz Wells died from the wound

Danny Kerrigan's cable splicer inflicted on Wells's carotid artery. In law, we call that the proximate cause. The proximate cause is an event sufficiently related to an injury that the court deems the event to be the cause of the injury. But there's another kind of causation in the law. It's called cause-in-fact. Cause-in-fact is determined by the 'but for' test. But for the action, the result would not have happened. For example, but for running the red light, the collision would not have occurred. If x had not happened, y would not have happened. Cause-in-fact is where things get tangled.

"So the cause-in-fact that directly led to Buzz Wells's death was Danny running into the commissionaire, who told him where he could find Ainsley," I said. "If Danny hadn't learned where Ainsley lived, he never would have knocked on the door of the College Avenue apartment. And if Danny hadn't lost his phone on his way to work, he would have received Ainsley's message about the shutdown and he would not have freaked when he saw that the production studios were empty."

"And this is where I come in," Zack said. "If I hadn't tried to spook Buzz by convincing Ainsley to shut down production until further notice, work at the production studios would have gone on as usual, and right about now, Danny would be finishing his shift. But Danny did lose his phone and because of that, Buzz Wells is dead and Danny is facing an uncertain future."

The note of self-reproach in Zack's voice alarmed me. "This wasn't your fault," I said. "If Danny had never embraced the doctrines of a church that filled him with fear and hate, he wouldn't have been convinced that he had a holy mission to save Vale from hell and damnation because she loves another woman."

"And if Danny hadn't felt the need for what that church offered, nothing that happened today would have occurred," Vale said softly.

"I imagine that, as part of their treatment, the psychiatrists at North Battleford will try to discover the events in Danny's life that made him so vulnerable," Zack said. "Fred C. Harney would tell them that navel gazing is a waste of time, that once you're on the train of events, there's no getting off until you arrive at your destination."

Vale reached across the table until the tips of her fingers touched the tips of Zack's. "Is that what you believe?" she asked.

For the first time since the young women arrived, Zack smiled. "It's been almost thirty years since Fred C. Harney introduced me to the train of events, and for me, the jury's still out. But Vale, I am certain of one thing: you are in no way responsible for what happened this morning."

CHAPTER TWENTY-ONE

In the early months after Gabe Vickers's death, *Sisters and Strangers* had seemed star-crossed, but Fate is capricious, and by June 11, the first day of principal photography, every department was prepared for the next step. Rosamond Burke, the last of the actors to appear, arrived in Regina on June 6, D-Day, as she crisply noted. The first three weeks of the shoot would take place at Emma Lake, and by June 11, actors, crew and equipment were within a stone's throw of the island and prepared to make a six-part series.

Miraculously, they had a locked script with which to work. Georgie and I resisted the urge to feed the pages of Buzz Wells's script to the flames in the nearest firepit and discovered that some of Buzz's ideas were worth developing. Together she and I produced a script that we felt was true to Roy's vision and, even more miraculously, satisfied Ainsley.

Georgie and Nick's wedding took place on May 5 as scheduled. They had talked briefly about postponing the ceremony because of Buzz Wells's all-too-recent death, but when Chloe showed them the Day of the Wedding scrapbook that she had created with elaborately drawn frames for the pictures they would take on the Big Day, starting with the appointment at the hair stylist and culminating in the cutting of the wedding cake, Georgie and Nick agreed a delay was out of the question, and their elegant, intimate wedding was even lovelier than the photos online suggested. On June 10, Georgie travelled north with her new husband and stepdaughter, and they were sharing Henry Chan's cottage on Anglin Lake with Taylor and Vale. From all reports, everyone was happily settled in.

Zack and I were happily settled in too. On June 11 we were at Lawyers' Bay with the twins, Charlie and Colin. The trial that Maisie and Angus were working on was in its second week, and June was a busy time on the farm for Pete and his new partner, Vince, so Maisie and Pete's long-delayed honeymoon continued to be on hold. However, there was good news. Maisie and Pete had decided to buy Blake Falconer's house. It was in our neighbourhood and the Crawford-Kilbourns would begin moving in as soon as the trial ended.

Katina Posaluko-Chapman kept us informed about Danny Kerrigan, and the prognosis was not good. Danny was despondent because he was convinced he had failed God by not saving Vale from eternal damnation. Danny's psychiatric team included a spiritual adviser, a young chaplain who had been at seminary with the dean of our cathedral, and the chaplain was already playing a key role in Danny's treatment.

As Katina explained, Danny had, in layman's terms, been brainwashed by Pastor Kirk and his cohorts, and the chaplain was attempting to give Danny a broader perspective so he could challenge the beliefs about God's will with which he'd been indoctrinated. The process would be long and painstaking, but the psychiatric care at North Battleford was excellent, and Danny's team was guardedly optimistic that he would make progress.

Kyle had been luckier. The police had tracked down the arsonist who set the fire at the production studios. He lived in L.A. and had learned how to stage a controlled fire from his work in movies. He was having money problems and Buzz had offered him cash and future employment in return for a few hours' work and a return ticket to L.A. Because Kyle had approached the police voluntarily, they had been receptive to his story that in giving Roy the LSD, he believed he was acting on the advice of Roy's therapist. Unlike Buzz Wells, Kyle had nothing to gain from destroying Roy. The absence of motive, Taylor's description of Kyle's suffering after Roy's death and my statement that I had witnessed Kyle's earlier desire to confess bore out Kyle's story, so there were no charges.

Taylor had been concerned about the effect returning to the island on Emma Lake would have on Kyle, and everyone was apprehensive about how Ainsley would react, but according to Nick, Kyle had offered his hand to help Ainsley out of their boat when it docked, and Ainsley had linked her arm with Kyle's as they walked to the site where the shooting would begin. Seemingly, Ainsley and Kyle were helping each other confront the memory of that dark March day.

* * *

When I awoke at Lawyers' Bay on the morning of June 11, the anxiety that had dogged me for months was gone. I had slept well, and I was ready to resume my old life. When Charlie and Colin bounced in with the dogs and clambered onto our bed, I felt a wash of relief. I was home again.

We weren't alone at the lake. Noah Wainberg, the husband of Zack's late partner, Delia, always spent the last two weeks of June at Lawyers' Bay getting everything ready for Falconer Shreve's big Canada Day party. Zack and I were very fond of Noah, a gentle giant of man who had loved his wife deeply and who was now raising their three-year-old grandson Jacob, with the help of Rose Lavallee, a no-nonsense seventy-ish dynamo from Standing Buffalo Dakota Nation. I had come to know Rose through Taylor's friendship with Gracie Falconer. Rose had cared for Gracie since the day she was born, and what Rose didn't know about raising children wasn't worth knowing. After Blake Falconer's death and Gracie's departure for university, Rose was at loose ends, but Jacob Wainberg was in need of a nanny, and Rose was in need of a child to care for and teach.

When the Falconer family was at Lawyers' Bay, Rose and Gracie always stayed overnight at Rose's house next door to her sister Betty's on Standing Buffalo. Gracie's mother was Nakota, and the sisters made certain Gracie grew up aware of her Nakota heritage.

Although they were sisters, Betty and Rose were, as my grandmother would say, as different as chalk and cheese. Rose was lean, limber and energetic. She loved the outdoors and rode her Trek bike everywhere. Her personal style was no frills; steel-grey hair tightly permed; wash-and-wear wardrobe and straightforward skincare regimen — sunscreen by day, Vaseline overnight. Like Rose herself, her house was neat as a pin with a decorating approach that placed function ahead of frippery. Rose's house was a place to sleep, eat and retreat to if the weather was too miserable to be biking, hiking, swimming or cross-country skiing.

Betty was Rubenesque, voluptuous and languid. Her home — a snuggery filled with plump silk-covered pillows, deep cushy chairs and an impressive collection of Beanie babies — was a castle through which Betty moved in a cloud of White Diamonds eau de toilette. She was a beauty, with gently waved jet-black hair, deep-set brown eyes and a wardrobe chosen to reveal just enough of Betty to leave a man wanting more. She took pride in the fact that none of her three husbands had ever seen her without makeup and that, except for time spent in bed, no man had ever seen her without high heels.

That first night we had dinner on the Wainbergs' front porch, and as we sat down to a meal of Betty's bannock, Rose's moose chili and Jacob's favourite cookies, I realized how much I needed the peace and familiarity of Lawyers'

Bay. Charlie and Colin's day had been an active one, running along the shore, throwing sticks in the water and digging in the sand. As a child, Taylor described the way she felt after a busy day outdoors as "good tired." The boys were good tired, and we were eating early to make sure they were fed before they fell asleep.

Moose chili was a new item on the twins' menu, and they were tentative as they took their first spoonful, but Rose's moose chili was generally acknowledged to be the best on Standing Buffalo, and after a few seconds of deliberation, Colin and Charlie dug in. It was a time to experiment with the new. For the next two and a half weeks, except for unavoidable commitments in Regina, Zack worked from the lake, and for once, he didn't push himself. More often than not, when Rose, Betty, Noah and I set out with the three little boys for an adventure, Zack joined us. Revelling in the quotidian was a new path for Zack, and I was hoping it would become a habit.

July 1, Canada Day, was always a red-letter day for Falconer Shreve Altieri Wainberg and Hynd. The summer after they opened their law office, the young partners invited friends and the firm's small but growing list of clients to a BYOB barbecue bash at Lawyers' Bay. The invitation suggested that guests bring blankets and pillows because, in all likelihood, they would end up sleeping on the beach.

Times had changed. Over the years, the party had evolved into a very large affair for clients, would-be clients, partners, staff, friends and families. Everything about the day, from the beach towels to the fireworks, was now organized by an event planner. Progress. The Canada Day party was always a hot ticket, but this year there was a special cachet — the cast and crew of *Sisters and Strangers* were joining the group.

Except for Rosamond Burke and Vale, I hadn't met any members of the cast. Usually at the Canada Day party, Zack and I split up to welcome guests and make certain they had everything they needed, but sensing my apprehension about meeting the actors who were playing the people who, for good or ill, had shaped me, Zack stayed close as cars began pulling up.

The first guests to arrive were Taylor and Vale, and they were dressed to wave the flag. Taylor wore very white, very short shorts and a red crop top; Vale, a white T-shirt and a red-and-white-striped miniskirt. Both young women sported red baseball caps with visors, and in my opinion, they were perfect. They'd flown in from Prince Albert the night before, so Zack and I hadn't seen them in three weeks. There was much news to catch up on, but in the way of big parties, everyone suddenly arrived at once. Vale and Taylor sprung into action, helping *Sisters and Strangers'* cast and crew get the lay of the land and introducing them to other guests, and Zack and I followed suit.

With a couple of notable exceptions, Falconer Shreve had good luck with Canada Day weather, and that July 1 it seemed the firm's lucky streak was continuing. The day was sunny, clear and warm but not hot — in short, a perfect day for water-skiing, swimming, canoeing, beach volleyball and croquet on the lawn. I'd been keeping an eye out for Georgie and when she, Nick and Chloe arrived, I joined them. All three were tanned and beaming.

"Northern Saskatchewan was obviously good to you," I said. "You look great."

Nick grinned. "Hard not to look great when you've spent three weeks in paradise."

"I know what you mean," I said. "We used to go to Anglin Lake when Taylor was little. At dusk when the loons start calling to each other, the lake seems primeval."

"Calling is how the loons find each other," Chloe said. "Taylor told me one loon says, 'Where are you?' Then the other one says, 'I'm here.' Then they can be together to go to sleep."

"Did Taylor tell you about the time she was treading water and a loon came right up to her?"

Chloe nodded vigorously. "Taylor said for a while she and the loon looked at each other, and then the loon swam away. She said it was one of her bests."

"One of my bests too," I said. "I was on the beach when it happened, so I got to watch."

"Well here's one of my bests," Georgie said, then with the half proud, half embarrassed at being proud smile I remembered from my own pregnancies, she patted her baby bump.

Chloe was quick off the mark. She reached into her beach bag and pulled out an ultrasound photo. "This is our baby," she said. "He's a boy. We're naming him Erik after my dad's dad, and Lewis after Georgie's dad. So his name will be Erik Lewis Kovacs. And right now Erik weighs . . ." The look she gave Georgie was questioning. "I forget."

"He weighs 140 grams," Georgie said. "Mrs. Szabo says that's the size of a small turnip."

"She didn't come today because there are three things she doesn't like," Chloe said. "Crowds, water and . . ." She frowned.

"Loud music," Nick said.

Chloe's attention had wandered. "Is Taylor here?"

"She is," I said. "She's down by the lake, helping organize the water-skiing."

Nick turned to his daughter. "Why don't you and I go down to help Taylor and give Georgie and Joanne a chance to talk?"

"Thanks," I said. I turned to Georgie. "Let's go to the cottage. That way we won't get interrupted."

"And I'll be close to the bathroom," Georgie said. "A pressing concern these days."

We settled in what had become my favourite place for reading, a room with floor-to-ceiling windows that faced the woods behind our cottage. The chairs were deep and comfortable, and when the windows were open, as they were that day, I could smell the sharp scent of evergreens and once in a while, the faint tang of skunk.

Georgie inhaled deeply. "I've always been a big-city girl," she said. "But I'm starting to feel the allure of cottage life. When we were at Anglin, Nick and I started talking about buying a cottage. We've decided to stay in the house on Winnipeg Street, but it would be nice to have a place like this not too far from the city for weekends."

"Then I guess it's time for you and me to hit the real estate listings again," I said. "Georgie, it just occurred to me that your work on *Sisters and Strangers* will be over soon. Have you decided what you're going to do next?"

"I've had offers," Georgie said, "but I'm not rushing into anything. A year ago I couldn't have found Regina on a map. And now here I am with a husband, a daughter, Mrs. Szabo, a house and a baby on the way. I think I'm just going to focus on making everything work for all of us. Writing is a portable skill, and if the urge overwhelms me, I'll open my laptop."

"Good call," I said. "Sometimes it takes a while to realize that we don't have to do everything at once."

"To everything there is a season?"

"Something like that," I said. "And when it's time for you to write again, you'll have a truckload of fresh insights and new perspectives to bring to your work."

"And I need that. I'm tired, Jo. *Sisters and Strangers* was a tough row to hoe, but we made it through. I'm proud of that, and I'm proud of the script we wrote. From what I've seen and from what Nick tells me, the series is going to be everything we hoped it would be." Georgie suddenly narrowed her eyes, looked puzzled and then touched her stomach. "I think I just felt the little dude move."

"How far along are you?"

"Nineteen and a half weeks."

"That's in the ballpark."

Georgie was on her feet. "I'd better find Nick and Chloe in case it happens again."

I smiled. "It will happen again. And again, and again. At the end you'll feel as if there's a roller derby going on in there."

I walked down to the lake with Georgie and stood aside as she told Nick and Chloe about Erik making his presence known. It was an intimate moment, and Nick's and Chloe's faces were soft with wonder as they rested their fingers on Georgie's belly.

I had turned away to give the Kovacs family time to savour the experience privately, when I heard Rosamond Burke's rich full-timbered voice call my name. Tall, commanding and elegant in a floaty white crepe de Chine maxi dress, she was striding towards me. When she reached me, she took both my hands in hers. "Joanne, before we start filming again. I wanted to thank you for the script, not just as an actor but as Sally's friend. Only someone who loved her as you did could have recognized her courage and her honesty. She never lied to anyone, including herself. That's a rare virtue. She had a huge capacity for love, but she told me that after her father died, you were the only person she ever allowed herself to love."

"That's because she knew that, no matter what, I'd never stop loving her," I said.

"Exactly." Rosamond squared her shoulders. "Now Zack has asked if I will be his spotter as he drives the water-skiers around the lake, and I see that he's already waiting." She picked up the ends of the pale orange crepe de Chine band on her broad-brimmed sun hat and tied them under her chin. "That's the ticket," she said. "This hat is an old friend, and I would hate for it to end its days on the bottom of a Canadian lake."

* * *

Rosamond's hat survived, and much, much later when I saw the close-to-finished first two episodes of *Sisters and Strangers*, I noticed how skillfully Rosamond adjusted the hat on her handsome head to make certain her features were always benevolently lit.

By the time I saw the rough cuts, the snow was on the ground; our Christmas lights were on the tree, and the rhythm of our lives seemed to have permanently slowed. At the beginning of August, Zack announced that he was taking the entire month off work. I was certain that he made the promise in good faith; I was equally certain that he would be unable to stay away from Falconer Shreve. He loved the law, and during the years when he was mayor, he honoured his commitment to the city, but I knew he was like a penned bull, head lowered, shoulders hunched pawing the ground, itching to get back in the ring.

That August Zack surprised me. He seemed perfectly content simply to enjoy life at the lake. There was always family around. Taylor had inherited the first cottage built on Lawyers' Bay from my long-time friend and Zack's late partner Kevin Hynd. She and Vale loved the old place, and no matter how late shooting finished on Friday, they drove out to the lake and left for the city in the early hours of Monday morning. We had a guest cottage, and Charlie D,

Mieka and the girls were there for the first two weeks in August, and Maisie, Peter and the twins stayed at the lake till Labour Day. Most weekends Angus was there too. The Wainbergs and Rose and Betty were at Lawyers' Bay all summer, and it was a treat for us all when, in mid-August, Gracie Falconer flew back from Indiana to participate in the jingle dance event at the Standing Buffalo Powwow.

Gracie, a pre-med student at Notre Dame University, and a guard for the Fighting Irish women's basketball team, was spending the summer on campus taking a class in human biology and shadowing one of the physicians with the Notre Dame's athletic programs. Gracie had inherited her father's red hair and pale skin, but Rose and Betty had schooled her in the old ways, and Gracie was not only fluent in the Dakota language, she always placed in the top three in the jingle dance event.

A powwow is a celebration in music, dance, food and crafts of First Nations culture. The drums, the singing, the traditional dances, the extravagantly beautiful and significant regalia of the dancers, and the smells of fried bannock and barbecued game combine to draw dancers and watchers into a single community driven by the powerful central heartbeat of the drum.

On that sizzling August day, Georgie, Nick and Chloe had joined the Wainbergs, Rose, Betty, Taylor, Vale, Zack and me to watch the Grand Entry of the veterans, flag carriers and dancers as they were drummed in by the host drums. After all had entered, we opened our folding chairs and as the drumming continued and the singers raised their voices, we sat mesmerized by first the male, and then the female dancers.

Rose and Betty had braided Gracie's flaming red hair in the traditional way, and they had sewn every stitch and attached every bell to the skirt of her green jingle dance dress. Gracie danced with precision and beauty and when she was awarded first prize, Betty burst into tears and Rose swallowed hard and handed her sister a tissue.

Every summer has one indelible memory, and mine came when, after the dancing ended, we all trooped outside the tent and, at their request, Gracie began teaching Madeleine and Lena the basic steps of the jingle dance. The girls stood single file behind Gracie, carefully mimicking her movements. For a minute or two Chloe watched and then she moved into line behind Lena, then Charlie and Colin joined the procession. As the drumbeat from the centre of the tent reverberated, and the singers' voices rose in pitch and intensity, Gracie and the five children danced. It was what Virginia Woolf would have called "a moment of being," as self-contained, fragile and shimmering as a teardrop — a flash of awareness of the pattern beneath daily life.

CHAPTER TWENTY-TWO

The last day of shooting for *Sisters and Strangers* was October 31, Halloween. That evening, Vale and Taylor, dressed as Teletubbies, handed out treats to trick-or-treaters. As always, we ran out of candy, and Zack had to drive to the Golden Mile for supplies, and also as always, after we blew out the candles in the jack-o'-lanterns, Zack sat at the kitchen table with whoever had handed out the candy and divided the leftovers.

The next morning, Taylor drove Vale to the airport to start the North American publicity tour for *The Happiest Girl*. Originally, they had planned to travel together, but the movie was attracting a great deal of interest — cities with significant media markets were being added to the schedule, and it became clear that the time Taylor had allotted for visiting galleries would now be spent in airports or TV green rooms. The two women respected each other's work, and when Vale suggested Taylor's time would be better spent making art, Taylor was quick to agree.

Early in December, Vale would return to Regina, and after a week of visits, she and Taylor would fly to London, where they would stay with Rosamond at her home on Cheyne Walk, the eighteenth-century street that was once home to Henry James, T.S. Eliot and Mick Jagger. Vale and Taylor would celebrate Christmas with Rosamond and then the tour would continue in Europe. It would be a true Henry James adventure for Taylor and Vale, and Zack and I had finally accepted the fact that it was time to let our daughter experience life an ocean away from us.

Until then, we were simply grateful that Taylor would be with us to celebrate her nineteenth birthday and to welcome Erik Lewis Kovacs to the world. Erik arrived on November 22, American Thanksgiving, and Nick brought Georgie a deli turkey sandwich to commemorate her first Thanksgiving as a mother. Erik was a healthy, handsome ten-pound boy, with his mother's blond hair and cleanly defined features and his father's blue eyes and expressive mouth. When we visited Erik and his family the evening of the day he was born, Georgie had trouble taking her eyes off her son's face. "I can't believe any of this is happening," she said. "This little guy really does belong to us."

Chloe's forehead creased. "But we're glad, aren't we?"

"Very glad," Nick said, and the hug Nick gave his daughter was warm and solid. "Very glad and very grateful."

***

The Wainberg family, including Isobel who was in pre-med at Johns Hopkins, and Gracie Falconer, Rose and Betty were having Christmas at Lawyers' Bay. Since Taylor and Vale would be in London, Zack and I decided to break with tradition and spend the holiday at the lake too.

On the Sunday before Christmas, Zack and I attended church, had a quick lunch and carried the last-minute purchases out to the Volvo. Except for cajoling Pantera and Esme into the back of the station wagon, we were ready to rock. I'd just put the dogs or their leashes when a cab pulled up in front of the house, and Ainsley Blair emerged.

It had been weeks since I'd seen Ainsley, and I was struck by how well she looked. Both Georgie and Vale reported that, throughout the shoot, Ainsley had been the consummate professional — calm but exacting and unfailingly patient and courteous with cast and crew. As she walked towards us that day, Ainsley moved with the easy energy of a vital woman at peace with herself.

"I'm so glad I caught you," she said. "I knew you were going out of town for the holidays, but I didn't realize you were leaving today." She handed me a package. "These are copies of the first two episodes of *Sisters and Strangers*. They need some tinkering, but they're close. As you know, Roy saw the first two episodes as the place where we reveal the roots from which all the stories in the series grow. It's critical that the audience sees how deeply those roots are planted and how inextricably they are connected to one another. I haven't separated the two episodes here. They comprise a whole, and as soon as the network people get back to their desks in the new year, I'm going to New York to see if I can convince them to show the first two episodes together." Ainsley gave us a winningly dimpled smile. "My charms are a little rusty but I'll give it my best shot."

Zack was gallant. "Your charms are still in good order."

Ainsley rewarded him with another dimpled smile, but her face grew serious when she turned to me. "Roy would have been proud of this series, Joanne. It would never have existed without you. I'm very grateful, and I'm sorry I wasn't the supportive colleague you deserved."

"We all did what had to be done," I said.

She nodded. "Maybe when I'm here for post-production, you and I can make a fresh start."

"I'd like that," I said.

"So would I," she said, then she turned and headed for the cab. When Ainsley's taxi disappeared onto Albert Street, Zack took my hand. "Do you want to watch the show here or at the lake?"

"At the lake," I said. "And I want to watch it in bed next to you, propped up by lots of pillows and with a bottle of Jack Daniels in easy reach."

The two episodes Ainsley brought begin with the raft scene of Sally and Joanne at fourteen, cover the events of that summer and end with Joanne going to the Loves' cottage and discovering the family in their dining room — Des, still sitting at his place at the table but with his head lolled back and his mouth hanging open, Nina in her chair with her head resting on her arm as it lies on the table and Sally lying face down in vomit on the floor. The segment ends with Joanne standing alone on the dock, watching her father drive the boat carrying Sally and her parents back to the mainland.

Roy's script for the first two episodes was everything it had to be. Played out against the colour-drenched world of high summer in cottage country, Roy's rendering of the inner lives of Sally and Joanne as they teetered on the cusp of womanhood was by turns funny and poignant. Camryn Hanson, the actor playing the young Joanne, had a way of stepping back into stillness that suggested she was wary of action, but her face registered every emotion. Camryn's Joanne was the perfect foil for Vale's Sally, who strode into life gloriously confident, fearless, ready to tackle anything and everything.

Sally and Joanne's last summer together had been idyllic: a time of glorying in the changes of their young bodies, breathlessly reading aloud steamy passages in novels and cringing in disbelief at clinical descriptions of intercourse in a medical book Joanne found in her mother's closet. Roy's script had captured the quicksilver emotional shifts of adolescence as Sally and Joanne dreamed their big dreams and gloried in the promise of their lives to come.

But Nina had put an end to all that, and the moment Tessa Stafford, the actor playing Nina, came onscreen was a body blow for me. I had glimpsed Tessa at the Canada Day party, but even from a distance her physical similarity to Nina rattled me, and I had avoided her.

Now, Tessa Stafford's face filled the screen, and the resemblance to Nina took my breath away: the raven-black hair, the widow's peak, the heart-shaped face, the violet eyes, the deceptive fragility. It was easy to underestimate Nina because she was so slight and so beautiful, but the old Chinese proverb she was fond of quoting revealed the truth: "The sparrow is small, but it contains all the vital organs of the elephant." Nina might have seemed as delicate as a Dresden doll, but she was strong enough to destroy any obstacle that stood in her way.

The first scene between Nina and Joanne was familiar to me. After a particularly bruising encounter with her mother, Joanne runs to Nina, tearful and dishevelled. Nina wipes Joanne's face with a cool cloth, rubs her temples and wrists with a soothing lotion and brushes her hair until Joanne's breathing slows and she's able to talk.

I had written very little of the dialogue in the first two episodes, but the dialogue in this scene was mine. The task had been an easy one. I had carried the words with me for decades, but hearing the words and watching the dynamic between Joanne and Nina was not easy. It was unbearable. As I watched Nina cultivate Joanne's need for her love, I knew I was witnessing a master class in the art of manipulation. When Joanne tells Nina that she wishes Nina was her mother, and Nina smiles wistfully and whispers, "I wish that too, but we don't always get the mothers we deserve," I winced.

In retrospect, that sentence chilled me to the marrow, but for years I clung to Nina's words.

At the end of the second episode, Joanne stands alone on the dock, watching the boat carry away Sally, Nina, Des and life as she has known it. The sun is setting and the only sounds are lake sounds: waves splashing against the dock, the low sighing of aspens in the wind and the eerily beautiful tremolo of loons calling to each other as night falls. The action freezes and words appear on the screen.

IN LOVING MEMORY OF
ROY BRODNITZ (1974–2018)

"There is no end to anything. The horizon is only an apparent division. As we move forward, it keeps moving away. There is no end to anything. There is only change."
— Ernest Lindner

After the screen went dark, neither Zack nor I spoke. We simply held each other close. Finally, I broke the silence.

"That was perfect," I said. "If the rest of the episodes are as extraordinary as this, Roy's legacy is assured. Audiences will see Sally in all her glorious complexity, and they'll know the power of Des's art."

"And Nina?" Zack said. "What will the audience's takeaway be about her?"

"I don't know," I said. "Nina will always be the big question mark in my life. Des had two daughters: Nina killed one of them and saved the other."

"That sounds very Old Testament."

"It does," I agreed. "I've spent much of my life trying to reconcile what Nina did for me with what she did to Sally. I still haven't come up with an answer, so I guess audiences are going to have to figure that one out for themselves."

"Maybe that's the lesson," Zack said. "We are all a mixed bag when it comes to morality. The only thing we can do is sort through the bag, acknowledge that the dark side exists and figure out where it comes from before it swallows the person we have the potential to be."

"That's an answer I just might be able to live with," I said. "You're not just a pretty face, are you?"

"No, I'm the guy who loves you, and I've seen the toll this has taken on you," Zack said. "I'm glad *Sisters and Strangers* gave you what you needed, Jo, but I'm relieved that it's finished."

"I am too," I said. "I want more August in our lives, Zack."

Zack's face creased in a smile at the memory. "August was great — day after day of kids, grandkids, dogs, the lake and you."

"August has always been a good month for us," I said. "Our first August together was transforming. July was all hot summer nights and great sex."

Zack raised an eyebrow. "Nothing wrong with that."

"No, but August was when we realized that we belonged together. By the time the leaves turned, we both knew that we'd been given something better than anything we could have wished for or imagined."

Zack took my hand. "And we're not going to squander

what we've been given. Jo, I was going to surprise you with this on Christmas morning. But I've told my partners that as of January 1, I'll be in the office three days a week, max. The rest of the time I'll be wherever you and the dogs are."

"Are you serious?"

"I am. On New Year's Day, we will have been married seven years — the best seven years of my life."

"And mine," I said. "Every so often I take off my wedding ring and read the inscription. 'A deal's a deal.' It always makes me smile, and it always makes me feel safe."

"It's the best deal I ever made," Zack said, but his smile was shadowed. "I just wish there wasn't a catch. The vows we took at the cathedral that morning make it clear that death ends the deal."

"I don't believe that," I said. "Nothing will ever part us, Zack."

Zack's voice was husky. "I defer to your judgment," he said. "And who knows? Now that we have more time to love and to cherish, you and I might just beat the odds and last forever."

"Remember those kisses that Kevin Costner talked about in *Bull Durham*?"

Zack grinned. "The long, slow, deep, soft, wet ones that last for three days?"

"Those are the ones." I moved in close. "Let's get started."

ACKNOWLEDGEMENTS

Thanks to:

Emily Schultz, my editor for her uncanny ability to know what needed to be done and for her boundless enthusiasm for the work we were doing together.

Jennifer Smith, who read the manuscript as soon as it arrived at ECW and said all the right things.

The ECW team, who were consummately professional and kind.

Hildy Bowen and Brett Bell, for their love and endless patience with my temperamental MacBook Air and me.

Max and Carrie Bowen, for their love and support.

Kai Langen, Brittany Scheelhaase, Madeleine Bowen-Diaz, Lena Bowen-Diaz, Chesney Langen-Bell, Ben Bowen Bell, Peyton Bowen and Lexi Bowen who are a constant source of delight.

Naima Kazmi, MD, for her gentle manner and her professionalism.

Wayne Chau, BSP, for his wise counsel and great sense of humour.

Ron and Cindy, our loving and generous neighbours.

Ted, for fifty-two years of love, laughter and friendship.

At ECW Press, we want you to enjoy this book in whatever format you like, whenever you like. Leave your print book at home and take the eBook to go! Purchase the print edition and receive the eBook free. Just send an email to ebook@ecwpress.com and include:

- the book title
- the name of the store where you purchased it
- your receipt number
- your preference of file type: PDF or ePub

A real person will respond to your email with your eBook attached. And thanks for supporting an independently owned Canadian publisher with your purchase!